Praise for
Love, Lucy

★ "*Love, Lucy* hits all the right notes. . . . This is a great
coming-of-age story, perfect for Sarah Dessen fans or
those who enjoy books with a summer romance."
—*VOYA* (starred review)

"A contemporary romance with surprising depth in
its coming-of-age elements, this modern update of
E. M. Forster's *A Room with a View* will appeal to
fans of Sarah Dessen, Stephanie Perkins, and
Lindner's reimagined classics."
—*SLJ*

"This intelligent love story will resonate with readers
who are themselves balancing the thin line between
making lives of their own and seeking parents' approval."
—*Booklist*

"April Lindner brings on the feels with her usual charm.
Love, Lucy is another romantic winner from this
amazingly talented writer."
—Meg Cabot, author of The Princess Diaries
and the Heather Wells mystery series

LOVE, Lucy

APRIL LINDNER

POPPY

LITTLE, BROWN AND COMPANY

NEW YORK   BOSTON

Poppy

Hachette Book Group
1290 Avenue of the Americas, New York, NY 10104
Visit us at lb-teens.com

Poppy is an imprint of Little, Brown and Company.
The Poppy name and logo are trademarks of Hachette Book Group, Inc.

The publisher is not responsible for websites (or their content)
that are not owned by the publisher.

First Paperback Edition: July 2016
First published in hardcover in January 2015 by Little, Brown and Company

The Library of Congress has cataloged the hardcover as follows:

Lindner, April.
  Love, Lucy / April Lindner. — First edition.
    pages cm
    "Poppy."
  Summary: After accepting a trip to Europe as a bribe from her parents to attend the college of their choice as a business major, seventeen-year-old Lucy discovers she is unwilling to give up her dream of being an actress—or Jesse, the boy she met in Italy.
    ISBN 978-0-316-40069-5 (hardcover) — ISBN 978-0-316-40065-7 (ebook edition) — ISBN 978-0-316-40066-4 (library ebook edition)   [1. Love—Fiction. 2. Theater—Fiction. 3. Colleges and universities—Fiction. 4. Voyages and travels—Fiction. 5. Assertiveness (Psychology)—Fiction.]   I. Title.
  PZ7.L6591Lov 2015
  [Fic]—dc23

                                                                      2013042984

Paperback ISBN 978-0-316-40068-8

10 9 8 7 6 5 4 3 2 1

RRD-C

Printed in the United States of America

For Dorothee Heisenberg,
la mia amica di una vita

PART ONE

Italy

I

*A*fter a sleepless night on the train to Florence, Lucy Somersworth and Charlene Barr checked into the Hostel Bertolini groggy and disheveled but with high expectations. The Bertolini's website had promised lace curtains, wide brass beds, and a vase full of sunflowers on the dresser. But their room on the second floor turned out to be dark and cramped, with two twin beds pushed together and no sunflowers in sight.

"At least the bathroom's all ours." Lucy darted through a narrow door to inspect the shower, which wasn't bad, considering. "We won't have to wait in line." Despite having sunburned shoulders and a bad case of bedhead, she was determined to be a good sport. After all, this stay at the Bertolini was supposed to be their last big splurge—a highlight of their backpacking trip-of-a-lifetime across Europe. After three weeks of

1

roughing it, a private room—no matter how tiny—seemed downright luxurious.

Charlene wrinkled her nose. "The bathroom's okay," she conceded. "But I told them we wanted queen-size beds."

"Twin beds aren't so bad. We can push them apart." Lucy peeled back a bedspread to take a peek at what lay beneath. "Look! The sheets are clean."

"Humph," Charlene said, too tired to even complain properly. Like Lucy, she was still dressed in the rumpled tank top and shorts she'd worn all day yesterday. The cheerful German family with whom they'd shared a sleeper car had thought to tuck pajamas and toothbrushes into their daypacks—another valuable travel lesson learned too late. Despite her having chewed an entire pack of gum, Lucy's teeth still felt fuzzy; the chance to brush them and take a hot shower sounded like the most luxurious thing in the world. If only she could convince Charlene to relax and make the best of things. In a little more than a week, their vacation would be over and Lucy would be back in Pennsylvania, packing for her freshman year at college. More than anything, she wanted to make the most of her last few days in Europe.

Charlene strode over to the window, flung open its dark green shutters, and froze, her body rigid. In her e-mail correspondence with the hotel manager, she'd been promised a view of the Piazza Santa Maria Novella. She'd shown Lucy a picture of the black-and-white church, the stone walkways, and a lawn where tourists strolled, licking cones of gelato. It wasn't the most beautiful spot in Florence, but it was the one they could afford, and the photos on the website had looked charming.

But instead of the piazza, the room's single window looked out on a dark little courtyard—actually more of an alley—with the buildings behind the Bertolini completely blocking both view and sunshine. As she joined Charlene at the window, Lucy could feel her friend's agitation growing. Three weeks in Charlene's presence had alerted Lucy to the signs—flared nostrils and arched eyebrows—that her friend was about to charge into battle, in this case, probably with the baby-faced guy who had just checked them in.

"It's just a place to sleep," Lucy murmured. "It doesn't have to be paradise."

"I wasted hours yesterday making arrangements," Charlene insisted. "I must have sent ten e-mails."

So you keep telling me, Lucy thought, biting her lip to keep the words from coming out. As tired as she was, she could feel herself on the verge of saying something she wouldn't be able to take back. She and Charlene had gotten along so well for the first few weeks of the trip. Though the two of them could hardly be more different, they'd balanced each other out—Lucy with her cheerful enthusiasm for every item on their to-do list, Charlene with her talent for reading maps and figuring exchange rates. But lately their money had started running low, and things between them had grown tense. Or at least that's how it seemed to Lucy. Now she gave Charlene's shoulder an awkward pat. "You tried your best. If we really want to see the piazza, we can just go out and stand in it."

But Charlene was in no mood to be cheered up. "No." She held up a hand like a crossing guard signaling *stop*. "They promised us a view. I'm not afraid to knock some heads together if that's what it takes." Charlene was two years older than Lucy, about to start her junior year in college, and everything about her broadcast neatness and efficiency—her blond bob; her lean, muscular build; her perfect posture; her sharp nose and determined chin. Next to her, Lucy always felt a little unkempt.

"I'll just go have a little talk with that guy at the check-in desk," Charlene concluded.

"Please don't." Lucy knew how easily a little talk could escalate into a very big talk, and she hated causing a fuss. "This room is nice, considering how cheap we got it. Only fifty dollars a night, right?"

Charlene sighed. "Fifty euros. Apiece. You do know that's a lot more than fifty dollars, right?"

Lucy had to concentrate hard to avoid rolling her eyes. Money had become a sore subject between them lately. Was it Lucy's fault that her parents were well off? It wasn't as though Lucy's father made a habit of sending her on glamorous vacations. He hadn't gotten where he was in life by throwing money away hand over fist, as he liked to say.

It's not like I'm spoiled, Lucy thought. *I earned this trip. I traded my whole future for it.* Tears sprang without warning into her eyes, and she blinked them back.

But Charlene noticed. "I know how much this trip means to you," she said, her voice kind. "Think of the sacrifice you made to get here!" With a flick of her wrist, she closed the shutters on the dim courtyard. "You *should* have a view."

"It's *your* vacation, too." Lucy sank to the bed and sighed, untangling the ponytail holder from her abundant light brown curls. When she looked back up, Charlene was still hovering near the door, looking expectantly down at her.

"What's wrong now?" Lucy asked, trying not to sound as impatient as she felt.

"The guy at the desk doesn't speak much English." With two semesters of college German and three years of high school French, Charlene had done all the talking in Munich, Vienna, Salzburg, and Paris. Now that they were in Italy, it was supposed to be Lucy's turn. Not that she spoke much Italian, except for a few random phrases she remembered from Signora Lucarelli's third-period class.

"His English was fine," Lucy countered. Maybe she couldn't stop Charlene from haranguing the poor desk clerk, but she really didn't want to be dragged into an ugly scene. "He'll understand you."

"If you say so."

"It's true," Lucy said.

"Just don't unpack."

Charlene shut the door briskly, and Lucy flopped onto her back, relieved to be alone for the first time in days. With nobody looking, she sniffed her armpits and grimaced. Maybe she couldn't shower yet, but what would it hurt if she brushed her teeth?

Afterward, teeth tingling reassuringly, she pulled out her copy of *Wanderlust: Europe* and turned to the chapter on Italy. This was the part of the trip she'd most looked forward to, and now Charlene was wasting their precious time. Besides, they still needed to run errands. At this rate, the whole day would be over before they'd squeezed in any fun. As Lucy riffled through the battered guidebook, she tried not to think about the bargain she'd made with her father, the one that had gotten her here in the first place.

Charlene knew the whole story, of course; Lucy had regaled her with it on the long transatlantic flight. "You're lucky," Charlene had said. "Your parents are so generous, flying us both to Europe."

"Well, yes," Lucy said, doubt in her voice.

"Aren't you thrilled? I can't think of a better graduation gift."

"But it's not a gift," Lucy said. "More like a bribe, in exchange for enrolling at Forsythe U. It's my dad's alma mater. He bought me my first Forsythe T-shirt before I was even born, and he's given me a new one for Christmas every year since. I've got seventeen of them, from baby sizes to adult. It's crazy."

"Forsythe's not so bad," Charlene assured her. "It might not be the Ivy League, but I'm happy there."

"Oh, I know." Lucy blushed faintly. "I'm sure Forsythe is a fantastic school. The real problem is...." She paused for effect. "I have to major in business."

"That's a problem?" Charlene asked.

"I don't really want to. I'm not good at things like math and money. My dad likes to say I don't have a practical bone in my body."

"Oh." Charlene frowned slightly, as though uncertain what to say next.

"It's okay." Lucy crinkled her nose. "I'm used to it. All my life he's wanted me to be things I'm not. Like a sports star. Or one of those kids in the Gifted program." She rolled her eyes. "But, you know. It's messed up that he wants me to major in something so not me."

"What would be you?" Charlene asked.

Lucy stared off into the clouds beyond the airplane window. "I wish I knew."

Not long ago, her answer to that question would have been very different. Strangely enough, for the daughter of such practical parents, Lucy Sommersworth was a born actress. When she'd stepped onto the high wooden stage to audition for the sixth-grade play, she'd been terrified, her knees almost buckling beneath her. But as she opened her mouth to speak her lines, her stage fright evaporated. When she sang the song her class had learned for the occasion, she felt the auditorium go still around her, everyone listening in surprise.

She'd won the title role in *Alice in Wonderland*, earning an instant enemy: Ashley Beauchamp, whose long, silky blond hair should have made her a shoo-in for the part. But Lucy's snub nose and wild curls didn't matter; when she was onstage she *was* Alice. She projected her lines to the back row, and her singing voice echoed from the rafters. At the end of the play, when the audience jumped to their feet in applause, Lucy felt her whole body flood with their love and approval. Nothing in her life had ever felt so good. She wanted to have that feeling again and again and again.

Lucy went on to land the lead in nearly every school play after that, and even in summer stage productions, where she had to compete with girls from other districts, she was often cast in the ingénue role—Sandy in *Grease*, Hope Harcourt in *Anything Goes*, Liesl in *The Sound of Music*. In her junior year, after she'd

7

nabbed the role of Kim McAfee in *Bye Bye Birdie*, she'd spent hours each night poring over her lines and practicing her dance moves. One night, as she was doing the Twist in the living room, she'd overheard her parents arguing in the kitchen. Well, not arguing—her mother never yelled—but discussing in that intense way they had when they were worried about something.

"Of course she's got talent," her father was saying. "More than the other kids in her school. But talent's not enough. Do you realize how many girls run off every year to Hollywood or New York? The competition is cutthroat, Elise. Odds are that Lucy will fail."

Lucy had frozen in mid-Twist, hurt that her father could say such a thing. She remembered him beaming from the second row the previous spring when she'd played Hope Harcourt. He'd brought her a huge bouquet of yellow roses, and her mother's eyes had sparkled with happy tears as Lucy took her curtain call. Hadn't they been proud of her then?

"Girls like Lucy wind up unemployed—or on some director's casting couch," Lucy's father continued. Didn't he realize she could hear him? "She has to go to college. It's nonnegotiable."

"Of course, sweetheart," Lucy's mother said in the voice she used to soothe her worked-up husband. "But she could study drama in college. That would make her happy, and give her time to find herself...."

"Find herself? She's not lost, Elise. She's got us to guide her; that's our job. We're not her friends; we're her parents."

Can't you be both? Lucy wondered.

Then Lucy's mother murmured something Lucy couldn't quite catch.

"But majoring in drama? In this economy?" He sounded as though his wife had just proposed that Lucy become a mermaid or a fairy queen. "Absolutely not. Our daughter needs to give up playacting for good."

"Are you saying she should drop out of *Bye Bye Birdie?*" Lucy's mother sounded as shocked as Lucy felt. She couldn't let her cast-mates down. Besides, Ashley Beauchamp—her hair as silky and golden as ever—was her understudy. The thought of how thrilled she'd be to take over the lead made Lucy see red.

"Of course not," Lucy's father said, and his daughter exhaled in relief. "High school's the time to get all that out of her system. But college will be another story. It had better be."

The very next night, over pot roast and mashed potatoes, Lucy's father offered her a deal. If she applied to his alma mater, got accepted, and agreed to major in business, her reward would be something really stunning. "How about a car of your own?" Lucy's father made a little tent out of his fingers and smiled enticingly above it. "Maybe one of those MINI Coopers?"

Lucy's mother clicked her tongue. "Those are so small. Would it be safe?"

"Something a little bigger, then. A Honda Civic?"

But cars weren't Lucy's thing. She would have much preferred to be an actress. She looked down at her plate for a minute, studying her peas and carrots, and then back up at him.

Her father's smile got slightly smaller. "Or what about a trip? To Florida? You could stay with your aunt. Visit your cousins."

Lucy wrinkled her nose. The last time she'd seen her cousins she'd been six. The oldest one had face-slammed her with a kickball. "How about Hollywood?" she tried. She'd always wanted to tour the celebrity mansions and stand in the stars' footprints in front of Grauman's Chinese Theater. In fact, she'd been hoping to live in Hollywood herself someday.

Lucy's father and mother exchanged a meaningful look, and he cleared his throat. "I have a better idea. What about Europe?"

"Europe?" Lucy's thoughts instantly flashed to *Roman Holiday*, her absolute favorite of all the old romantic movies in her mother's DVD collection. She imagined herself as Audrey Hepburn, zipping on a Vespa through the streets of Rome. Though it wasn't Hollywood, it did sound glamorous.

"You could take a month, do the whole grand-tour thing, like I always wanted to when I was in college. Wouldn't that be exciting?"

And Lucy had to admit that it would be.

But Lucy's mother was none too pleased. "Do you really think it's such a good idea, sending her off to another continent?" Lucy overheard her mother ask later that night. As the months passed, she became pretty sure that her mom hoped the deal would fall through, that Lucy would remain on U.S. soil, safe. But the idea of Europe grew on Lucy, especially after she watched *Roman Holiday* five times in a row, falling a bit more in love with Gregory Peck—and Italy—with each viewing.

Right around that time, Lucy tried out for a community theater production of *Thoroughly Modern Millie*. The audition was a disaster, with Lucy completely blanking on the monologue she'd rehearsed for weeks. After that, she started wondering if maybe her father was right. Maybe raw talent wasn't enough; maybe she wasn't competitive enough to be an actress. Suddenly the thought of never having to try out for another role seemed like a massive relief. So in her senior year, Lucy applied to the business program at Forsythe University.

Her parents had seemed so pleased. But when her acceptance letter arrived, Lucy's mother immediately started to fret. "She's only seventeen. Anything could happen to a young girl traveling all by herself. Why don't we go with her, Harry?"

"I can't take a whole month off from the business. And I can't spare you for that long, either."

At her mother's urging, Lucy tried asking her friends from school if maybe they would like to come with her, but Anna's dad had been laid off in November, and Serenity's folks had already planned a family vacation to Yosemite. When it seemed the promised trip to Europe might just evaporate into thin air, Lucy grew mopey, already feeling nostalgic for the drama career she'd abandoned. Lucy's mom volunteered at the high school library where Charlene's mother was the head librarian, and when the two women came up with the plan of sending their daughters off to Europe together, everyone involved was relieved.

Lucy had been hearing about Charlene for years, but the two girls hadn't yet met. "Charlene will be the perfect traveling companion," Lucy heard her mother tell her father. "She's so level-headed. I know we can trust her to look after our Lu."

Though Lucy's father had grumbled about not being made of money, before long Lucy's mother had talked him into springing for plane tickets and Eurail passes for both girls. She took Lucy to the mall to shop for a backpack, full of chatter about how much fun Lucy and Charlene would have together, how traveling for a whole month would bond them as friends for life. Which had seemed to be the case until basically a day ago, when Charlene became short-tempered and snappish and weirdly obsessed with the perfect room she and Lucy would have at the Bertolini.

Lucy sighed and tossed *Wanderlust* aside, wondering what was taking Charlene so long. She reached for her Italian phrasebook, flipping through it in search of words that might prove useful if she ever got out of the hostel and into the world. *Buongiorno. Scusi, signore. Dove sono la toilette?* When she spoke the phrases out loud into the quiet room, she felt like a different person—worldly and glamorous rather than an ordinary, sheltered seventeen-year-old from the suburbs of Philadelphia.

She was practicing "Where is the nearest ATM?"—somehow, even that question managed to sound gorgeous in Italian—when the door burst open. From the smile on Charlene's face, Lucy could tell she'd achieved victory. "You got us a penthouse suite?" she asked without enthusiasm.

"Not exactly, but the guy behind the desk has a room with a view. He and his roommate offered to trade."

"The guy who checked us in? He lives in the hostel?"

Charlene's long fingers played with the chain around her neck. "Maybe he works in exchange for room and board."

"And we're kicking him out of his room? He seemed so nice."

"He *is* nice. Turns out he's fine with the trade. He said he was happy to give us his view. And he should be. We were promised...."

"But maybe not by him," Lucy said.

Charlene hoisted her backpack on decisively. "It's too late to back down now."

When the girls arrived at their new room on the third floor, they found the door ajar. Charlene pushed it open and they came face-to-face with a guy—not the one from the check-in desk—stuffing rolled-up shirts into a backpack. Dark-haired and with olive skin, a Roman nose, and the scruff of a two-day beard, he regarded the girls with steady brown eyes.

Lucy thought she saw disdain in his expression, as if to say he'd seen their type before—ugly Americans throwing their weight around. She couldn't stand to be looked at like that. One of the useful phrases she'd just practiced popped into her head. "*Mi dispiace*," she told him—Italian for "I'm sorry."

The guy cocked his head and removed an earbud from one ear.

"*Mi dispiace*," she repeated. She wanted to explain that this whole trading-rooms thing wasn't her idea, but she couldn't come up with the right words. The best she could do was "*Possiamo aspettare*," which meant "We can wait." Or at least she hoped it did.

A pile of battered paperbacks stood on the floor beside one of the twin beds. The guy bent to gather them up, his longish hair falling into his eyes. Tall and angular, he wore jeans despite the heat. Lucy, who was particularly fond of dark Italian eyes, might have found him attractive under other circumstances. This made it even worse that he seemed annoyed with her. As if the fuss Charlene had made was somehow her fault.

"*Possiamo aspettare*," Lucy said again. She wanted to say something like *We'll go away and come back later*, but she was too flustered to remember how.

The scorn she'd seen in his eyes when they arrived now gave way to something like amusement.

Another useful phrase popped into her head. "*Non parla Italiano?*" she tried, beginning to think that maybe he wasn't Italian at all.

Now he straightened up and grinned down at her like she was the funniest thing he'd seen all day.

Lucy elbowed Charlene discreetly in the ribs. "You try. Maybe he speaks German."

"He doesn't look German."

"Try anyway," Lucy urged.

"What should I say?"

"Say we're sorry. That we don't mean to kick him out of his room."

"But we're *not* sorry," Charlene declared. "The hostel took our down payment. They promised us a view. This is our room now."

Lucy threw up her hands, and just then, the sweet-faced guy from the front desk poked his head through the door, his eyes twinkling behind blue-framed glasses. "Bad Jesse. You are giving these beautiful young ladies a hard time?" And before anyone could answer, he swept into the room, smiling at Lucy and Charlene. "I'm Nello," he said. "Please excuse my rude friend."

"Who, me?" The roommate took out his second earbud and spoke up at last, sounding every bit as American as Lucy. "I haven't said a word. Who's giving who a hard time?" He even had

14

an accent she recognized—from New York, maybe, or possibly New Jersey.

Lucy inhaled sharply as the American's eyes met hers. Clearly, he had enjoyed making her look foolish.

She turned her back on him and focused on Nello. "Thank you so much for swapping with us."

He shrugged. "No problem. Jesse and I stay in Florence for the whole summer. It's nothing for us to exchange rooms for a few days. Right, Jesse?"

Jesse didn't respond.

To fill the silence, Lucy addressed Nello. "You're not from Florence?"

"I'm from Torre Annunziata. Near Naples. But my man Jesse here is from the Jersey Shore." He tilted his head toward his roomie. "Like the TV show, no?"

In no mood to acknowledge Nello's smirking friend, Lucy turned instead to the large picture window. The curtains had been flung back, the pane thrown open. She stepped over to it and took in Piazza Santa Maria Novella—quieter than she'd expected, but as charmingly Italian as she could have hoped. She might not have realized how badly she wanted a view, but now that she had one, she had to admit that it was a little bit thrilling.

"We've been here so long I forget to look out the window. I like to give this view to someone who will enjoy it." Nello's eyes scrunched up so kindly that between his big smile and the view, Lucy felt herself forgiving Charlene after all.

II

*To give Nello and Jesse time to pack up, the girls wandered downstairs. They needed to check out the Internet situation, anyway. Both girls had promised to write home as soon as they arrived at each stop on their trip, and the one time Lucy had forgotten, her mother had sent about forty frantic e-mails. A computer sat on a desk in a common room off the lobby, but a girl with white-blond braids frowned behind it, too busy typing to look up when they entered the room. Lucy and Charlene settled on a nearby sofa, trying not to look like they were breathing down her neck.

Unable to stand the silence for very long, Lucy whispered, "Our new room is great."

Charlene nodded, looking pleased with herself.

Lucy felt annoyed again. "But wasn't that Jesse the rudest?

Letting me go on and on like that. Pretending not to speak English. How long does it take to pack a knapsack, anyway?"

"He just wants to be sure we know how much we're inconveniencing him," Charlene agreed.

"He's spoiling our whole afternoon." And though she'd been happy about the new room just a second before, Lucy felt the tip of her nose tingle, a sure sign that she was about to cry. She laughed it off. "Look at me. I'm a total mess. We'd better hurry up and run our errands before I have a meltdown."

Charlene checked her watch and shook her head. "All the stores will be closed. It's siesta time."

"That depends on what you're looking for." This interruption came from the blond girl, who kept typing as she spoke. Her voice was crisp and distinctly American.

"Food. And ibuprofen," Charlene said. "I've got the mother of all headaches." She shut her eyes and tipped her head back.

"There's a pharmacy just a couple of blocks from here," the blond girl said. "And a grocery store. Both stay open all day. Are you two waiting for the computer? I'll be off soon. I'm just filing an entry on the Uffizi."

"An entry? What kind of entry?" Charlene's eyes opened.

"For the next edition of *Wanderlust: Europe.*"

"You write for *Wanderlust*? That's the guidebook we're using." Charlene sounded excited. It was almost as though they'd just discovered they were talking to a celebrity.

"Everyone uses *Wanderlust.*" The blond gave her head a shake and sent her bangs flying. This was more or less true; all over Europe, Lucy and Charlene had seen American backpackers poring over the paperback with its distinct orange cover, looking for a decent hostel or someplace to get a good but cheap meal.

"Do you get paid to write?" There was something like awe in Charlene's voice. Lucy, who wanted the girl to finish up and hand the computer over, bristled with annoyance.

"*Wanderlust* pays my travel expenses." She said this too casually, clearly trying to make it sound like she wasn't bragging. "Airfare, room, board."

"How on earth did you get a job like that?" Charlene asked.

The girl turned from the computer completely, launching into a speech about how important it is to know the right people. Lucy crossed and uncrossed her legs, trying not to show her growing impatience. Just beyond this room, its windows blocked by heavy drapes, Florence lay shimmering in the sun. When the girl started explaining how she'd been editor in chief at her school newspaper and had won some kind of journalism award, Lucy jumped to her feet, unable to sit still a minute longer.

"Why don't I go find that pharmacy and bring you back some ibuprofen?" she said brightly.

Charlene looked confused. "But what about writing to your parents?"

"Could you maybe drop them a line for me?" Lucy edged toward the door. "Just so my mom doesn't contact the American Embassy?"

Before Charlene could say another word, Lucy slipped from the room and burst through the lobby's glass double doors. On the fringes of the Piazza Santa Maria Novella, she blinked in the Italian sunshine. The square was empty but for a few stray tourists browsing at a souvenir kiosk and a couple splashing each other at the edge of a fountain. Lucy patted her pockets, but in her hurry to escape, she had left her map behind. *That's okay*, she told herself, unwilling to go back inside for even a second. *I'll find my way.* She stood for a long moment in the piazza, trying to decide which direction to take.

I can go anywhere I want, she realized, and the thought made her feel about a hundred pounds lighter, the way she felt whenever she shrugged off her heavy backpack. *For once I don't have to worry about what Charlene wants.* Three short weeks earlier, when the girls had touched down at Charles De Gaulle Airport in Paris, she'd been so thankful to have Charlene along. How would she have survived without Charlene, who could convert euros to dollars in her head, who spoke fluent French and knew how to decipher train schedules?

But getting around had grown easier. As the girls made their way from Paris to Zurich, from Interlaken to Salzburg, from Vienna to Munich, Lucy got better at reading maps and street signs in French and German. She learned how to make sense of exchange rates, and how to figure out what side of the street to stand on to catch a bus going in the right direction.

Even so, she'd been happy to have Charlene's company. The endless whirl of cities as glamorous as stage sets was made even better by having a friend to share it with. Together Charlene and Lucy had climbed mountains and bell towers to marvel over the views. They had traipsed through museums and sculpture gardens and hung out in courtyards with Australians, Brits, Swedes, Canadians, and Argentineans, swapping travel stories. In front of every major tourist site along the way they'd asked strangers to photograph them, arms draped around each other's shoulders, grinning matching grins.

What's changed between us? Lucy asked herself as she paused on the street corner, trying to decide which way to go next. Charlene had been so strange, so difficult, ever since they left Munich.

On a whim, Lucy chose a random street because she liked its name: La Via delle Belle Donne—the Street of the Beautiful Women. All but empty, the road was lined with small, pretty shops, giving her hope that a pharmacy would pop up in her path soon. But the street fed into Via della Spada, then Via degli Strozzi, and soon she seemed to be in a ritzy part of town, passing all sorts of upscale boutiques—Gucci, Armani, Pucci, and Prada—with no pharmacies or grocery stores in sight. Lucy slowed her pace, peeking into one window, then another, a smile playing on her lips. She was finally in Italy, the country she'd been most looking forward to, seeing as how she was Italian on her mother's side and had grown up listening to Frank Sinatra and *La traviata* and eating her mother's spaghetti Bolognese.

Up ahead, the buildings fell away, and Lucy's pulse quickened. Without meaning to, she'd made it almost to the Arno, the river she'd seen in so many pictures of Florence. Errands forgotten, she hurried toward it.

The Arno wound picturesquely into the distance, sparkling in the sun. Lucy lifted her sunglasses, wanting to see the scene's actual colors—the blue-brown of the river, the peach, gold, and cream of the city's buildings. She let a string of impatient motorbikes and taxis buzz past, then crossed the street to get even

21

closer, leaning against the stone wall for a better look. To her left was the Ponte Vecchio—Florence's famous old bridge. It wasn't terribly far away—just a few blocks, really. Despite how long she'd been gone, Lucy couldn't help wanting to see it up close.

As she hurried toward the bridge, a man so handsome he could have been a model crossed her path, a jacket slung over one shoulder and a smile on his lips. His mirrored sunglasses made it impossible to tell where he was looking, until he smiled right at her—a quick white dagger of a smile that made it clear he'd been looking at her the whole time.

Feeling quite unlike her usual self, Lucy smiled back and kept on grinning. In real life, she didn't usually turn heads. With her delicate, pale features, she could look pretty under the right conditions—made up for the stage or the prom—but most of the time Lucy thought of herself as ordinary. And yet she'd caught the stranger's eye. Maybe she looked the way she felt—exhilarated. Hungry for adventure. Though she knew she should finish her errands and get back to Charlene, Lucy was seized by the desire to keep walking.

What if I don't go back to the Bertolini? I could just disappear—lose myself in Florence. The thought gave her a delicious little shiver. She could go anywhere, pick a new name for herself, become a whole new person. She could learn Italian, apply for a job in a café, and never go home again. *I could be whoever I wanted to be. An actress, even.* The thought made Lucy's heart leap for a split second, until she remembered the disastrous audition that had ended her career—not to mention the promise she'd made to her father.

The Ponte Vecchio turned out to be a row of charming little

jewelry shops strung together along a wide bridge crowded with tourists. Lucy imagined what she would buy if money were no object. One bracelet in particular—a glittering string of topaz the color of the sky above the Arno—was the most gorgeous one she'd ever seen. And that was saying a lot, considering her father owned a chain of three jewelry stores.

Lucy knew what her father would say if he were here: *You have expensive taste.* It was what he said whenever she asked for an advance on her allowance. *You'd better study hard and get yourself a good job.* If he were with her now, he would remind her that all vacations have to end, that a person can't just flit around like a butterfly, following her heart.

Lucy loved her father, she really did. He had a temper and liked to get his way, but as long as she didn't cross him, he was a total sweetheart, bringing her carefully chosen presents from his business trips, his black eyes bright with pleasure at her reaction. But now, as Lucy caught her reflection in a jewelry store window—nose sunburned, hair wild, arms muscular from three weeks of the backpacking life—she wished that for once he would turn out to be wrong.

When Lucy returned to the Bertolini, she found Charlene sleeping on top of the covers, her lavender-scented satin eye mask blocking out the afternoon light. The new room *was* bigger and brighter than the old one had been. As quietly as she could, Lucy set her bags down, opened the window, and leaned out of it, drinking in the happy sounds of children playing soccer. At the base of a white obelisk sat a couple, their arms slung around each other's shoulders. From the window, Lucy could spy on their happiness, undetected, for as long as she wanted.

When she turned back around, Charlene was propped up on her elbows, eye mask in hand.

"I'm back!" Lucy said with forced cheer. "Look what I brought." She built a still life atop the bureau: soft cheese, a loaf of crusty bread, olives, cherries, and bottled water. "Supplies." She handed Charlene a bottle of water.

"You're so sweet." Charlene took a sip and settled back onto her pillow.

Lucy perched on top of her own bed, waiting to see what Charlene would say or do next. She supposed she should hang around while Charlene recovered from her headache, but what a long, dull night that would be! Cross-legged on her bed, Lucy ate cherries straight out of the bag. Like just about everything she'd eaten in Europe, they tasted shockingly fresh and vivid, like the best possible version of themselves. She had just made up her mind to take her long-postponed shower when Charlene spoke again.

"What should we do tomorrow?"

So Charlene really was in for the night. Lucy felt her spirits sink. "Isn't it your turn to choose?" she asked.

"That's okay. I know how excited you are to be in Florence."

Lucy rummaged in her daypack. *Aren't you excited to be here, too?* she almost asked. Lately, even when Charlene was trying to be nice, she found ways to get on Lucy's nerves. "I made a list of all the places we should go while we're here," Lucy said, pulling it out. "The Mercato Centrale. The Pitti Palace. The Boboli Gardens. Oh, and the Accademia. That's where Michelangelo's *David* statue is."

Charlene heaved herself back onto her elbows. "Ellen says we need a reservation to get into the Accademia. Otherwise we'll waste our whole day waiting in line."

Lucy blinked. "Ellen?"

"The girl who writes for *Wanderlust*. Remember? From the common room this afternoon?"

"Maybe she's wrong," Lucy said.

"Somehow I doubt it."

Lucy glanced back down at her list. "What about the Duomo? You know, the cathedral in all the pictures? We could climb to the top and look out over the whole city."

"I hate to break it to you, Lucy..."

"What does Ellen have against the Duomo?"

"That's another place with a long line. We'd have to get there by eight in the morning. Which I wouldn't mind, but I know how you like to sleep in."

"Great." Lucy felt like ripping her list into little pieces. "And what does Ellen recommend we do tomorrow?"

"She mentioned Santa Croce," Charlene said.

Lucy stared at her blankly.

"It's a medieval church, with all sorts of important art, plus the tombs of lots of famous Italians. Michelangelo, for one."

"Famous *dead* Italians?" Lucy said.

If Charlene heard the sarcasm in her voice, she didn't let on. "You know, Ellen is really helpful. She's a good connection to have.

25

Wouldn't it be great to write for *Wanderlust*? Then you could come back to Europe for free."

Remembering the B she'd gotten in her high school creative writing class, Lucy shrugged. Somehow she didn't think *Wanderlust* would be breaking her door down with plane tickets and cash anytime soon.

"They accept photographs, too," Charlene said.

Lucy turned away to hide her impatience. Charlene's photos always came out better than hers. "*You* should submit something."

"You should, too," Charlene said, but Lucy could tell she was just being polite.

After her shower, Lucy settled back onto her bed and stared up at the ceiling. It wasn't even dark out yet. From the piazza just beyond the window, voices wafted up, calling to one another in rapid Italian. Listening to them, feeling the seconds ebb away, Lucy once again felt restless. *My vacation is almost over,* she thought. *I traded away my future as an actor for it, and soon it will be in the past.* She reached over to the nightstand for her copy of *Wanderlust,* managing to knock it to the floor with a noisy *thwap.*

Charlene sighed. "How can you not be tired?"

"I honestly don't know." Then, as though the idea had just occurred to her, she added, "Maybe I should go out for another walk? So you can get some peace and quiet."

"You wouldn't mind?" Charlene asked.

"Not at all." And as though she'd been granted a leave from prison, Lucy dressed quickly, ducked out into the hallway, and hurried down the stairs, not knowing where she was going but wanting to get there as soon as possible.

26

The lobby was quiet. On her way out, Lucy caught sight of someone familiar behind the check-in desk. It was Nello's roommate, still with his earbuds in, restlessly tapping the desktop as if it were a piano keyboard. When he caught sight of her his fingers froze and he looked at her expectantly, as though he hoped she might say hello. Should she?

Lucy recalled how unfriendly he'd been just a few hours earlier. *Too bad he's such a jerk,* she thought, taking note again of his dark-lashed eyes and glossy hair. Flustered, she looked down at the map in her hands. Before things could get any more awkward, she darted out through the glass double doors into the night.

III

—◆◆◆—

The next morning, after the best night's sleep they'd had in weeks, Lucy and Charlene felt a lot less cranky. They lingered over breakfast in the Bertolini's dining room—croissants, Nutella, and cup after cup of coffee with warm milk—then headed up Via de' Tornabuoni, toward Santa Croce and their first full day of sightseeing in Florence. The morning air cool on her skin, Lucy felt hopeful and energized, even as she struggled to keep pace with her long-legged friend.

"So what did you do last night after I passed out?" Charlene asked when they paused on a street corner, waiting for the light to change. Her pink T-shirt picked up the hint of sunburn on the bridge of her nose.

"Not much," Lucy said. "I just kind of wandered." Being out in Florence again had made her feel calmer. She'd returned to the Arno, crisscrossed its bridges, and gazed into store windows, admiring the displays of handmade paper and leather jackets. Every so often, when her feet began to ache, she would find a place to sit and watch the world pass by—the tourists with their complicated cameras, the families, the young couples hanging on to each other's hands.

When it arrived, the sunset—orange with streaks of red—was so beautiful it made her heart ache. She found herself longing for someone, anyone, to watch it with. After dark she'd wandered back to the Bertolini, hoping to find fellow travelers to hang out with, but the common area was empty and the front desk had shut down for the night. Later, as she listened in the dark to Charlene's steady breathing, she couldn't shake the feeling that somewhere nearby, something exciting was happening without her.

"There's one thing I'd absolutely love to do tonight," she told Charlene. "Let's find a nightclub and go dancing."

Charlene didn't answer.

"I know clubbing's not your thing," Lucy added. They'd had this conversation before, more than once. Charlene hated loud music and having to shout in order to make small talk. She didn't like dancing, or crowds, or being around drunk people. But Lucy, who had never even been to a club, couldn't help wanting to try it at least once. And when would she ever get another chance to go to a real European nightclub? Probably never. "It would just be one time. We can leave right away if you hate it."

"I already know I'll hate it," Charlene said.

"We might even meet some guys. Wouldn't that be nice?" For a second, Lucy thought Charlene would have to agree with her, at least on this one small count. Along the way they'd met and hung out with so many cute guys that they'd come up with a name for the experience: *vacation flirtation*. And Charlene had seemed to enjoy flirting every bit as much as Lucy had.

So Lucy was shocked to see Charlene grimace. "I'm really not in the mood."

"Since when?"

Charlene didn't respond.

Then Lucy remembered the last time she'd seen a genuine smile on her friend's face: the day before yesterday. The two of them had been wandering the streets of Munich with Simon, an easygoing, jokey Brit, Charlene's most recent vacation flirtation. In fact, he'd been more of a full-fledged romance, or so it had seemed from the outside. Lucy, whose own flirtations had never advanced even so far as a first kiss, had been a little jealous, but also happy to see her friend having so much fun.

Lucy and Charlene had met Simon at the Tent, a hostel made up of white circus tents strung together by party lights. When they arrived, they found a huge crackling bonfire surrounded by backpackers. One strummed a guitar, playing an old Cat Stevens song, while the others sang along. Lucy's heart had warmed at the sight. Staying at the Tent had been her idea. She'd read about the place online; travelers who had stayed there raved about how funky and colorful it was. Though funky wasn't exactly Charlene's style, Lucy somehow had convinced her to give the place a try. As they scouted out a quiet spot in the main tent, Charlene was ominously quiet. *She doesn't like it*, Lucy thought. *She'll have a miserable time and it will be all my fault.*

But just as they were spreading their bedrolls out, a tall, red-headed guy on the next mat over turned to introduce himself. "I'm Simon," he'd said, holding out a big, warm hand for each of them to shake. "Welcome to the Tent."

"Are you the official greeting committee?" Charlene had asked with a sultry smile. Given Charlene's usual businesslike manner, it had surprised Lucy to learn what a good flirt she could be when she felt like it. With her long legs and sleek blond hair, she turned heads everywhere they went, a fact Lucy tried hard not to resent.

"At your service." Simon had scooched his bedroll closer to theirs, and from that point on he'd been their sightseeing buddy. The next morning he'd taken them to Marienplatz to see the famous glockenspiel strike the hour. They stood in the crowd, oohing and aahing while the bell tower's life-size knights jousted, and he'd seemed to enjoy it as much as they did, even though he'd already seen the show more than once. While he was friendly with both of them, by lunchtime it was pretty clear that he and Charlene were clicking.

"You two go have lunch together," Lucy said when Simon went off to buy them each a water. "I don't mind seeing Munich by myself."

"What?" Charlene asked, her eyes sparkling in a way Lucy hadn't seen before. "I would never desert you."

"I wouldn't feel deserted," Lucy had replied, but Charlene waved her off. Simon squired the two of them all over Munich and then to dinner, and though he and Charlene tried to include her in their conversation, Lucy felt more and more like a third wheel. That night at the Tent, she excused herself and wandered over to the campfire sing-along. When she got back, she found Simon's bedroll parked side by side with Charlene's, the two of them cuddling under a single blanket.

"Simon wants us to have more time together," Charlene confessed to Lucy the next morning as they waited in line for a shower.

"But we're leaving for Italy tomorrow night."

"That's what I told him," Charlene said.

"I know! He could come with us to Florence," Lucy offered after a moment's consideration. "How romantic would that be?"

"No." Charlene looked uncomfortable. "He wants us to be *alone* together."

"Oh," Lucy said.

"He's leaving tomorrow for Mittenwald, where some friends of his have a house. They're out of the country and they said he could use it." She delivered this information quickly, as though it were somehow embarrassing.

"Oh," Lucy said again. She thought a moment. "You said yes, I hope."

Charlene's nostrils flared. "Of course not."

"But you *like* him." Lucy gaped at her friend. "This is your chance to have a real vacation romance!"

"We've only just met," Charlene said. "I hardly know him."

"That's what a vacation romance *is*," Lucy said.

"Besides, what kind of friend would I be if I just left you?"

Lucy shuffled her feet, her flip-flops squeaking on the bathhouse floor. "I would be fine," she said. "We could meet up later in Rome. Or even at the airport."

Charlene didn't reply.

"In your shoes, I would go," Lucy said.

"You're just saying that," Charlene said. "I know for a fact you wouldn't."

"But I absolutely would."

Charlene's mouth twisted. "Well, I'm not going to ditch you. Especially not for some guy I'll never see again after we fly home."

"You might see him again," Lucy said. "You never know. Maybe he'll come to Philadelphia someday. Or you could do a semester in London."

"Oh, Lucy." Charlene's tone implied that Lucy was being naïve and impractical. And Lucy, whose father often accused her of being both, looked away, annoyed. *I tried*, she thought as she showered in water that could have been a lot warmer. The rest of that day, Lucy tagged along after Simon and Charlene, looking politely away as they held hands, and even as they made out in the English Garden. *Get a room, you two*, she was tempted to say, but she figured Charlene probably wouldn't appreciate the joke.

The next morning at the train station, Lucy guarded Simon's luggage as he and Charlene shared a long good-bye kiss. After the train pulled away, Simon waving out the window like a hero in a black-and-white movie, Charlene refused to talk any more about him. Instead, she spent the long walk back to the Tent hatching her plan to book a private room at the Bertolini.

Remembering all this, Lucy slowed to a stop on the crowded sidewalk. "Are you upset about Simon?"

"What?" Charlene looked shocked. "No."

"Because you've been..." Lucy searched for an inoffensive word. "Different. Ever since he left for Mittenwald."

34

"Different?" Charlene asked, hands on her hips.

Bitchy, Lucy thought. "Less happy," she said.

"I've been *sleep deprived*," Charlene said. "And homesick."

"You've been homesick?" Lucy asked. Charlene had never seemed homesick before. "Are you sure this isn't about Simon?"

Charlene's nostrils quivered. "Stop trying to turn something little into some kind of big deal."

"I wasn't," Lucy said. "I just thought..." But she couldn't seem to finish the thought. "In your shoes..."

"You've never been in my shoes," Charlene said. Then, without warning, she stomped off, faster than Lucy could follow.

And Lucy, who had meant to be nice, stood for a long moment in the middle of the sidewalk while people flowed around her. By the time she reached the corner, Charlene had vanished, taking the street map with her.

Does she expect me to run after her? Lucy thought. *I never even wanted to go to Santa Croce in the first place.* For the first time on her trip, Lucy felt a bit homesick herself.

IV

───∞∞∞───

*B*ecause she couldn't stand alone on a street corner forever, Lucy picked a direction at random and took it. *I might as well do whatever makes me happy*, she told herself, though *happy* wasn't exactly the word for how she was feeling. Each time she reached a corner, she looked both ways and chose whichever direction looked more inviting. On Via del Corso, she paused before a boutique window of haute couture jumpsuits and imagined Charlene pacing in front of Santa Croce, looking at her watch and wondering when Lucy was going to catch up.

Before long, Lucy found herself in a piazza she hadn't seen before, with a massive stone archway on one side. Cafés lined the other sides. She lingered, watching a child run with a balloon, scattering pigeons into flight. A glint of mirrors caught her eye—the decorations on an oddly silent carousel. Its wooden horses were almost empty. Lucy fumbled for her camera. The piazza swirled, all light and heat and motion, on her screen. *I bet I'm having more fun than Charlene*, she told herself glumly.

Somewhere in the crowd, a street musician was singing and playing an acoustic guitar—a song Lucy vaguely recognized but couldn't name. She wandered in the direction of the music, taking snapshots as she went. As she approached, the song ended and another began—one she'd heard just a few weeks ago, back home on the radio in Philadelphia.

Lucy smiled for the first time that morning and moved in closer, stepping through the shifting crowd. Street musicians— buskers, Simon had called them—were one of the things she liked most about Europe. She had been drawn to the old man with the violin who had played on the Champs-Élysées in Paris, and to the Bolivian panpipe players and cellists she'd heard on the streets of Munich. How many times had she dug in her pocket for change only to have Charlene tug at her arm?

"They're begging," Charlene would say.

"They're working." And Lucy would toss a twenty- or fifty-cent piece in the violin case or nearby hat, even though Charlene had made her feel foolish for enjoying the show.

Today, though, Charlene wasn't there to spoil her fun, so Lucy drew closer to the source of the music. A smattering of people surrounded the young man with the guitar. She maneuvered her way through the crowd, hiding out near the back, then slipping a bit closer, her camera at the ready.

The singer had a warm, deep voice, and Lucy had to hold herself back from singing along. The song ended and she was

38

reaching into her pocket for loose change when the couple in front of her picked up their daypacks and slipped away. Nudging forward into their vacated place, Lucy lifted her camera. She got a shot or two as the musician bent to gather up a five-euro note somebody had flung at his feet. Dark, longish hair obscured his face. Just as she emerged from behind the camera, he straightened and caught her eye.

Shockingly, it was someone she knew. How could that be, in a city where she knew hardly anyone? From his expression, she could tell he recognized her, too. It was Jesse—Nello's roommate. He looked as surprised to see her as she was to see him.

"You," she said. She didn't mean to be rude, but that was the first word that popped into her mind.

"You," he replied. "How's your new room?"

Was this a reproach? She wasn't sure. "I like it," she said.

"Good." Then he smiled—a wary smile, but not at all sarcastic. He might not be her favorite person in the world, but bumping into him like this when she'd been arguing with Charlene made him feel, oddly enough, like an old friend.

Lucy dimpled in return. "The view's great," she added. "Thank you for trading with us." Bystanders were watching them now. Somehow she'd become part of Jesse's act.

"You're all by yourself?" Jesse scanned the crowd. "Where's your friend?"

"I lost her." But this wasn't the whole truth. "Or maybe she ditched me. I seem to be driving her crazy. Actually, it's mutual."

Jesse cocked his head to one side and looked at her intently, as though hoping she would say more. With his dark, long-lashed eyes and Roman nose, he really did look Italian; it hadn't been as stupid a mistake on Lucy's part as she'd feared.

Feeling shy, she changed the subject. "You're a street musician? I thought you worked at the hostel." Around them, the crowd was losing interest and moving away. "I'm sorry. I should let you play."

But he seemed in no hurry to go back to work. "I busk for fun. Not that the extra money isn't useful." He strummed his guitar and the chord shimmered through the square. "But I can take a break and help you find your friend."

Lucy felt the niceness of this offer spread through her like warmth. Had she read him wrong? "I'd rather stay lost," she said. "Please play another song."

So he did, a Nico Rathburn tune that just happened to be one of Lucy's favorites, and the crowd assembled again, a few of them coming up close to drop coins in Jesse's gig bag. When the song was over and the people started to disperse, Jesse began packing up his guitar. "Let's get out of here." He pocketed his earnings and slung the gig bag over his shoulder. "This heat is killing me. How about a gelato?"

Gelato was yet another thing Lucy adored about Europe. Here in Florence, every other storefront seemed to be a gelateria, with colorful mountains of ice cream—melon, coconut, strawberry, dark chocolate, hazelnut, pistachio, lemon—glistening inside glass cases, the perfect antidote to the torpor of late July. Lucy could have eaten it for breakfast, lunch, dinner, and dessert. "That would be wonderful."

Jesse led her down a narrow side street, straight to a gelateria. He ordered hazelnut and she ordered raspberry. Over her objections, he paid from his pocketful of coins. They sank down on the stone steps in front of yet another church and sat for a while in silence, both of them licking around the edges of their cones to keep rivers of melting gelato from streaking down their arms.

"Oh my God," Lucy said when her body temperature had cooled back to something like normal. "I'm starting to feel human again." She looked around. "Where are we, exactly?"

"I'm not sure, but we were just in Piazza della Repubblica." Jesse pointed back toward the square. "Were you looking for the Bertolini? When you bumped into me?"

"Not exactly. I was just...wandering. Without a map. Or a destination."

Jesse nodded, as though this were the most normal activity in the world.

Lucy found herself wanting to tell him her whole life story: how she'd given up on acting and this trip was her consolation prize, and how things had been going so terribly wrong with Charlene lately. "My trip's almost over," she said instead. "I wanted my time in Florence to be special. I mean, I love it here; I really do. But all I seem to be doing is wandering around in circles."

"Almost," Jesse said.

Lucy looked at him, perplexed.

"Your trip is *almost* over. Which means there's still time." He nudged her arm with his elbow. "What would you like to see?"

Lucy remembered the list she'd made and left behind, folded in her guidebook. "The Duomo." Again and again, she'd glimpsed the cathedral—the famous one in all the photos of Florence—its grand red dome appearing at the ends of streets, impressive even

41

from a distance. She wanted more than anything to see it up close, to climb up to its roof and look out over the city. "But Charlene says the line's super long."

"So?" Jesse asked. "I don't know about you, but I've got nothing but time."

Lucy followed Jesse on a winding tour through the streets of Florence to the Piazza del Duomo, where the cathedral rose abruptly into the air before them, enormous and ornate as a wedding cake, its white exterior frosted with pink and green. They wandered along its outer walls, weaving through the crowd to the end of the line. Within seconds, a batch of tourists glommed on, and soon the line behind them snaked out of sight. Nearby, a street artist drew a portrait of two little blond boys, who wriggled and bounced despite their parents exhorting them to stand still. A bicyclist rang his bell and cut through the piazza, scattering pedestrians and pigeons.

"It will be worth the wait," Jesse said, unstrapping the gig bag from his shoulder and setting it down beside his feet.

"You've done this before?" Lucy shaded her eyes with her hand to see him better in the sharp sunlight.

Jesse nodded. "The first thing I do when I'm in a new city is climb to the highest point. To get a sense of where I'm at." His slight New Jersey accent reminded Lucy of home.

"How long have you been traveling?" she asked.

"Just over a year." Jesse lowered himself to the pavement, and Lucy followed suit.

"A year," she repeated, trying to fathom such a thing. "Has it been amazing?"

"Mostly."

Lucy waited for him to say more. When he didn't, she tried to draw him out. "Where have you been so far?"

"I flew into Amsterdam and bummed around there for a while. Prague, Berlin, Munich, Vienna. But then I got to Rome and fell in love."

"In love?" Lucy asked. "Who with?"

"Italy," Jesse said. "I decided I had to stay. I found a job in a hostel in Verona. On my days off, I would hop a train and see someplace new. Then I moved on to Florence, and here we are."

Lucy hugged her knees. "That sounds so wonderful. Where will you go next?"

Jesse shrugged.

"When will you go home?"

He thought a moment before speaking. "I don't have plans."

No plans? Lucy thought. The idea struck her as peculiar—how could a person not have plans?—but also enticing. Though the Jersey Shore wasn't all that far from her hometown, in some ways he was the most exotic person she'd ever spoken to.

The line into the Duomo seemed to be moving pretty quickly; every so often she and Jesse inched forward. When they ran out of things to say to each other, he drummed on his knees, humming softly to himself, as though any minute without music was a wasted minute. Somehow the silence felt more companionable than awkward. When he wasn't looking in her direction, she stole a closer look at his strong nose, his full lips, his long and graceful hands. When she felt his gaze returning to her, she glanced away. Lucy had always been a little shy and clumsy around boys she found attractive. You'd think she would know how to fake confidence with guys in real life the way she could onstage, but no; offstage she blushed and fumbled and could never manage to be anything other than herself.

But something about Jesse made her feel at ease. When she dared to look at him again, she caught him watching her. Then she couldn't help smiling, and he grinned back, bashful in a way good-looking guys usually aren't. Wordlessly, he held out his half-full bottle of San Pellegrino, and Lucy, who had drained her own water a while back, accepted it gratefully.

Before long, they entered the dimly lit basilica. The climb to the roof was steep, the circular stairway becoming increasingly narrow the higher they climbed, the air stuffy to the point of claustrophobia. Lucy counted the steps as she climbed, but lost track at 286. Just when she thought she couldn't take another step, she and Jesse reached the top. Gasping for air, Lucy stepped out onto the observation deck and was overcome by a mixture of dizziness and joy. The building's red-tiled dome curved steeply away beneath her feet, the city streets far and tiny below. Lucy clutched the low metal fence that stood between her and certain death, looking down at the swarm of tiny tourists in the piazza.

"Not bad, right?" Jesse asked, the corners of his lips turned up in a mischievous smile.

"I can't believe I almost missed this."

From where Lucy stood, she could see all of Florence—its

labyrinth of red-tiled roofs stretching out in all directions and, beyond that, a carpet of rolling fields, and still farther, the pale blue hills of Tuscany meeting the bright sky. A crisp breeze lifted her hair from her shoulders, whipping it into her face. Lucy released her death grip on the fence to dig out her camera, though she knew no picture would capture the sweep and the beauty of what she was seeing. Then she let Jesse take *her* picture, posed in front of that breathtaking landscape.

"You ready to brave the stairs again?" Jesse hoisted his gig bag to his shoulder.

But Lucy wasn't ready. They lingered a while longer, drinking in the view, before starting back downstairs to solid earth.

Back at the hostel, Lucy found Charlene sitting cross-legged in a chair by the window. A paperback lay unread on the table beside her as though she'd been watching the door, waiting for Lucy to come through it.

She exhaled sharply at the sight of Lucy. "Oh my God. Where have you been? I was just about to call your parents and break the news that I'd lost you."

Lucy, who'd been dreading this moment, stood awkwardly in the doorway with no idea what to say.

"I waited in front of Santa Croce for an hour," Charlene said. "I can't believe you blew me off like that."

"*I* blew *you* off?" Lucy stepped in and shut the door behind her, a little too hard. "You left *me* in the dust."

"You knew where I was going." Charlene sounded exasperated. "Didn't you even think to come find me?"

"You took the map with you." Lucy slipped her money pouch from around her neck and dropped it onto the bed. "Besides, maybe I didn't feel like chasing you down the street."

Apparently unable to come up with a retort, Charlene reached for her book and opened it in front of her face.

"I'm going to take a shower." Feeling as though she'd won that last round, Lucy grabbed a towel and a change of clothes, then locked herself in the bathroom, letting the water wash away the city dust and sweat.

When she came back out, Charlene hadn't moved. "You're right," she told Lucy in a small, clenched voice. "I shouldn't have left you like that."

Lucy unwrapped the towel from her hair and slung it over the windowsill to dry, all the while trying to come up with a response. "It doesn't matter," she finally said, matching her tone to Charlene's. "I had an okay day without you." In fact, the day had turned out much better than okay, but she didn't feel like letting Charlene off the hook just yet.

To Lucy's surprise, Charlene dropped the paperback and burst into tears. Alarmed, Lucy ran to her side. She'd never seen her friend cry before. "What is it? What's wrong?"

Charlene buried her face in her hands and sniffed, the tear storm gone as quickly as it had rolled in. "It's nothing," she said, then dug in her bag for the pack of tissues she always kept handy.

Lucy sat down on the edge of the bed. "I can see it's *something*."

Charlene blew her nose. "I don't mean to be so horrible to

46

you," she said in a small voice. "You've been so nice, taking me on this trip. Putting up with my moods." She pulled out another tissue and meticulously wiped her eyes. "Even offering to let me go off to Mittenwald with Simon."

"Is he why you're so upset?" Lucy asked, pretty sure that she knew the answer.

But Charlene pursed her lips. "No," she said. "That was no big deal."

"You know, it's still not too late," Lucy said. "You've got his cell-phone number, right? You could catch up with him at his friends' house, and then meet me in Rome for our flight out."

"Of course it's too late. How pathetic would it look if I chased him all the way to Germany?"

"He invited you," Lucy insisted. "You wouldn't look pathetic."

"I'd *feel* pathetic." Charlene gathered up her tissues and crumpled them in her hand. "Besides, by now he's probably moved on to some other girl."

"I doubt it," Lucy told her. "He really seemed to like you."

"It was just a fling, and now it's over." Charlene crossed the room to where the wastebasket stood and dropped her tissues in. "Slam dunk," she said, laughing a little too noisily for the occasion. Then she looked over at Lucy. "Oh, well. Thanks for listening. You're great, you know that?"

Was the conversation really over? Lucy watched as Charlene bustled around the room, setting out a change of clothes. "I'm tired of wearing the same five shirts," Charlene declared. She held one up to her nose. "No matter how hard I scrub, nothing smells clean." Then she looked over at Lucy. "Your hair's drying all crazy."

Though nothing between them seemed truly settled, Lucy got up to examine herself in the mirror. The sight of her disheveled hair brought back the memory of the wind whipping it as she stood beside Jesse on top of the Duomo. She sighed happily and reached for a hair elastic.

"We'll go someplace fun tonight," Charlene said. "To make up for what a pain in the ass I've been today."

Feeling generous, Lucy turned back to Charlene. "You've been fine," she told her friend. "No worries, okay?"

They spent the evening popping in and out of boutiques on the Via de' Tornabuoni, trying on clothes they couldn't afford and spraying themselves with perfume testers. Charlene's good mood lasted through dinner, a shared pizza at a nice outdoor café in Piazza Santo Spirito. Still, Lucy answered warily when Charlene asked where she'd gone that morning. Lucy described wandering around in Piazza della Repubblica, taking pictures of the carousel and the children playing in the square. She told Charlene about the view from the top of the Duomo—how breathtaking it had been. But she didn't mention Jesse. She was careful to say *I* when it would have been more honest to say *we*. And when Charlene apologized again for leaving Lucy to wander around all by herself, Lucy didn't correct her.

Over dessert—panna cotta with blueberry sauce—Lucy wondered why she was keeping Jesse a secret. There was nothing all that unusual about spending the day with him, was there? *You're being ridiculous*, she told herself. *It's no big deal. Just tell her. She won't care.* More than once she opened her mouth to speak, but then shut it again.

"You're quiet tonight," Charlene finally said. "Is everything okay?"

"Everything's fine." Lucy pushed away her plate with its last half bite of dessert. "I'm just glad we're friends again."

Charlene leaned back in her chair, looking more relaxed than she had in days. "We never weren't friends," she said, patting down a single strand of golden hair that had gone astray.

V

‌———∞∞∞———

The next morning, Lucy looked around the Bertolini's small, sunlit dining room to see if Jesse was on duty. A woman in a white smock was cleaning the tables and refilling the serving trays. Equal parts disappointed and relieved, Lucy sat down beside Charlene. She was midway through her second mug of coffee when she felt a presence just behind her.

"Hey," a familiar voice said.

Lucy's stomach did a flip-flop. She turned in her chair to find Jesse smiling down at her. Across the table, Charlene blinked up at Jesse as if trying to place him.

"Hey." Lucy patted the empty chair beside her.

"I can't. I'm working," Jesse said. "But I get off at noon. What's your plan for the day?"

Lucy glanced over at Charlene again and then looked away,

flustered. "We were just talking about that," she said. "We might go see the Boboli Gardens this morning, then maybe we'll visit the Mercato Centrale."

"The Boboli's one of my favorites," Jesse said. "Great place for a picnic. Maybe I could meet up with you there. After that, we could check out the market together. How does that sound?"

Lucy could feel a smile spread across her face. "Perfect." She dared another look at Charlene. "As long as you don't mind."

Charlene paused a heartbeat too long before replying. "Sure. Of course." When Jesse was barely out of earshot, she asked, "What was *that* about? Just yesterday you said he was the rudest person you'd ever met."

"Shhh!" Lucy checked over her shoulder to make sure Jesse hadn't heard. "That was *two days* ago. Anyway, I was wrong. He's nice, actually. If you just give him a chance."

Charlene made a face.

"He is! I bumped into him yesterday. He helped me get back to the Bertolini." Aware that she was leaving out the part about spending half the day with Jesse, Lucy tried changing the subject. "You want some more fruit? We could smuggle it out in our pockets for later."

"And now we're going to hang out with him all day?" Charlene asked.

"You didn't have to say yes."

"Of course I had to. You put me on the spot. I wasn't going to say no right to his face." Charlene frowned at her empty plate. "Despite how rude he was to us the other day."

"I think we misread him," Lucy said. "He had his earbuds in, remember? Maybe he couldn't really hear us...."

"Ohmygosh." Charlene stared at Lucy. "You *like* him."

Lucy looked around again to make sure nobody was listening. "I do," she hissed. "So what?"

Charlene didn't answer.

"I don't see why that's a problem," Lucy continued.

"It's not a problem," Charlene said. "No problem at all." Then she stood abruptly and walked away.

Lucy followed her out to the lobby and up the staircase. "Good," she said, a little louder than she meant to. "I'm glad we agree. It's not a problem."

"There's no reason you shouldn't hang out with someone you like," Charlene said over her shoulder.

"Right," Lucy said again. "So why are you acting all mad at me?"

"I'm not mad." Charlene fumbled her key in the lock, swearing softly. She flung the door open so hard it banged against the wall. "What makes you think I'm mad?"

When Jesse turned up at the Boboli Gardens—carrying grocery bags, a blanket, and his guitar—Lucy was tremendously relieved to see him. By the time they'd left the Bertolini, Charlene had calmed down. In fact, she was working hard to be friendly and nice, walking extra slowly so Lucy didn't have to hurry to keep up, and pointing out shoes and dresses Lucy might like in the store windows they passed. All of which made Lucy feel like she had to be super polite, too. Before long, her cheeks started to hurt from all the fake smiling she was doing.

But Charlene's mood soured when she learned that entry to the Boboli Gardens wasn't free. Though she handed over ten euros to the guard, Lucy could tell she was miffed. They wandered past the garden's statues and fountains without saying much of anything to each other.

So Jesse—with his hair ruffled from the walk across town— was a welcome sight, to Lucy at least. "You brought your guitar," she observed, taking one of the bags from him.

"Everywhere I go," he said. "Let me show you my favorite spot for a picnic." He led them along a winding path to a shady spot in a grove of pine trees, spread his blanket among the fragrant needles, and motioned for them to sit. Then he unpacked the grocery bags, laying out soft cheese, crusty bread, artichoke hearts, apricots, and prosciutto.

"How much do we owe you?" Charlene reached for her money belt.

"My treat." Jesse joined them on the blanket. "Here." He handed a Swiss Army knife to Charlene, who looked at him blankly. "To spread the cheese," he said. "You first."

"Oh. Thanks." Charlene took the knife gingerly, as though it might have germs, and Lucy shot Jesse a quick apologetic look. He wasn't smiling, but she was pretty sure she saw a sparkle in his eyes.

Luckily, Charlene seemed not to notice. While they ate, she

asked Jesse the usual questions—how long he'd been traveling, where he'd been so far, when he would fly back to the States.

"I don't know," he replied to that last question.

"You don't know?" Charlene frowned.

"I don't believe in making plans," he said, biting into an apricot.

"I'm so jealous you've been over here for a whole year," Lucy said quickly, trying to create a distraction before Charlene could say something cutting. "If I tried that, my parents would flip out."

"Mine aren't exactly thrilled," Jesse said. "But it's my life." He took a big swig of water, then offered the bottle to Lucy. "They wanted me to go to college, but I told them not to waste their money. They still don't get it. Not everybody needs to go to school. There are other ways to learn about the world."

"I guess Lucy told you her story already," Charlene chimed in. "About how we came to be on this trip."

Lucy shot Charlene a warning look. After hearing how Jesse had stood up to his parents, the last thing she wanted was for him to know she'd bargained away her future. "Oh, it's no big deal."

"It's a very big deal," Charlene said. "Lucy's a talented actress."

"Not really." Lucy felt her cheeks tingle, a sure sign she was blushing. "You've never even seen me act."

"She's way too modest. My mom went to one of your plays, remember?"

Lucy didn't, but she nodded anyway.

"She raved about you for weeks. This was a while back, before we were friends." Charlene focused on Jesse again. "Lucy can sing, too."

Lucy felt her face go an even deeper shade of red. She looked away, up into the shifting pine boughs, off into the distance—anywhere but at Jesse—as Charlene filled him in. *Will he think I'm a sellout?* Lucy wondered. *Compared with him, maybe I am.*

Jesse's response set her at ease. "I'm sure you had your reasons," he told Lucy, his voice soft, as though it were just the two of them on the blanket.

"I did." Lucy's voice trembled as she spoke.

"Of course she did," Charlene said. "She knows college is going to be the best time of her life. Maybe that's a cliché, but it's true."

"No." Lucy's voice rose. "That's not why."

"Why, then?" Charlene asked.

But Lucy didn't want to say. That disastrous audition had been the most embarrassing moment of her life. Just as she'd stepped onstage, her father's words—*Odds are that Lucy will fail*—had rushed back to her like a sucker punch, and the monologue she'd spent hours memorizing had vanished from her mind. She'd stumbled off the stage, embarrassed and miserable.

Lucy really didn't want to tell Jesse any of this, but then again, she didn't want him thinking she was some obedient little Goody Two-shoes. So she gave him the abridged version. "I had a bad audition. I froze."

"A little stage fright's normal." He rubbed the palms of his hands on his knees. "Anyone who's serious about performing gets it."

"This was way more than a little stage fright." Lucy dared a glance at him. "I don't ever want to feel that way again."

Jesse didn't reply.

"Well, anyway," Charlene said brightly, "that's how we got to be here in Europe."

"I'm glad you're here," Jesse said, and from the tone of his voice, Lucy knew he was talking to her, not Charlene.

"Me, too," she said, hardly daring to meet his eyes.

Charlene's voice broke in on their moment. "So, Jesse, are you going to play for us?"

"He's eating," Lucy protested, though Jesse had barely touched the bread and cheese he'd brought.

"I don't mind." He reached for his guitar. "I've been working on something." He began to strum. "I haven't finished the words yet."

"It's pretty," Lucy told him, and she wasn't just being polite. Though the tune was up-tempo, the chord progression was bittersweet. Lucy allowed herself a small shiver and thought how she would miss this moment when it was over.

Jesse smiled and kept playing.

Before long, though, Charlene interrupted him. "Doesn't that look like Ellen?" She pointed up the path at a blond girl in a sunhat.

It took Lucy a few seconds to remember who Ellen was. "Oh. Yeah. I guess so."

Charlene got to her feet and waved. "Ellen! Over here."

Ellen waved back, hurrying in their direction. "Small world!" She looked from Charlene to Lucy to Jesse, an amused smile playing on her lips, and Lucy got the feeling that Charlene had invited Ellen to barge in on their picnic.

"Want to join us?" Charlene asked. "We've got enough food for a small army."

"I'm on my way to the Pitti Palace to do some research," Ellen said. "Have you guys made it there yet? I've got some extra passes."

"That sounds fantastic," Charlene said. "The heat out here is melting my brain. What do you say?" She looked expectantly at Lucy.

Heat or not, Lucy couldn't think of anywhere she would rather be than on a blanket in the Boboli Gardens, listening to Jesse play his guitar. "You go with Ellen," she said. "Have fun. I'll see you back at the Bertolini."

Was it Lucy's imagination, or did Charlene look hurt? She was gone before Lucy could decide. And anyway, Lucy had other, happier things on her mind. She listened as Jesse played the rest of his song. Might he have been thinking of her as he wrote it? At just that moment, anything seemed possible.

The rest of the afternoon passed in a flash. When he tired of playing, Jesse stretched out on the blanket to take a nap and patted his taut stomach, inviting Lucy to use it as a pillow. Delighted, she took him up on the offer. She shut her eyes, lulled by the oceanic rhythm of his breath and by his scent, which, despite the heat, was clean and already familiar. Though she only meant to pretend to sleep, she must have dozed off. When Jesse stirred at last, she was surprised to find the sun lower in the sky.

Lucy sat up, and Jesse checked his wristwatch.

"I have to get back to the Bert," he told her. "I'm supposed to work the front desk from four to ten."

"That's okay," Lucy said, though she was sorry their day together had to end.

"Want to hang out tomorrow?" he asked. "I'm free after breakfast."

Lucy hesitated. She could just imagine what Charlene would say. But Charlene had been in such a hurry to get away with Ellen; maybe she wouldn't mind. "Okay."

"We can go anywhere," Jesse said. "What haven't you seen?"

Lucy thought of her list of museums, monuments, and churches, more than she could ever get through in the little time she had left. Then a smile spread across her face. "Let's go somewhere that isn't in the guidebooks."

"Ah," Jesse said, thinking for a moment. "I have an idea."

"You aren't going to tell me where we're going?"

Jesse shook his head, his dark eyes amused. "No," he said. "I hope that's okay."

Lucy brushed a few stray pine needles from her T-shirt. The thought of having another day with Jesse, of his planning a surprise for her, made her happier than she cared to reveal. "Sure, it's okay." She tried to sound casual.

"Then it's a date."

VI

~~~

The next morning Lucy woke earlier than usual and pondered her drawer full of rumpled clothes. How nice it would be to have something brand-new to wear on her day out with Jesse. "A date," he had called it, but had he really meant it?

Lucy finally settled on a periwinkle-blue tank top and the iolite earrings her father had given her as a sixteenth-birthday present. She put on mascara and fiddled with her hair for a long time, putting it up in a ponytail and then changing her mind and taking it down. Her curls—wild, but for once not out of control—tumbled around her shoulders. *Not too bad, considering,* Lucy thought as she checked her smile in the mirror one last time.

In a strange role reversal, Charlene was still in bed, asleep—or pretending to be—when Lucy slipped out of the room. Lucy was relieved; things hadn't gone so well between them the night before, when she'd broken the news about her date with Jesse. Minutes earlier, Charlene had been recounting the great time she'd had with Ellen at the Pitti Palace, but suddenly her voice turned to acid. "You're going to leave me to wander around by myself all day tomorrow? Doesn't that break the first rule of friendship?"

Lucy set down her fork. "There are rules?"

"Rule number one is that you don't abandon your friends just because some guy comes along."

"He's not just *some guy*." Lucy's cheeks grew hot.

"That's two days in a row," Charlene said.

"I didn't abandon you today. You're the one who took off."

"Oh, please. I could tell you didn't want me around." Charlene speared a meatball with unnecessary force. "Admit you were glad when I left."

"I was not," Lucy lied. "Anyway, you can hang out with Ellen tomorrow."

"She has another deadline," Charlene said.

Lucy hesitated. "Or you could come out with me and Jesse."

"No." Charlene frowned down into her coffee. "You two want to be alone together. Just go."

Though she'd gotten what she wanted, Lucy couldn't help feeling bad. "It's only one day," she mumbled.

Charlene pushed her nearly untouched plate aside. "I'm full," she said.

"Already?" Lucy asked, though her own appetite had pretty much disappeared as well.

After a long silence, Charlene spoke again. "I hope you haven't made plans for Tuesday."

Lucy looked blankly at her. It was easy to lose track of the days.

"The day after tomorrow?" Charlene said. "Our last day in Florence?"

"I haven't," Lucy said, a bit warily.

"Ellen wants to take us to Fiesole. It's this hillside town out in the Tuscan countryside. She says it's absolutely gorgeous. It will be our grand finale, before we leave for Rome."

"Oh," Lucy said, wondering what Jesse would be doing that day. She didn't want to think about leaving Florence, or about flying home to Philadelphia on Sunday.

"Could you at least promise to come with us?" Charlene's voice grew softer, more persuasive.

Feeling slightly guilty, Lucy gave her word. Now, too excited to eat breakfast, she killed time reading in Piazza Santa Maria Novella, trying not to think about grand finales and trains to Rome. At five minutes to ten, she wandered back to the Bertolini.

Jesse was waiting for her in the lobby, looking freshly scrubbed, his dark hair still damp. "Hey," he said.

"Hey," she said back.

He surprised her with a quick hug, as though they hadn't just seen each other the day before. Lucy inhaled deeply, taking in his clean, delicious smell. *Almond and mint*, she decided. "I've been wondering all morning where you're planning on taking me," she said.

Without a word, Jesse ducked behind the front desk and emerged with two motorcycle helmets, one under each arm.

Lucy's pulse sped up. She followed him out into the square,

then down the street to a row of parked motorbikes. He walked up to a silver-blue scooter and pulled a set of keys from his pocket.

"A Vespa? Like in *Roman Holiday*?" Lucy was simultaneously thrilled and terrified. "Is it yours?"

"I wish," Jesse said, straddling the seat. "It belongs to Nello, but it's ours for the day." He handed Lucy one of the helmets, strapped the other on, and backed the Vespa out into the street. A chorus of horns and what sounded like Italian curses immediately started up behind them. "Aren't you going to get on?"

Lucy thought of what her mother would say, if only she knew. Lucy had never been on a Vespa before, and she wasn't exactly a fan of high speed. "Is it safe?" A motorbike zipped past them on the narrow street, so close it blew her hair back.

"I'll be careful," Jesse promised, his voice muffled by his helmet. Lucy hesitated, then thought of Audrey Hepburn zipping around Rome with Gregory Peck. She pulled on her helmet and slung a leg over the Vespa, leaning into Jesse's back. The engine's hum traveling through her whole frame, she wrapped her arms around his waist and shut her eyes tight. Several minutes went by before she dared to open them. By then they were zooming down a city street, people and store windows streaming past on both sides.

"Do we have to go so fast?" she yelped, her words drowned out by the engine. Jesse leaned into a turn and she gasped, putting all her concentration into hanging on. When they stopped for a red light, she allowed herself a look around. They were on the road that ran along the Arno; sunlight danced on its dark surface. Lucy clung to Jesse, adrenaline coursing through her veins. The view of the river had been beautiful before, but now it was thrilling.

After that, Lucy forced herself to keep her eyes open, to watch the city unfurl through the scratched plastic visor of her helmet. She didn't want to miss a thing.

Jesse took Lucy on the ultimate Vespa tour of Florence, tooling past many sights she recognized from the photos in *Wanderlust*. Then he parked near the Bargello, an imposing stone building that looked more like a fortress than a museum. "We won't have to stand in line," he said, tugging off his helmet. "A friend of mine works here. She'll get us in for free." The friend turned out to be Gianna, a fresh-faced girl with white streaks in her straight black hair. "We were in a band together. She plays bass," Jesse whispered to Lucy as Gianna waved them past the turnstiles.

"You're in a band?" Lucy asked.

"Used to be," Jesse said. "Then the rhythm guitarist went home to Scotland, and I decided to focus on my own music."

"Still," Lucy said, "it must have been so cool." The list of things to like about Jesse just kept getting longer. He'd been in a band, he could drive a Vespa, and he knew his way around the Bargello and could lead her straight to its highlights. Lucy's favorite object in the whole museum turned out to be a statue of David, but not the famous one by Michelangelo. This *David*, by Donatello, was naked except for a floppy hat and boots. Art students surrounded him, squinting up at him over their sketchpads, drawing furiously.

Lucy stepped around them, getting as close as she could. Light from the windows played across David's body, illuminating traces of gold leaf on his hat. She paused, surprised by the lush curve of David's bare behind, then hurried back around to the front, not wanting Jesse to catch her in the act of staring. But when she zoomed in for a closer look at David's face—his long nose and the full lips, his puzzled yet tender expression, she forgot about being watched. "He's amazing," she said, completely forgetting herself. Then she caught Jesse's eye and tried to sound more casual. "I wonder what he's thinking."

Jesse pointed. "He's feeling pretty proud of himself." She'd been so caught up in David's beauty that she hadn't noticed he was standing on Goliath's severed head.

"Ew." Lucy took a step back, and Jesse laughed.

"Seen enough?" he asked. "I wouldn't mind getting back outside."

"Me, either," Lucy said, and they burst from the quiet of the museum, back into the noise and bustle of Florence.

Their next stop was Piazza della Signoria, a sweeping square full of tourists. In the shade of the piazza's famous loggia—yet another sight Lucy recognized from her guidebook—Jesse sliced cheese and bread with his Swiss Army knife while she leaned back against the cool stone wall to people-watch.

"So what's your favorite place? Out of everywhere you've been?" she asked, digging into the fresh figs they'd picked up in the central market, a bustling indoor mall full of food stalls.

Jesse tipped his head back, deep in recollection. "Venice."

"Lucky," Lucy said. "I would love to see Venice."

"Why don't you go, then?"

"Not enough time." Lucy frowned. "What makes it your favorite place?"

"It's like another world. All the narrow, winding streets and canals. You can't help getting lost. But just when you're hot and exhausted and think you'll never find what you're looking for, you come to the end of a street, and turn a corner. Everything drops away and you're in Piazza San Marco, with the lagoon all silvery-green in front of you. A cool breeze wafts over you, and the architecture just blows you away."

This was the longest speech Lucy had heard Jesse give. She waited to see if he'd go on.

"I'll live there someday," he concluded. "Maybe I'll rent out an old, broken-down *palazzo* on the Grand Canal."

"Really?" Lucy felt a little pang. "So you're never planning on going back home? To the States, I mean?"

"Never is a long time," Jesse said.

That's not really an answer, Lucy thought, picking stray bread crumbs from her shorts. "You really don't ever want to go to college?" she asked finally.

"Probably not. I like making a living with my music."

"But you can't do that forever." Lucy regretted the words the moment they came out of her mouth. It was the kind of thing her father would have said.

"Why not?"

She considered the answers that popped into her head—that Jesse seemed more than smart enough to finish college, or that a person needed an education to get by—knowing how ordinary and boring she'd sound if she said them. Instead, she held out the box of figs toward him.

He fished in the box, took out a fig, inspected it. "I've been thinking," he said. "About what you told me the other day. That deal you made with your father."

Lucy felt her heart speed up. She looked down at her toes, peeping out of her sandals, her shell-pink pedicure gone dusty from the streets of Florence. "You have?"

Jesse returned the fig to the box as though it hadn't met his approval. "He made you trade away your whole future? In exchange for this trip you're on right now? That's just not cool."

Though she was still annoyed at her dad, it hurt to hear Jesse criticize him. "He's paying my tuition. I have to do what he wants."

Jesse didn't reply.

"The trip to Europe's just a bonus." She tried to keep her voice light, upbeat. "For doing what I was planning to do, anyway."

"But you wanted to act," Jesse said.

"I used to. I mean, I've been doing it forever...." Lucy felt herself growing increasingly flustered. "I loved being onstage."

Jesse waited for her to finish.

"Everybody always said I was pretty good at it. But it's so hard to break into the industry. There's so much competition in Hollywood, not to mention on Broadway." She heard herself channeling her father, but couldn't seem to stop. "I probably would have failed."

"How can you know that?"

"I just do," she said.

"Even if that's true"—Jesse rubbed his palms against his legs and squinted into the distance—"I'm not saying it is, but even if it is, you don't have to be a movie star. You can do what you love, anyway. Like me, for example. I'll probably never be famous. But I'm here, making music. Doing what makes me happy."

"And that's fine for you," Lucy said. She could hear she was losing the battle to keep her voice calm and light. "But if I can't be great, I don't see the point."

"So instead you're going to waste your life? Doing something you hate?"

"Waste my life?" Lucy felt like she'd been slapped. "Did you really just say that?"

Jesse looked embarrassed.

"Besides, maybe I won't hate being a business major. I haven't even tried it yet. For all I know, I might like it." Her forehead throbbed, and she felt it with the back of her hand. It was hot, of course. Even in the shade, everything here was hot. "I feel like you're judging me," she said, finally.

"I'm not," he said.

"Not everyone can just drop everything, buy a one-way ticket to Europe, and become a street musician."

"I'm not judging you," he said again. "It just bothers me to think you're..." His voice trailed off. "You know. Giving up on yourself."

Without warning, tears popped into Lucy's eyes. Embarrassed, she tried in vain to blink them away. She was remembering something she'd worked hard to forget: how she used to feel onstage, as everything fell away—everything but the make-believe world she'd stepped into. All that mattered was the audience

69

wanting to be entertained, holding its breath, waiting to laugh or cry or applaud. Waiting for her. Was Jesse right? Had she given up on her dreams too easily?

"Hey." Jesse sounded alarmed. "Did I do that? I'm sorry." He patted his pockets for tissues, apparently not finding any. "Here." He grabbed the bottom of his T-shirt and pulled it up toward her. "Use this."

Lucy wiped her eyes, smiling through her tears. "Even if you're right, even if I made a mistake..." Her voice came out wobbly. "It's too late. I promised."

"It's not too late." Jesse smoothed his T-shirt—now damp—back into place.

"It is." Lucy rubbed beneath her eyes, hoping her mascara wasn't running. "You don't know my dad."

They sat quietly side by side, watching tourists mill around and take photos of one another in front of the statues. Finally, Jesse broke the silence. "We should go."

"Where?"

But he still wasn't telling. "Our next stop. Someplace I think you'll like."

Wherever his mystery destination was, he didn't take Lucy straight there. First he took her to a sidewalk café for espresso, then to a bookstore where they browsed in the English section for a long time. Only after they'd watched the sun set over the city from Piazzale Michelangelo did he turn to her and, with mischief in his dark eyes, ask, "Are you ready for something that absolutely isn't in your guidebook?"

VII

After dark they pulled into a neighborhood Lucy hadn't seen yet, on an ordinary thoroughfare of restaurants and stores. "This is it?" she asked him.

Jesse didn't reply. Instead, he motioned for her to follow him down the street. In front of a mural—a colorful jungle scene in which lambs and tigers lay side by side—he stopped. "This is what you wanted me to see?" Lucy asked, hoping it wasn't. It was a nice mural, and a vivid contrast to the old stone buildings everywhere in Florence, but she'd been hoping for something a little more exciting.

"Look closer," Jesse said. Lucy scrutinized the bright leaves and flowers, the painted monkeys and jaguars, and then noticed a door-shaped crack in the wall. She looked at Jesse questioningly, her pulse quickening. He nodded, so she felt around until her hand landed on a doorknob camouflaged by paint. She gave it a turn.

The door opened into what looked like the dark lobby of a small theater, blue lights giving it an undersea glow. Though the room was empty, from behind a drawn velvet curtain Lucy could hear the deep throb of a bass, an electric guitar, and voices conferring—some kind of sound check. "What is this place?" she asked, excited. "Why isn't there a sign outside?" Before Jesse could answer, she connected the dots herself. "Is this an underground nightclub?" She glanced down at her dusty sandals, her shorts, and the rumpled tank top she'd been wearing all day. "I'm not dressed nicely enough," she said sadly.

"No worries," Jesse said. "We're casual here." Easy for him to say: In his jeans and black T-shirt, he would fit in wherever he went.

"But I'm a mess." Lucy reached up to assess the condition of her hair. "I have helmet head."

Jesse smiled. "Spoken like a girl who has no idea how beautiful she is," he said, and before she could absorb the fact that he'd said something so incredibly sweet, he'd turned and was heading through the velvet curtain.

Still reeling from his words, Lucy followed.

"What's this place called?" Lucy asked Jesse. They joined the edge of the crowd in a large room full of Italian hipsters waiting for the show to start. Despite what Jesse had said about the crowd being casual, she couldn't help feeling she stood out among all the skin-tight jeans, artfully draped scarves, dreadlocks, spiked hair, and biker gear.

"It doesn't have a name," Jesse told her.

"What about them?" Lucy pointed at the band. "Do they have a name?"

"It changes every week." Jesse folded his arms and inclined his head toward the bassist. "Recognize her?"

Lucy looked closer. It was Gianna, Jesse's friend from the Bargello, but she'd shed her museum-guard blazer in favor of black leggings, a long op-art T-shirt, and a fedora. "You know the band?" she asked, wide-eyed.

"So do you." Jesse pointed to the drummer, a baby-faced, curly-haired guy in prisoner stripes and severe blue glasses. Lucy looked closer and he turned into Nello, the desk clerk from the Bertolini.

"I do! I do know the band!"

"Let's get closer." Jesse hooked his arm through hers and started nudging through the crowd, pulling her toward the front row. Just as they got there, Nello spotted them. "It's my man, Jesse!" he called, playing a drumroll. "And you brought Lucy!"

Lucy waved, feeling like a celebrity despite her less-than-cool clothes.

"You coming onstage with us tonight?" Nello called to Jesse, whose only reply was a shrug.

"This is *your* band?" Lucy asked him.

"Not anymore," he told her. "Like I said, I dropped out to focus on my brilliant career as a street musician."

"But why?" Lucy asked.

"The money's better, if you can believe that. Besides, their new lead guitarist is a hotshot." He gestured toward a skinny-as-a-toothpick guy with his black hair gelled upright in a rooster comb. "They don't need me."

At that exact moment, Nello called from the stage again. "Get up here, my man," he shouted at Jesse.

"*Andiamo*, Jesse!" Gianna called, brandishing her bass in his direction. "Get onstage."

"See?" Lucy said. "They do need you. And I want to see you play."

"You've seen me play," he said.

"Not like this," she told him. She slipped behind him, grabbed both his shoulders, and pushed him toward the stage. "Please. Get up there." As cool as it was to be in the front row of a nightclub so underground it didn't even have a name, it would be even cooler to be the guest—possibly even the date—of a guy in the band.

He looked over his shoulder at her. "Don't go anywhere," he said.

Lucy grinned from ear to ear. "Where would I go?"

The band—whose current name Lucy never did catch—played American-style garage-band rock. Some of the songs seemed to be original, and some were covers Lucy recognized. Jesse played rhythm guitar and sang backup at first, but as the room filled up and the crowd grew rowdier, he began to switch places with the rooster-haired guitarist, taking over lead guitar and vocals every few songs. Lucy sang along with the songs she recognized, dancing as much as she could in the jam-packed crowd, which basically meant pogoing in place. Dark hair flowing as he played, face serious with concentration, Jesse was adorable. *And you're here with him,* she told herself, giddy with the adventure of it all. *You're with the band!*

Then came the moment when Jesse took the mike between songs. "I'd like to bring somebody up on the stage," he said, his gaze searching the front row and landing on her.

Lucy caught her breath. *This was a setup,* she realized, thinking back to their conversation in the Piazza della Signoria. *He's been planning this all along.* Panicked, she looked around for an escape route, determined to keep the promise she'd made to herself after that last audition: to stay away from stages of all kinds.

"Oh, no," she said, though she knew he couldn't actually hear her from the stage.

But Jesse was saying something into Nello's ear, then into Gianna's.

"Come on, Lucy," Nello said into the mike on his lapel. "Get up here."

"Lu-cy, Lu-cy, Lu-cy!" Gianna chimed in, and the crowd joined the chant, though of course they didn't have any idea who it was they were chanting for. What could Lucy do but climb the rickety steps onto the stage, legs trembling? Even back when she'd still considered herself an actress, when performing had been the one thing she truly loved to do, there had been a moment before each show when she'd been seized by stage fright. Each time she'd had to talk herself through it. She would close her eyes and tell herself, *You can do this.*

But ever since that terrible audition, she didn't believe she could. Not every time. Not anymore. Now Lucy stood in the shadows at the far end of the stage, unable to take another step forward.

"You can do this." Jesse took her hand and tugged her to center stage. "Share my mike."

"I don't know any of your songs," she hissed.

"You'll know this one. Trust me."

"What part do I take?" she asked.

"Just sing." He signaled to Nello, who counted off.

The band launched into the Beatles' "I Saw Her Standing There." Jesse was right; she did know the song. Her parents had just about every Beatles album ever recorded, and her mother had sung her to sleep with "Hey Jude" and "Norwegian Wood." But knowing the song wasn't the same as singing it for an audience. As the band played the familiar opening bars, Lucy considered bolting from the stage. When the time came to sing, though, she opened her mouth and her voice rang out, the way it was supposed to. "Well, she was just seventeen. You know what I mean...." She could hear her voice through the mike, blending with Jesse's. Below the stage, the crowd bobbed and sang along.

Lucy felt herself relax. As they launched into the bridge, she dared a glance over at Jesse and caught his eye. *This is fun*, she thought, surprised, though it hadn't been all that long since performing onstage had been the best thing in her whole life. When the song ended, the crowd erupted in applause, and she grabbed Jesse's hand and gave it a grateful squeeze. He squeezed back, his smile so bright it dazzled her.

"I knew you could do it," Jesse told her when the set was over. Clothes still damp from the heat of the stage, they'd slipped out of the club to a sidewalk café just down the street, the perfect vantage point for watching the hipsters stream past.

Lucy took a long sip from her lemon soda. "I wanted to kill you when you made me get onstage, but now I'm so glad you did," she admitted. "That was the most fun I've had in a long time. No... it was the most fun ever." Lucy had known every one of the songs the band played after she got onstage, and she had grown progressively more daring, taking the harmonies, her voice winding around Jesse's, lending the music an extra dimension.

"We sound good together," he said.

She grinned. She'd been thinking the same thing.

But the next words that came out of his mouth pulled her up short. "I really hope you'll reconsider that whole giving-up-your-stage-career thing."

Lucy set down her glass. "I don't think so." She looked away from him, at a couple that had just walked into her line of vision.

Tall, slender, and golden-skinned, they were matched bookends, the most beautiful couple she'd ever seen. Had they come from the show? Lucy wondered. She watched them wander past the sidewalk café, slow their pace, confer, and walk back to talk to the maître d'.

But Jesse persisted. "You've got an amazing voice," he said. "And you were so comfortable up there, once you started singing."

Lucy frowned. Why did everyone insist on trying to tell her what to do? Her parents. Charlene. And now Jesse. "Anyone can get up onstage and sing some Beatles songs...."

"Not anyone can sound good doing it."

"Not everyone should make it their life," she said. She lowered her voice as the maître d' seated the beautiful, happy couple at the table beside theirs. "Not everyone wants to," she whispered.

"I'm not talking about everyone," Jesse said, lowering his voice to match hers. "I'm talking about you."

"Please, don't." Lucy glanced over at the couple. "Let's talk about something else."

Instead they fell silent, watching the gorgeous couple slide their chairs side by side and share a single menu. Then he was kissing her, the menu forgotten.

Lucy tore her gaze from the couple and gaped at Jesse, trying to remember what she'd just been saying. He gaped back, just as distracted.

A moment later, it seemed the couple had forgotten they were in public. His hands were enmeshed in her blond hair; under the table, her long legs were entangled with his.

"PDA Italian-style," Jesse whispered, looking pointedly at a spot to the right of the couple.

Just then a cell phone rang, and the man broke from the embrace to answer it. The mood at the next table changed quickly. The girl listened to her boyfriend's half of the conversation, giving off waves of distress even Lucy could feel.

"Dinner and a show," Jesse whispered.

By the time the boyfriend pocketed his phone, the woman looked furious, her forehead wrinkled in frustration. She started yelling at him in rapid Italian, apparently not caring who was listening. Lucy could only catch a word here or there, so Jesse translated for her.

"That phone call was from another girl," he whispered to Lucy. "Now she's accusing him of cheating on her."

"Unreal." Lucy couldn't seem to stop watching the unfolding drama. Now the boyfriend was yelling back, a look of wounded disbelief on his face.

"He's saying she's crazy. He's always been faithful," Jesse whispered. "The girl on the phone is just a friend." Jesse paused to listen some more. "Now he says his girlfriend's jealousy is out of control and he just might cheat on her to teach her a lesson."

"Whoa," Lucy said.

"Tactical error," Jesse said.

The girl lunged at the boy, beating his chest with her fists. She screamed at him, calling him names—that much Lucy could tell without translation. He took her punches for a while, a look of pained forbearance on his handsome face, evidently hoping she'd tire out and give up. But she didn't, and before long he exploded, screamed a swear word or two, then jumped to his feet, pushing her off him, hard.

In what felt like slow motion, the girl's slender body fell, her golden hair billowing around her like a parachute. All Lucy could do was watch in horror as her head hit the concrete patio.

"Oh my God," Lucy said. "Should we call for an ambulance?" she asked Jesse, whose face had gone utterly pale.

Jesse pointed through the open doorway, where the maître d' was barking something into the house phone, gesturing wildly with his free hand. "He must already be calling one."

Lucy nodded, relieved.

A man from a few tables over was bent over the woman, listening for breath. Meanwhile, the boyfriend had thrown his head back and was wailing—an almost inhuman sound.

"Let's get out of the way," Jesse said, and they emptied euros from their pockets onto the table. "They'll need room when the ambulance gets here."

"Will she be okay?" Lucy asked. "What will they do with him?" The boyfriend dropped to his knees beside his girlfriend, screaming what must have been her name. "Marietta! Marietta!"

A siren screeched in the distance, getting louder. Jesse put his arm around Lucy's shoulders and moved her through the crowd. Once they got beyond the rubberneckers, they found themselves in a piazza with a fountain at its center. "Please sit down," he said. "You look like you might pass out."

"I don't faint. At least, I've never…" But she did feel a bit shaky, so she sat. "That was unbelievable. One moment, they're all…and the next…"

Looking pretty unsteady himself, Jesse sat down next to her. Though an ambulance had already passed them, a siren still shrieked. They watched as a police car pulled past, pedestrians scurrying out of its way.

"You don't think she's going to die?" Lucy asked.

Jesse rubbed his temples. "I don't know."

Lucy's hair clung thick and hot to the back of her neck. "I don't understand," she said as she gathered it into a ponytail and held it away from her skin. "How could they go from being so in love one moment to wanting to kill each other the next?"

Jesse didn't reply.

Lucy nodded, feeling completely wrung out. "Let's go now." As they trudged back toward where the Vespa was parked, she couldn't bring herself to make conversation. The woman had seemed to have everything—extreme beauty, a gorgeous boyfriend, a life in glamorous Florence—and a few minutes later she was lying on the pavement, unconscious, maybe even dead. Her boyfriend was probably on his way to jail.

On the ride back, Lucy clung to Jesse even harder than before. As he took corners, she bore down with her knees and arms to keep from flying off the scooter and into traffic. "Can we find out if she's okay?" she asked when they'd climbed off the Vespa.

"I'll ask around," Jesse said. "And we can pick up a newspaper in the morning, see if there's a story."

Lucy nodded, her head heavy. It had been such a long, full, intense day. All she could think of was getting into bed.

But just before they entered the lobby, Jesse touched her arm. "I've been thinking about tomorrow," he said. "I want you to sing with me. On the street." His words came out in a rush. "I'm not trying to convince you to, you know, change your life plan. I just think it would be fun to busk together."

"I can't," Lucy said. "It's a nice idea, but I've already promised Charlene and Ellen I would go on a day trip with them. Someplace with a view." She struggled to remember the name. "I think it starts with an *F*."

"Fiesole?"

"That sounds right."

"How about the day after?" he asked.

"We're leaving for Rome."

"Already?" Was it her imagination, or did he look disappointed?

"Come with us to Fiesole." The words tumbled from Lucy's lips.

Jesse brightened. "Okay," he said.

"It will be fun," Lucy said. She followed him into the dimly lit lobby, hoping that maybe he would turn and kiss her good night. For a moment he drew just a little closer, his dark eyes dreamy, and it seemed that he might. But then he was thanking her for the day they'd spent together and she was insisting that she should be the one thanking him, and then she was taking the stairs up to her room on shaky legs and wondering how Charlene would take the news that Jesse was coming along for their grand finale in Fiesole.

But why shouldn't Jesse come with us? she wondered as she let herself into the dark room. Too tired to change out of her clothes or even brush her teeth, Lucy crawled under the covers and fell asleep, into convoluted dreams. In the morning, though, she could remember only one: stepping out from behind a velvet curtain to find herself onstage, then looking down to realize she was utterly naked.

VIII

The orange bus to Fiesole was crowded, and the ride was more than a little tense. Of course, Charlene had been annoyed with Lucy for inviting Jesse along on their day trip. To make matters worse, Jesse's morning shift didn't end until eleven. When Lucy broke this news to her companions over breakfast, she saw them exchange a look.

"He can't help it," Lucy said, feeling defensive. "It's his job."

"Why does he need to come with us today?" Charlene asked with a wave of her butter knife. "He lives here. He can see Fiesole anytime he feels like it."

"Fiesole is for lovers," Ellen chimed in cryptically. The sunburn on her nose was peeling slightly, and today she had a straw hat on over her straw-colored hair.

"You two go on ahead. We'll catch up," Lucy said.

"Why don't we three go ahead and have *him* catch up with *us*?" Charlene countered.

Lucy considered giving in just to keep the peace. But then she thought of how let down Jesse might feel. "I'd rather wait." Her voice didn't come out quite as strong as she intended.

"If you insist," Charlene finally said.

After that, Lucy had picked at her breakfast, no longer hungry. *I got my way*, she thought as she half listened to Ellen's lecture on Fiesole—the museum, the restaurants, the five-star hotel, the mind-blowing view. *So why do I feel so terrible?*

When Jesse had arrived in the lobby, Charlene had been less than gracious. "Look who's here," she flatly announced to his face. The whole walk to the station, she and Ellen had hurried ahead. When the number 7 bus arrived, Charlene jumped on first, snagged the last remaining bench, and patted the seat beside her for Ellen, leaving Lucy and Jesse to hang on to the overhead straps.

As the bus wound its way through the city's outskirts, then uphill past rows of skinny cypress trees and high umbrella pines, Lucy felt uneasy. "I'm sorry for how she's acting," she told Jesse.

"Charlene?" Jesse grinned. "It's not your fault."

"I know," Lucy said. But the uneasy feeling lingered. "Did you hear anything this morning? About that girl from last night?"

Jesse's smile vanished. "I asked around," he said. "And I checked the paper. Nothing. But, hey." He stooped a little to meet her gaze. "That might be a good sign."

"I guess we'll never know." Lucy looked away, out the window, at the Tuscan countryside—the distant hills, sun-glossed leaves tossing in the breeze, the brilliant cloudless sky. *The world really is a beautiful place*, she thought, still a little sad for the lovely, injured girl.

Jesse's shoulder brushed hers. "*We're* here now," he said, and Lucy knew exactly what he meant. It was true; they were right there, together, at that pinpoint on the globe. The world would turn, the bus would move, and twenty-four hours later she would be on a train speeding away from him, but at least they had this moment.

Lucy managed a smile. "We are," she said, liking the sound of the word *we*.

Fiesole was the last stop on the line. The bus let them out on the edge of a quiet square. The morning air was cool and fresh. Ellen pointed out the archaeological museum, a monastery, and a few quaint little shops, then gestured toward an outdoor café. "That restaurant is supposed to be amazing. It's on my list of places to review."

"Well, then," Charlene said, "let's go. It's already almost lunchtime." Lucy knew that last part was for her benefit.

"But we just got here," Lucy objected.

"We could squeeze in a visit to the museum first," Ellen said. "I've got free passes."

"Sounds perfect," Charlene said, and she and Ellen immediately took off across the square, toward the museum. Only when they reached the other side did they realize that Lucy hadn't followed.

"Lucy," Charlene called from across the street, "what's wrong?"

Lucy searched for the words to explain. Spending even a minute inside a dusty museum was the last thing she felt like doing on a day like today, when Fiesole lay spread out all around her in the relentless sunshine. But it was more than that. She was tired of Ellen's bossiness, and she didn't like how rude Charlene had been to Jesse. But when she tried to explain all this, she grew flustered. Instead of answering, she bit her bottom lip and held her ground.

Charlene crossed the street to stand before Lucy, arms folded over her chest. Ellen followed at her heels.

"What is the matter with you?" Charlene glared down at Lucy.

"Nothing," Lucy said. "Nothing's the matter."

"Then why are you acting like this?" Charlene cast a quick glance at Jesse, a glance that said she wished he would go away so she could speak her mind. In response, Jesse took a step closer to Lucy's side.

"The museum's supposed to be fun," Ellen said, her voice big and cheery. "And it's not that big. We'll be out in an hour."

"Besides"—Charlene's nostrils flared—"we were going to spend today together. You promised."

Charlene was right. Lucy had promised. Even so, she couldn't seem to make herself take a single step toward the museum. She wasn't in the mood for paintings and pottery and the finger bones of medieval saints.

"I want to see the view," she heard herself say.

Charlene spoke through clenched teeth. "You gave your word."

"You go to the museum," Lucy said with as much firmness as she could muster. "I'll wait for you up there." And she pointed toward the right side of the square, where a path led uphill to what had to be a scenic lookout. Before Charlene could say another word, Lucy started in that direction, arms pumping, Jesse following along.

Only after they'd turned a corner and were out of Charlene's sight did Lucy slow her pace. "It's true," she admitted, already winded. "I did promise to spend the day with her."

"The whole day? Every single minute?"

"Apparently she thinks so." Lucy paused in the doorway of a gift shop. "But does that give her the right to be a total pill?"

"Four weeks is a long time to travel with someone."

"I'll say. We've been driving each other crazy lately. The thing is, I don't usually…" She struggled for the right words. "I don't want you to think I'm the kind of person who breaks my promises."

He looked surprised. "I don't think that."

They turned onto a narrow street that sloped sharply uphill. Climbing it stole all of Lucy's breath. At the top, they found a park full of trees but empty of people. The shade made Lucy think of something delicious to drink after being parched.

Lucy and Jesse wandered to where the park ended, in a cliff overlooking the valley below. "Look." She leaned against the low fence and pointed toward Florence. In the distance, its terra-cotta rooftops spread like a red star. "You can see the Duomo from here. Imagine: We were on top of it a few days ago." It was hard to believe they'd come so far in just a brief bus ride.

"We could climb even higher," Jesse said. "I think there's another ledge above us."

"But it's perfect right here." Lucy clung to the fence, relishing the thrill of being up so high; she had the sensation that if she leaned out too far she would tumble into the valley below. A breeze came out of nowhere to rustle her hair. She glanced over at Jesse, whose dark bangs were fluttering. When he met her gaze, she looked away, bashful. Just out of reach, a white-and-yellow butterfly wafted over the silvery-green tops of olive trees. Something sprang open in Lucy's heart, like a window flung wide on the first warm day of spring. "I can't believe I'm really here."

Jesse waited for her to say more.

"Yesterday, on your Vespa. And singing with you at that club. And now this place…" She swept an arm around to indicate the view. "It feels like we're in a movie." Without planning to, she reached for the sleeve of his blue T-shirt and gave it a playful tug.

Though later she would think she should have seen it coming, she didn't. Jesse's arms circled her, tightened around her, and drew her in, and a moment later he was kissing her, his lips soft and warm and searching. This wasn't Lucy's first kiss—there had been a few others—but it might as well have been. In a way—in the only way that counted—it was the first.

"Lucy! Lucy!" Someone had been calling her name for a while. She'd been hearing it, a distant sound like the buzz of insects in the underbrush or the rustling of olive leaves, without actually taking it in. "Lucy!"

Oddly, the sound seemed to be coming from above her, as if from a low-flying bird, but of course that didn't make sense. Though she didn't want to, Lucy planted her hands on Jesse's chest and pushed herself away, craning to see who was calling her name. It was Charlene, on the lookout point just above the park, a camera dangling around her neck.

"How can she be up there?" Lucy asked. "She's supposed to be at the museum."

Jesse just shrugged, looking as startled and disoriented as Lucy felt.

"Wait here," she told him. "I'll be right back." Shaking her head grimly, she stomped uphill toward Charlene. "What on earth are you doing here?" Lucy shouted.

And though she could hear the anger and frustration in her own voice—the sound of someone who has been pushed just about as far as she can stand to be pushed, and then a little bit more—Charlene didn't seem to be catching it. She hurried downhill, meeting Lucy in the middle of the path. "I felt bad about seeing the museum without you, when we said we'd spend the day together, so I told Ellen…"

But once she'd started fighting, Lucy wasn't able to stop. "First you were rude to Jesse," she said. "Then you tried to make me feel guilty for not wanting to go into some stupid museum. And just now you ruined the most perfect moment of my life."

Charlene went pale. "I didn't mean to."

"But you did," Lucy said.

Charlene pointed in the general direction of Jesse. "Can't you go back to him and take up where you left off?"

"That was our first kiss." Tears sprang into Lucy's eyes "We can never have another first kiss."

"Oh," Charlene said, as speechless as Lucy had ever seen her.

"We're leaving Florence tomorrow, and I don't know if I'll ever see him again after today. Like I said, the moment's ruined now, thanks to you."

Charlene raised an eyebrow. "Everything's always my fault," she said drily.

Lucy wiped her eyes with the backs of her hands. "Lately it is." Her voice came out small. She gulped, on the verge of apologizing, but before she could find the right words, Charlene's nostrils gave a warning flare.

"Jesse is just some random guy you met on the road." Her voice picked up volume as she spoke. "He's a vacation flirtation, Lucy. You have to know that. I can't believe you're actually crying over him. Do you think he's going to cry when you're gone?"

"Shhh!" Lucy glanced downhill. Jesse was out of sight, but that didn't mean he was out of earshot. "You're embarrassing me."

"Maybe you *should* be embarrassed." Charlene peered down her nose at Lucy. "You've been acting like this is some kind of great romance. And you've known him for how long? Three days?"

"Three and a half." Lucy sniffed. Audrey Hepburn and Gregory Peck in *Roman Holiday* popped into her head. That whole, gorgeous love story had unfolded over a mere twenty-four hours. "What does it matter how many days?" The hours she'd spent with Jesse had been so rich, so full; each one could have been an ordinary day.

"You're never going to see him again," Charlene said.

"You can't know that."

Charlene gave a little snort. "You do know what you are to him, right? A hookup. That's all. You could be any girl."

"You can't know that, either," Lucy said, fuming.

"Lucy. He works at a hostel. How many tourists pass through every day? You really think you're the first one he's locked lips with?"

"You're wrong," Lucy said. That kiss—and everything that had led up to it—had felt like more. It hadn't felt casual. Still, she knew if she tried to explain, Charlene would say she was fooling herself, believing what she wanted to believe. Despite the heat, a chill ran through Lucy. "I can't believe how cynical you are," she said when she could speak again. "You're…." She searched for the right word. "Coldhearted."

Charlene's eyes widened.

Emboldened, Lucy stood a little taller, hands planted on her hips. "And you're bitter," she said. "You could have gone off with Simon the way he wanted you to. I wouldn't have stopped you. I tried to talk you into going. And now you're jealous…."

"I am not jealous. And I'm not"—Charlene gulped, as though saying the word was hard—"coldhearted. Just because I don't believe in fooling myself, imagining my thing with Simon actually meant something."

"How do you know it didn't mean anything? You didn't even give it a try. You should have gotten on that train to Mittenwald."

"Oh, please." Charlene sounded exasperated. "Have you forgotten that your parents paid for my flight?"

"As if you would ever let me forget," Lucy said. "Anyway, what does that have to do with it?"

"They expected me to travel with you." Now Charlene was speaking slowly, as though to someone extremely stupid. "How would it look if I just abandoned you?"

"I wouldn't have told them. You could have gone. You *should* have," Lucy insisted. "It doesn't matter who paid."

"That's easy for you to say," Charlene said. "You've got money. You have no idea what it feels like not to get every single thing you want."

Lucy felt stung. "That's so wrong." She thought again of the thing she'd wanted most—to act. "I can't believe you would say something so mean."

"Did I hurt your feelings?" Charlene asked, sounding anything but sorry. "Poor spoiled little Lucy. The truth hurts, doesn't it?"

Unwilling to waste even another moment on someone so unreasonable, so downright cruel, Lucy spun away and stomped off down the hill. But when she reached the park where she'd left Jesse, she saw that Ellen stood beside him, rhapsodizing about the view. And though he made a point of catching Lucy's eye and shooting her a helpless look, it was clear their romantic moment had been spoiled, almost before it had even begun.

That afternoon, Ellen led them on a tour of the quaint monastery at the topmost point of Fiesole. They walked down a plain wooden hallway, peeking into the cells where monks once slept. The rooms were only big enough to hold a narrow bed and a desk, but in each one a window opened onto the same view that had so recently filled Lucy with bliss. Though Jesse walked by her side, the mood between them had changed. Self-conscious now, they barely spoke two words to each other the rest of the day. And as hard as she tried to ignore Charlene, Lucy could feel her ice-blue eyes burning into the back of her head.

She's ruined everything, Lucy thought as they followed Ellen through the echoing hall. At every moment, she could sense exactly where Jesse's body was in relation to hers, could feel the warmth of it radiating toward her. Though she could still taste his kiss on her lips, she couldn't help feeling sad. Soon that kiss would be nothing but a memory—a small, bright window surrounded by thick gray stone. But how could it be otherwise?

IX

Are you all right?" Jesse asked Lucy after they sat down together in the back row of the bus. Luckily, Charlene and Ellen had grabbed seats up front. The bus was fairly crowded, which gave Lucy and Jesse the illusion of privacy.

"I'm okay," Lucy said.

"You don't seem okay," he replied. "What did she say to you up there?"

Though Charlene's words echoed in Lucy's head, she didn't want to repeat them. "It doesn't matter," she said. "I'm just sorry she ruined our afternoon together."

"We still have tonight," Jesse said. Then he put an arm around her shoulder and pulled her in closer, and she relaxed into him. Breathing in his scent—wind and crushed mint leaves, almonds and earth—she felt a little better.

Unfortunately, Jesse had to work the front desk from four to eight. Back up in her room, Lucy pretended to nap while Charlene bustled around, changing clothes for dinner. Only after Lucy was alone did she get up and survey the contents of her drawers. The pickings were slim. Luckily, she had one nice item in reserve: the sundress she had brought along in case of a special occasion, white splashed with red poppies. Lucy held the dress up to her shoulders and checked out the effect in the full-length mirror.

I'll make sure I look my best tonight, she thought, doing a little twirl. *Even if this is just a fling, tonight will be the best, most romantic night of my entire vacation.* She practiced her widest, brightest smile. Tonight she would play the part of the girl in a romantic comedy. She would be charming and flirty, and she'd make herself forget that this movie couldn't possibly have a happy ending.

The sight of Jesse pacing in front of the hostel, freshly shaved and wearing a crisp white shirt and black trousers, brought a smile to Lucy's face. He looked handsome and just a bit nervous, the streetlight beaming down on him like a spotlight.

Eyes wide, he took her in. "Hey," he said.

Lucy had taken her time getting ready, pulling her curls

into a high ponytail, leaving a few tendrils free. She even put on makeup and perfume. "Hey yourself," she said. "Where shall we go?"

Jesse suggested a walk down to the Arno. Lucy agreed, and he took her hand. As they walked back to the river, she realized that she now knew the way by heart. The streets were still busy. Lucy and Jesse took the first bridge they came to, the Ponte alla Carraia, stopping in the middle to take in the view. All along the water, a string of streetlights sparkled, the reflection glittering like the second strand of a necklace. Two bridges over, the Ponte Vecchio basked in a warm golden glow.

Lucy sighed deeply. Just then she caught sight of something— some kind of flickering light—floating toward them above the velvety black river. It looked like a candle flame riding the breeze. "What's that?"

"I don't know," Jesse replied. They watched as it soared slowly toward them. A moment later, a second light appeared behind it, then a third. "Paper lanterns?" he guessed.

"I wonder how they fly," Lucy said. "And how they keep from burning up."

They stood there, side by side, in silence. *I hate so much for this to be over*, Lucy thought. The words echoed so loudly in her head that she said them out loud. Immediately she wished she hadn't. Though she'd been talking about her trip, about Florence, she saw right away how Jesse might have misunderstood her words, might have thought that by *this* she meant something else: the two of them. The last thing she wanted was to seem clingy. *I don't mean us*, she considered saying. But the words wouldn't have been entirely true, so she didn't speak them.

In the silence that spread between them, Lucy had time to feel disappointment and embarrassment, time to wonder if maybe Charlene had been right after all. Just then an evening breeze kicked up, and she hugged herself for warmth.

She was just about to suggest they head back to the hostel when Jesse spoke up. "So, I asked Signora Bertolini if I could have the rest of the week off. I thought for sure she would say no, but she surprised me. I pulled a lot of double shifts last month. I guess she feels she owes me a favor."

"Oh?" Lucy said, unsure of why he thought she should care. She turned her attention to the last of the floating paper lanterns quivering in the distance.

Jesse looked at her closely, as though trying to gauge her reaction.

"Were you planning to travel?" she finally asked, fixing her gaze on his forehead, trying very hard to be polite.

Jesse's mouth twitched in what looked like a nervous smile. "That depends," he said. "I was thinking—well, hoping, really— that I could come to Rome with you," he explained. "If you want me to."

"Oh," Lucy said again. All the blood seemed to rush to her face at once. *Charlene was wrong!* she thought. "Oh."

"I'm not trying to be pushy." Jesse's words came out in a rush. "I'll understand if you don't want—"

"But I do."

Jesse reached for her and she melted into his arms.

"You don't think Charlene will mind?" he said after a while.

"I don't care what she thinks anymore," Lucy said, with more certainty than she felt. Then she rested her cheek against his crisp cotton shirt. "Where will you stay?"

"I can get us a room," he said. "You and me. Would that be okay?"

Lucy nodded. The thought of sharing a room with Jesse made her tremble, and her trembling made him tighten his arms around her in a gesture that felt protective. She'd never spent the night with anyone before. Her first time would be with Jesse, in Rome. What could be more perfect?

"'I'll need a train ticket and a reservation," Jesse was saying. "So I'll go to the station with you in the morning. If your train's full, I might need to take a later one. We could meet up at the Termini Station in Rome...."

But Lucy couldn't concentrate on the logistics. As she and Jesse walked hand in hand back to the Bertolini, chatting about the sights they would see in Rome, it took effort just to keep her voice steady. *Is Charlene going to freak out when I tell her?* she was thinking. Also, *What if I'm not as ready as I think I am?* Their shoes echoed against the pavement of Florence's hushed streets, and their voices bounced against the darkened storefronts, making even the lightest conversation feel momentous.

Just before midnight, they kissed good night in front of the Hostel Bertolini. Rehearsing the words she would say to Charlene, Lucy took the stairs up to her room two at a time, but when she let herself in she found the lights off and Charlene already asleep. Lucy felt her way around the darkened room, fumbling for her nightgown. In the bathroom, she switched on the light and examined her face in the mirror—her brown eyes were brighter than she'd ever seen them before. *Jesse's coming to Rome to be with me*, she thought. And, *What will Charlene say when I tell her?* And, *I probably won't sleep even a wink tonight.*

Which turned out to be 100 percent true.

X

―∞∞∞―

*L*ucy broke the news to Charlene as they were dressing to catch the train, and the conversation went about as badly as she had feared. "You're going to do *what?*" Charlene, who had been searching under the bed for her sneakers, looked up in alarm.

Lucy had no choice but to say it again. "I'm going to stay with Jesse in Rome."

Charlene got to her feet, a sneaker in each hand. "I guess I shouldn't be surprised," she said, her voice ten degrees chillier. "You've been trying to ditch me for days."

"What?" The word came out in a squeak. "I have not."

"Ever since you met *him*." Charlene's nostrils did that flaring thing Lucy dreaded so much. "No, even before that, when you wanted me to go off with Simon."

"That wasn't me trying to ditch you. I wanted you to be happy. Just like I would think you'd want me to be happy now."

"*Happy.*" Now Charlene's voice was mocking.

"Yes," Lucy said. "What's wrong with that?"

"And now I'm going to be alone in Rome while you and Jesse are off being *happy.*"

"We can all meet up and do some sightseeing together," Lucy said.

"Oh, please."

"Why not?" Lucy asked.

Charlene didn't answer.

"Well, then, if you'd rather be alone, that's your choice. Not mine." Even as she said the words, Lucy tried to determine how Charlene was taking them. Her blue eyes were brighter than usual. She wasn't about to cry, was she? A wave of guilt washed over Lucy. "You'll meet people at the hostel. Everywhere we've gone, we've met people."

But Charlene's only reply was a little snort, and Lucy saw she'd been wrong about the crying. Annoyed, she began yanking out her dresser drawers to make sure she hadn't left anything behind. Sure enough, she'd overlooked a pair of balled-up socks in the bottom drawer.

"You know, I promised your parents I would stick by you this whole trip," Charlene said. "I gave my word."

"I don't need a babysitter." Lucy held back the rest of what she wanted to say: how sick she was of Charlene always acting like she was so mature, so superior, so sensible. Treating Lucy like a child.

"Well, that's not what your mother thinks, apparently." Charlene busied herself with gathering the jewelry from the top drawer of her dresser, sorting it into the many little ziplock bags she'd brought along for that purpose. When she spoke again her tone was more guarded. "What will she say when you tell her?"

"About getting a room with Jesse?" Lucy felt the blood drain from her face. "Why would I tell her that?"

"My mom always holds you two up as an example. She says you tell each other everything."

Lucy bit her lower lip. "Not everything," she said, though it was true that she'd never needed to keep many secrets from her mother. Until now. She was pretty sure her mom wouldn't approve of her going off with Jesse, and even more sure that her father would be furious. If he found out, that was. To hide her face, Lucy fussed over the contents of her pack, as though where she tucked her last pair of socks was the most important decision in the world.

"If you told her about this, it would make me look bad," Charlene continued. "Like I failed to do my duty."

"Your *duty*?" Her back still turned, Lucy allowed herself a small, relieved smile. "You don't have to worry. I promise not to say a word if you don't."

Though Lucy and Charlene had struck a kind of truce up in their room, the rest of the morning was every bit as awkward as Lucy might have expected, and then some. When Jesse met them in the lobby with his guitar and duffel bag, Charlene aimed a gruff hello in his direction, then refused to say anything more. The three of them trudged to the station in grim silence. As Jesse had predicted, Lucy's train was sold out, but he was able to reserve a seat on a later one. Their good-bye kiss was rushed and awkward. How could Lucy not feel Charlene's death stare as she waited three feet away, leaning against a concrete pillar, all their baggage at her feet? For the whole train ride, Charlene glowered in the window seat, blocking Lucy's view of the landscape streaming past.

When they arrived in Rome, Charlene turned her back on Lucy and stalked off without a word.

"I'll see you at the airport on Sunday morning," Lucy called after her, trying to sound cheerier than she felt. "We can meet up at the gate."

Charlene turned reluctantly. "You'd better be there."

"Of course," Lucy replied. "Why wouldn't I be?"

But Charlene simply started off again, her shoulders hunched under the weight of her pack. After that, Lucy checked her own knapsack into a locker and spent the next few hours wandering the streets around the train station. Rome was bigger than Florence, a bit grittier and more intimidating, and Lucy hesitated to go far, afraid of missing Jesse's train.

I'm really in Rome, she told herself, trying to shake off the cloud Charlene had cast over her morning. In the booth of a small pizzeria, she picked at her lunch and paged through *Wanderlust*, making a mental list of things she wanted to see. But her mind kept flitting back to Jesse, to the hotel room they'd soon be checking into, and to what would happen next. *Will Jesse bring a condom with him?* she wondered. *Or should I find a pharmacy? And is the Italian word for* condom *even in my phrasebook?* Feeling shaky at the very thought, she decided Jesse would be prepared. *He has to be, or I won't…we won't…* She pushed aside her half-empty bottle of San Pellegrino and snapped *Wanderlust* shut. Too anxious to sit still a moment longer, she resumed walking, heading vaguely back in the direction of the Termini Station.

Jesse's train arrived on time. Lucy, standing on tiptoe for a better view, watched the crowds of travelers pour out. When he appeared at last—the first familiar face she'd seen in hours, scanning the crowd for her—Lucy waved with both arms, feeling as relieved to see him as if they'd been apart for weeks. Jesse smiled at the sight of her, dropped his bag unceremoniously to the platform, and scooped her up in a hello kiss. Not minding the crowds of strangers milling around them, Lucy kissed him back.

When he released her, she felt flustered. "You're here" was all she could think of to say.

"Were you afraid I wouldn't show?" he asked.

"Of course not." Lucy glanced down at her feet and then up into his dark eyes. "I was a little worried I might be standing at the wrong track. This station is so confusing."

"You figured it out," Jesse said.

"Yay, me." Lucy mimed shaking pompoms in the air.

"Ready?" Jesse bent to retrieve his bag. In contrast with the weathered, well-traveled blue fabric of his duffel bag, Lucy's red pack looked brand-new. *I'll never catch up with him,* she thought as she followed Jesse out of the station and back into the busy streets of Rome.

When they came to a corner, Jesse unfolded a street map and pored over it. "We're just a few blocks from the hotel," he said.

Lucy nodded. Making small talk was suddenly too much for her. In a few minutes, she and Jesse would be checking into a room together. She'd never done anything like this before—not with Adam, who'd taken her to the senior prom, or Patrick, the lacrosse player she'd gone out with for a few awkward months in the middle of junior year. Between the afternoon heat, the weight of her pack, and her jitters, it took all her concentration just to put one foot in front of the other.

Not that I'm having second thoughts, she told herself. *Jesse and Rome: What could be more romantic?* Still, as she waited while Jesse studied his street map, she had to admit that one small thing was less than perfect: They would have a few days together, and then she would get on a plane and probably never see him again.

I can't fall in love with him, she told herself as sternly as she could manage.

"You okay?" Jesse asked, folding the map. "We're almost there."

And though his words made her pulse speed up, Lucy gave him what she hoped was a cheery little smile. "I'm fine."

The Albergo della Zingara was easy to miss. Only a small gold plaque beside an iron gate gave its location away. Jesse pressed a button and said a few words into an intercom, and a moment later they were buzzed into the hotel's lobby. He greeted the tiny, red-haired woman behind the desk in Italian too rapid for Lucy to follow, though she caught the words for *reservation* and *double bed*. The woman took Jesse's cash and handed over a heavy key. "You have a lovely stay," she told them in heavily accented English.

The elevator was barely big enough for the two of them and their bags. Somewhere around the third floor it slowed and then stopped. For a moment, Lucy thought they might be stuck, but a second later they lurched back into motion.

"Phew," she said to Jesse, mostly because it had been a long time since she'd said anything at all.

The hotel room was small but clean, its double bed taking up most of the space. Lucy stepped in and hesitated, unsure of where to stand. Jesse ventured to the window, brushing back a white curtain. "It's not too fancy, but we've got a street view."

Could he be as nervous as she was? Lucy wondered. She joined him at the window, both of them looking down at the street four stories below.

Lucy reached to give the sleeve of his T-shirt a tug. "I don't care about fancy."

A moment later, Jesse's arms were around her. "I'm glad," he said. Lucy rested her head against his chest, breathing in his familiar scent of almonds, crushed mint, and, somehow, even though he'd spent the whole day on a train, fresh air. She drew back to look at him, and he kissed her, gently at first, and then deeply, his hands warm on her bare arms. She felt herself tremble again, the way she had the night before. "I'm sorry," she mumbled.

"What for?" He sounded surprised.

"It's just...I've never...I mean..." Lucy inhaled sharply. "This is the first time I've ever..." She shut her eyes and burrowed against his neck.

Jesse stroked her hair, his fingers tangling in her curls. "That's not something to be sorry for."

"I know," she said. "It's just that I'm feeling so..." She struggled for the right word. "Shy," she said finally. "It's silly, I know...."

"It's not silly." He kissed the top of her head. Then he sighed and released her. "I don't want to rush you into anything."

"You're not," she said.

With a swift backward spring, Jesse was prone on the bed. "Why don't we take a nap?" He patted the white voile spread beside him, and Lucy climbed into the crook of his arm. She shut her eyes and forced herself to breathe deeply, just as she would to calm herself before stepping onstage.

"I don't think I can sleep," she said.

He brushed her hair away from her face. "Don't sleep, then."

"I won't." And she didn't, at first. But the steadiness of his breathing must have lulled her. When she opened her eyes again, the room had darkened slightly, the sun having slipped behind the buildings across the street.

Lucy tipped her head back to find Jesse watching her, a smile playing on his lips. "Hello," he said.

"Did I sleep long?" she asked.

"Not very," he said. He twirled one of her light brown ringlets around his finger, then gave it a tug so that it bounced back like a spring. "I've been dying to do that. And this..." He brought the curl up to his face, holding it under his nose like a mustache.

She giggled. "You're easily entertained."

"My needs *are* pretty basic," he agreed.

A moment later they were kissing, though Lucy couldn't have said which of them had started it. When his lips found her neck and his hands slipped under her tank top, gently easing it over her head, she couldn't help trembling, but this time she didn't apologize.

"Did you bring..." she began, hesitant to ruin the mood.

Luckily, though, he knew what she meant. "Yes." He patted the pocket of his jeans.

Lucy let herself exhale. "Good," she said. A moment later, when he reached for her again, she didn't hesitate. She slipped her hands under his T-shirt, then helped him pull it off over his head, leaving his dark hair crackling with static electricity. Any trace of shyness vanished the moment his skin met hers and she felt that he was trembling, too.

XI

~∞~

When Lucy and Jesse finally made it out of the hotel, the sun was just about to set. Ravenous, they ate dinner in a trattoria not far away. "Where shall we go after dinner?" Lucy asked, her fork hovering over her order of *cacio e pepe*.

"What would you like to see?" Jesse asked.

Lucy tried to remember the list of sights she wanted to see in Rome. "Everything," she said finally. "I don't want to miss anything."

"That narrows it down." Jesse's grin implied that the two of them now shared a secret, which in a way they did.

Lucy couldn't help but smile back. She was just about to suggest that he pick the evening's destination when a thought occurred to her. "Have you ever seen *Roman Holiday*?" she asked. And when Jesse shook his head, she grabbed his arm excitedly. "It's the reason I came to Italy."

There was that grin again. "Thank you, *Roman Holiday*."

Over tiramisu, she related the plot to him: A bored princess tours Europe and, sick of her long days of public appearances, runs away to enjoy a day of freedom. When a broke newspaperman recognizes her, he knows he's stumbled onto the story of the year, so he takes her all over Rome to do everything she's always dreamed of.

"He doesn't tell her he knows who she really is," Lucy explained. "And the whole time his friend is taking photos of her for the newspaper."

"Let me guess," Jesse said. "He winds up falling in love with her."

"Of course! It's a romantic comedy. And she falls in love with him, too." Self-conscious, she looked down into her little cup of espresso. "But then she's got to choose between love and duty. And he's got to choose whether or not to turn in his story."

"And?" Jesse reached across the table for her hand.

"I'm not telling," Lucy said. "You'll just have to watch the movie."

Jesse signaled for the check. "So where does this princess go while she's in Rome?" he asked. "Because I'm thinking we should invent our own *Roman Holiday* tour."

"Really?" Lucy bounced a little in her chair. "You would do that?"

He nodded.

"Well, first she goes to a salon and has her hair cut short."

"Can't we skip that part?" He brushed the long, wild hair back from her face.

"Audrey Hepburn looked adorable with short hair," Lucy

said. "But okay." Then she wrinkled her nose, thinking. "Next she goes to the Spanish Steps."

A long, breathless walk later, Lucy led Jesse to the exact spot on the Spanish Steps where Audrey Hepburn ate gelato with Gregory Peck, and looked out over the same view they must have seen. Above them, the Spanish Embassy towered, and below, a little boat-shaped fountain burbled. Though it was well after dark, the steps and the nearby square were still crowded with people enjoying themselves.

"Is it what you expected?" Jesse asked finally.

"It's even better," Lucy said. A breeze—the first she'd felt all day—played over her skin.

Jesse leaned in a bit closer, his arm rubbing hers. "This is one of my favorite spots in Rome," he said.

"You've been here before?" Lucy asked.

"Once or twice."

With someone else? Lucy wanted to ask. Instead, she bent to pick out a pebble that had worked its way into her sandal.

"Where's the next stop on our *Roman Holiday* tour?" Jesse asked.

Lucy thought. "The Trevi Fountain. And then the Colosseum."

"We could squeeze in a visit to the Trevi Fountain tonight," Jesse said. "Or we could go back to the hotel now, and save the rest for morning." He rubbed his cheek against her bare shoulder, then gave it a kiss.

"Mmmm," Lucy said. *So what if Jesse has been to Rome with other girls?* she thought. *He's here with me now.* And right there, in front of about a hundred tourists, she kissed him with great concentration, as though one amazing kiss could wipe out his memories of those other girls, whoever they had been.

Lucy's last few days in Europe were spent crisscrossing Rome on foot and by subway, taking in all the sites from *Roman Holiday*. They returned to the Spanish Steps just so they could have a stranger take their picture together, Lucy with a cone of vanilla gelato in hand, pretending to be Audrey Hepburn, and Jesse smiling down at her, doing his best impression of a bemused Gregory Peck. In the midday heat, they hiked past the Roman Forum—those gorgeous ruins that had somehow lasted more than two thousand years—and wandered in a big loop around the Colosseum. By then their money was running out, and they couldn't afford the admission fee. But even from the outside, just the sight of it—familiar from so many films and photographs—thrilled Lucy.

They paid a visit to the Castel Sant'Angelo, where Audrey Hepburn had gone dancing on a river barge. They wandered into a sixth-century church to see the huge, scary stone face Gregory Peck called the Mouth of Truth. They even visited the Piazza Venezia, though it had made only the most fleeting of appearances in the movie's credits. Each stop on their tour was like glimpsing a movie star on an ordinary city street—otherworldly but utterly familiar.

They tossed coins over their shoulders into the Trevi Fountain because the superstition said that meant they'd come back someday. *Let me come back with Jesse,* Lucy thought, squeezing her eyes shut, as she released her twenty-cent piece into the air. The crowd in front of the fountain was so noisy with tourists she could barely hear her coin plop into the water. To be safe, she tossed in another, and another.

"I can't believe I'm really here," Lucy told Jesse again. *With you,* she added silently, but, still trying to keep things light, she didn't let herself say the words out loud.

At the end of each day, they hurried back to their little room at the Albergo della Zingara and undressed each other in the moonlight that filtered in through the gauzy white curtains. Each night, as their time together dwindled, they returned to the hotel a bit earlier and slept a bit less. Though she'd taken about a hundred pictures of Jesse, Lucy still found herself trying to memorize the line of his jaw, the full curve of his lower lip. Not to mention the things her camera couldn't capture, like the scent of his hair and the feel of his skin.

By their next-to-last day together, Lucy and Jesse were almost broke, so he carried his guitar to Piazza Navona and she set out her sunhat—the one her mother had made her pack but that she'd never bothered to wear—to collect coins from passersby. On the long walk over, they'd worked out a list of songs Lucy already knew. She and Jesse took turns singing harmony. In the middle of the Nico Rathburn song Lucy had heard Jesse playing back in Florence, she let herself look at the crowd gathered around them, their faces rapt and eager to be entertained. Of all the memories she'd been storing away of Europe, she already knew this would be one of her favorites.

The last night of Lucy's trip came all too soon. She and Jesse dressed up in their best clothes, took the metro to the Via Veneto, and blew their earnings on a fancy dinner in one of the little glass-walled cafés that lined the wide and shady street. Afterward, they walked hand in hand back to the hotel. Though Lucy wanted very much to be happy, she couldn't help thinking how every minute that passed brought her that much closer to the end of their time together.

"I just remembered the Catacombs!" she exclaimed out of the blue.

Jesse looked at her quizzically.

"And Vatican City. And Trastevere. They were all on my list of things to see in Rome."

Jesse looked as though he was about to say something but didn't speak.

"I'll just have to come back someday." *Though it won't be the same without you*, she thought. Then she forced a smile. "Good thing I threw a coin into the fountain."

Jesse still didn't reply. In fact, he'd been quieter than usual the whole evening. Now they walked on through the darkening streets, not talking. Just a few blocks from the hotel, Jesse's step slowed, until the two of them were standing in front of the wrought-iron gates of some kind of government building. Lucy reached for her camera, thinking it must be a historic site, but when she looked up at him, she saw that he wasn't looking at the building at all.

"The movie has a happy ending, right?" he asked.

Puzzled, Lucy looked at the building, then back at him.

"*Roman Holiday*," he added. "Tell me the princess chooses love over duty."

Lucy didn't respond. And though she waited for him to start walking again, he remained frozen in place, his arms folded over his chest.

After a long and awkward pause, he spoke again. "I've been thinking about how maybe you could stay." His words sounded casual, but he was looking at her in a way that made her stomach flip over.

Lucy stammered, "S-stay?" Was he saying what she thought he was saying?

"How you could maybe come back to Florence," he said. "With me. And stay there."

A cool evening breeze lifted Lucy's hair, and she rubbed her bare arms.

"For how long?" she asked.

"As long as you want."

Lucy struggled for the right words: *That's so romantic*, or *There's nothing in the world I would like more*. But what came out of her mouth was "I wish I could."

"You can," Jesse said. "If you want to."

"Of course I want to. I do." She allowed herself another glance at him, and the look on his face—intent, expectant—made her heart speed up.

"Then stay," he said, unfolding his arms and taking a step

toward her. Before she could answer, he had gathered her up and was kissing her. *He really does care about me*, she thought. *I'm not just some hookup.*

He released her. "Will you at least think about it?" he asked.

Lucy could hardly believe this conversation was happening. Jesse wanted her to stay! And though she was glad—giddy, even—to know that he'd been feeling the same things she'd been feeling, the reasons she couldn't stay began flooding into her mind. "But my flight leaves tomorrow."

"So miss it." His lips brushed her forehead.

"Where would I sleep?"

"In my room," he said. "At the Bertolini."

"But what about Nello?" As stunningly unromantic as all her objections were, Lucy couldn't seem to stop herself.

"He can room with someone else. He'll understand."

"What would I do for money?"

"I could talk the signora into hiring you," he said. "She likes me. I'm sure she'll like you, too. And we could sing on the streets. Together."

Lucy rested her head against his chest. *I should be so happy*, she thought. She felt like a kite that had reached the limits of its string and was being yanked back to earth. "I want to stay. I really do," she heard herself say, her words muffled by his shirt. "It means everything that you want me to."

"Does it?" Jesse mumbled, his lips close to her ear.

Lucy nodded, not wanting to say what came next. But it had to be said. "I'm supposed to start college in a few weeks."

"That's why it would be so perfect." He stroked her hair as

he spoke. "You wouldn't have to. If you stayed here, you wouldn't be dependent on your parents, and they couldn't manipulate you anymore."

Lucy drew back, surprised. "You've never even met my parents. You don't know anything about them."

"I know they're trying to bully you out of doing the thing you love most."

Her voice came out in a squeak. "Bully me?"

"What would you call it?"

She shut her eyes and imagined her mother's face—young and still pretty. And her father—his proud smile when she made him happy. Was it so wrong that she wanted to please them? And was it so wrong that they wanted her to be safe and successful? "They just want what's best for me," she said.

"What *they* think is best. But what do *you* want?"

"I don't even know anymore," Lucy said, but then all at once she *did* know. She wanted to start college, and she wanted to be with Jesse. And, while she was at it, she wanted not to disappoint her parents. She pictured Charlene having to face them at the airport and explain how she'd left their daughter in Italy. Then she imagined trying to call home and explain why she was breaking her part of the bargain and dropping out of Forsythe University before she'd even started. Her father would have every right to be furious. She'd promised. And he'd already paid her tuition.

"I *need* to go to college," she said finally.

"Because they want you to?" he said.

"No! Because *I* want to." That much was true. She wanted to move into a dorm and make new friends, and walk around

121

campus in a red sweater, backpack slung over her shoulder. And she wanted her degree so that someday she could make decent money at a job she might even like. "I love being here with you, but my life is back in Pennsylvania."

"Okay," he said, sounding defeated. "I get it. But—" He broke off and stared over her shoulder, into the distance. "I don't understand how you can just give up acting. You've got such a great stage presence, and your voice...it's amazing."

Lucy's eyes grew wide. This was a beautiful compliment, the best he could possibly have given her.

"I just hope you'll make your own choices," he added.

"I'll try," Lucy said, but the words came out sounding tentative, not terribly convincing.

"I just want you to be happy," he said finally. "That's all. Whatever happiness means to you, I want you to find it." He reached for her hands, interweaving his fingers with hers, pulling her toward him, kissing her again, and after that, how could Lucy even think straight?

Back at the hotel, they exchanged e-mail addresses. "I don't check my messages very often," he said. "I'll try to get better about it." Then Lucy suggested they program their numbers into each other's cell phones, but Jesse shook his head. "I'm between phones."

"How is that even possible?"

"I've got more important things to spend my money on," he said. "What little money I have."

More important than calling me? she wondered.

"Nello says I'm living in the wrong century," Jesse volunteered.

Lucy bit her lower lip, working up the courage to say what she really wanted to ask. "I don't suppose you ever plan to come back to the States?" As they'd walked back to the hotel, she'd realized what she really wanted: for Jesse to fly back to his home in New Jersey—for him to want her badly enough to give up his travels. "Not even for a visit?" she added.

"I wasn't planning on it."

Lucy hid her disappointment behind her bravest smile. "Oh, well," she said lightly.

"Maybe someday," he relented.

But *someday* sounded so far away. Lucy didn't want to think about it, not really. If she was never going to see Jesse again, she at least wanted him to remember her as the girl who got away. She undid her ponytail holder, letting her hair fall loose over her shoulders, and smiled at him again, this time trying for flirtatious, trying for sultry. Then she reached for the lamp switch, and in the light of the waning full moon, she slipped the straps of her sundress from her shoulders.

After a night that passed too quickly, Jesse kissed Lucy good-bye on the platform at the Termini Station.

"Send me a postcard from college," he said. "Care of the Bertolini."

"You, too," Lucy said. "Write me from everywhere you go."

123

Because the airport train cost fourteen euros, they had agreed it didn't make sense for Jesse to make the trip. Lucy chose a window seat so she could see him standing on the platform as the train pulled away, so she could wave and call to him through the open window. But those last few minutes before the train took off—knowing she could still change her mind and jump off, back into Jesse's arms—were sheer torture. When the train at last started into motion, Lucy blew him one last kiss and then watched his form grow smaller and disappear.

Now that it was too late to change her fate, she resigned herself to looking through all the photos she'd taken in Italy. There was Jesse, hanging from a strap on the subway, grinning beside the Mouth of Truth, leaning against a wall overlooking the Trevi Fountain. And there the two of them were, posed *Roman Holiday*–style on the Spanish Steps. Lucy clicked back in time to the picture she'd taken of him on the Ponte alla Carraia, the night of their first date, the Ponte Vecchio gleaming behind him, golden in the twilight. Looking at it, Lucy could recall his aftershave and the crisp feel of his shirt. Already she could imagine showing this picture to her friends at school, friends she hadn't made yet.

"He was my boyfriend for a couple of days," she would say. "Just a really great guy from New Jersey who I met in Florence." Though that was the truth, it didn't do justice to how she was feeling.

As the train hurtled forward in space and time, away from Jesse, toward Charlene and the airport and Philadelphia, toward her parents and Forsythe University and her future, Lucy gave herself a pep talk.

I've just had the most perfect vacation ever. As soon as I start college, I'll meet all sorts of new people, but this will always be the best, most romantic time of my life. Even if it hurts, I'll always remember Jesse.

PART TWO

—∞∞∞—

Philadelphia

XII

⟨∽∽∽⟩

*Y*ou're wearing *that?*" Lucy's new suitemate Glory looked her up and down, clearly not approving of the black jeans and gauzy blouse Lucy had changed into for her very first college party.

Lucy felt herself flush. "What's wrong with what I'm wearing?" But the answer was standing right in front of her. Glory had changed into platform heels, a tight black cocktail dress, and dangling earrings that sparkled against her dark skin. Though Lucy had known Glory for only a week, she already knew her suitemate had some very definite ideas about life. Since Glory's boyfriend, Armand, was a sophomore, she'd been to plenty of college parties. Tonight's bash was at Armand's off-campus apartment, and Glory had wrangled her suitemates a special invitation that, to hear her talk about it, was kind of a big deal.

"I think what Lucy's wearing is fine." Still in her terrycloth bathrobe, her honey-blond hair damp from the shower, Lucy's roommate, Brittany, spoke up. "I'm going to wear jeans, too."

"I don't even own a cocktail dress," Lucy added. Even with all the back-to-school shopping she'd done since getting home from Europe, she hadn't foreseen the need to buy anything quite so dressy.

But Glory chewed on her lower lip, assessing Lucy. "You could borrow one of mine." She led Lucy to her closet. "You don't want to stick out like a sore thumb."

"What does it matter?" Brittany asked from the doorway. "Why can't we just be *ourselves*?"

"Because." Glory emerged with several hangers' worth of skimpy dresses. "You're my guests, and I want you to look right."

"Who decides what *right* is?" Britt grumbled. "I'd rather be comfortable, thanks."

"Armand's whole team is going to be there," Glory said. "Have you seen how hot rugby players are? Don't you want to look your best?"

"I *have* a boyfriend," Brittany reminded her. "Maybe I should just stay home and watch a movie." She shook her head, scattering water droplets.

Glory turned her attention back to Lucy. "You want the full college experience, right?"

Lucy thought for a moment. She didn't want to desert Brittany, who was turning out to be the best roommate she could possibly have imagined. And though she knew she should be meeting people—meeting *guys*—it had been just a few weeks since she had kissed Jesse good-bye on the train platform.

Glory read her hesitation. "This isn't about that Italian guitar player you've been obsessing over, is it?"

"He's from New Jersey." Lucy felt her cheeks grow hot. Apart from the nights they'd stayed up late swapping their romantic histories, Lucy had hardly mentioned Jesse to her suitemates at all, or so she thought. "I haven't been obsessing. Have I?" she turned to Brittany.

"Just a little," Britt said.

"Oh, come on, Lucy," Glory said. "The photo? We've all seen you staring at it."

Of course Glory meant the snapshot Lucy had printed out, framed, and hung above her desk—the one of her and Jesse on the Spanish Steps, posing as Audrey Hepburn and Gregory Peck.

"I don't stare," Lucy mumbled. She hated to think she'd been obsessing about Jesse, especially since there was very little evidence that he was thinking of her. Since she'd gotten back to the States, she'd had only three e-mails from him, and none of them had been particularly romantic. Of course he'd warned her that he hardly ever checked his e-mail, so maybe that didn't mean he wasn't missing her. But it was hard to tell for sure.

Lucy hesitated, then reached for a pretty plum-colored strapless dress. "Of course I want the full college experience," she said, holding it up against her body and casting an apologetic smile in Britt's direction. "You could think of it as a costume party."

Britt made a face, then relented. "Don't you have any that aren't strapless?"

Back in their room, the girls changed into their borrowed dresses. The plum one was a bit long, but otherwise fit fine. Lucy, who loved playing dress-up, smiled at herself in the full-length mirror, then fished in the closet for her favorite heels.

Britt tugged at the skirt of her dress, as though she could magically make it longer, despite the fact that—with her long legs and runner's body—she looked stunning.

"Don't tell Glory I said so, but I'll bet you look better in that than she does," Lucy said.

"Stop buttering me up." Britt scowled. "I feel foolish." She dropped to her bed. "Do you think I should tell Rich about this?" Every night that week she'd slept with her cell phone, texting back and forth with her boyfriend, who was at a school four hours away.

"Why wouldn't you?" Lucy wriggled her feet into black wedge heels. "It's just a party. Don't they have parties at Penn State?" She examined her hair in the mirror. Luckily, for once, she was having a reasonably good hair day.

"You'll look after me, right?" Britt said. "If somebody slips me a roofie, you'll drag me home?" She bent to rummage under her bed. "I'm wearing flats," she declared, emerging with a mismatched pair. "Glory had better not give me crap about it, either."

"I'd wear the black satin ones," Lucy said, spreading her earrings out on top of her bureau, looking for her favorite dangly crystal ones.

"I think I'll carry pepper spray in my purse," Britt said. "Just in case."

Lucy laughed. Next to Britt, who came from rural Pennsylvania and had never even been to Philly before she left home for Forsythe, Lucy sometimes felt downright worldly. "Maybe you should wear a superhero costume under that dress," she said.

Britt sighed. "I hate the thought of Rich at a party, flirting with some girl."

Lucy sat down beside her on the bed. "I know." She rested her head on her roommate's shoulder.

"No, really," Britt said. "I really hate it. Really."

Lucy shut her eyes and heaved a sigh of her own. "I really, really know," she said.

At the front door of Armand's row house, Lucy, Britt, Glory, and their fourth suitemate, Sarah, paid five dollars apiece and were each given a red Solo cup. They squeezed their way through the hallway and into a living room that was already packed. "Come and meet Armand," Glory shouted to be heard over the house music pounding through the stereo, then disappeared into the crowd surrounding the keg. Sarah followed, but Lucy and Britt hung back.

"I can tell I'm going to hate this night," Britt shouted. "Are you planning to drink?"

"Maybe just one," Lucy screamed back. "I don't actually like beer much. Too bad they don't put strawberry daiquiris in kegs." They got in line. "Looks like there's dancing." Lucy pointed toward the next room over. "Let's go, after this."

A panicked look crossed Britt's face.

"You don't have to dance *with* anyone," Lucy said. "We can dance together. It will be okay."

The dancing room was less congested than the keg room had

been, its only furnishings a couch pushed up against a wall and Christmas lights strung from the ceiling. Just as Lucy and Britt arrived, the DJ swapped out the house music for a Rolling Stones song. Lucy gave a little whoop, grabbed Britt's hand, and pulled her into the middle of the dance floor, looking for a clearing.

"See! This isn't so bad," Lucy said, always glad for a chance to dance.

Britt tipped her head in the direction of a sweaty guy doing the Running Man. "Dude just splashed beer all over my new shoes," she said.

"We'll clean them later." Lucy took another sip from her drink.

Just then a hand grabbed Lucy's arm. It was Sarah, in a bright turquoise dress, her wispy yellow hair piled high. "I'm so glad I found you," she said. "Glory's in the basement watching Armand play beer pong. Not my scene."

"Hang with us," Britt said.

Sarah nodded gratefully and fell in step, bouncing along to the music. "Have you seen all the hot guys here?"

Britt shrugged, taking another sip from her cup.

"Look at that one, in the Eagles jersey. And that red-haired one in the corner." Sarah pointed discreetly.

"It's like you've got radar," Lucy said, impressed.

"And then there's Dream Boy over there on the stairs, talking with his friend." Britt and Lucy followed Sarah's gaze to a tall blond leaning against the wall. "He's scrumptious, no?"

Even Britt had to agree: With his chiseled profile and broad shoulders, Dream Boy was easily the best-looking guy they'd seen that night.

"He's in my sociology class, but I can't get up the nerve to say hi," Sarah said.

"Maybe you could accidentally spill beer on him," Britt said.

"Or trip over something and land in his lap," Lucy said.

"Shit!" Sarah grabbed their arms and jerked them in the other direction. "He caught us staring."

"He's probably used to it." Lucy peeked over her shoulder and saw Dream Boy smiling and shaking his head.

"Now he thinks I'm an idiot," Sarah said.

"Just keep dancing," Britt advised. "Ignore him."

So they did. The Rolling Stones gave way to the Doors, then to more electronic house music. Soon some guys Lucy didn't know had broken into their little dance circle. Before long, Sarah was making out with one of them in a corner.

"I guess she decided not to hold out for one of the hot ones," Britt said. "I'm getting back in the beer line. You want another?"

Lucy shook her head.

"I'll find you." And before Lucy could offer to tag along and keep Britt company, she whirled and disappeared into the crowd.

With Britt gone, Lucy stood around for a moment or two, feeling too awkward to dance. Her borrowed dress was sticking to her skin, and her shoes were starting to pinch. She edged her way off the dance floor, into the kitchen, in search of Glory and the beer-pong tournament. As she was thinking about descending into the basement, a cool breeze passed over her arms, and she decided to find out where it was coming from.

Just past the kitchen, a door was propped open. Lucy stepped through it onto a deck. A handful of people sprawled across it, all of them deep in conversation. When Lucy passed, nobody even looked up. She draped herself over the rail, gathered her heavy curls away from her neck, and wondered when Britt and Sarah would be ready to leave. So far, her first college party was turning out to be something of a bust.

Just then, another breeze kicked up, caressing her bare shoulders. Something in the air—maybe it was the scent from the trees next door—reminded her of Fiesole, of standing at the edge of the park overlooking the red roofs of Florence. *Will I ever stop missing Jesse?* Lucy wondered.

"So this is where the beautiful people hang out," a voice said from behind her, startlingly close.

Lucy jumped. Of all the people it might have been, it was Sarah's Dream Boy, grinning down at her. Had he followed her out onto the deck? "You scared me," she said.

"I didn't mean to," he said. "I just felt like talking to someone. Not screaming at them over the music or crushing their feet on the dance floor or pouring beer on them."

Lucy tucked a stray curl behind her ear, relieved to have someone to talk to. "I was just thinking how this doesn't seem to be my scene."

"Mine, either," he said. "But I let my friends drag me here."

"Are you on the rugby team with Armand?"

He shook his head. "I tried out for rugby freshman year. But then I decided I liked my teeth too much." He flashed them at her.

"I can see why," Lucy said without thinking, then blushed.

Dream Boy took mercy on her and changed the subject. "This is your first off-campus party?"

"My first *college* party," Lucy said. "If you don't count popcorn parties with my suitemates. Are they all like this?"

Dream Boy shrugged. Up close he was even better-looking than he'd been from across the room, with steely silver-gray eyes and carefully tousled ash-blond hair—so good-looking that being close to him made Lucy feel the tiniest bit dizzy. "I've been to better. But this one's pretty typical." He took a step closer. "Let me be your guide through the underworld."

"Um, okay." Lucy smiled up at him, hardly able to believe her luck.

"First, whatever you do, stay away from the jungle juice. The red stuff in the punch bowl. It's always lethal."

"Steer clear of the jungle juice," Lucy said. "Check."

"Also, it helps to be familiar with the kinds of characters you'll meet at one of these things. First there's Sloppy Drunk. He's basically harmless. Unless he's big—and then you don't want to let him stand too close. If he falls over he could crush you flat."

"Sloppy Drunk," Lucy said, wishing she could summon the wits to do more than repeat everything Dream Boy said.

"Closely related to Sloppy Drunk is 'I Love You, Man' Drunk."

"Sounds pretty harmless," Lucy said.

"Until he gets you in a death-grip hug. 'I Love You, Man' Drunk won't release you until he's sure you truly understand how much he loves you."

"Yikes," Lucy said. "What other stock characters are there?"

"Well, you'll want to steer clear of Violent Drunk, and also Scary Drunk. And Talkative Drunk can be a terrible time suck." Dream Boy took his chin between his thumb and index finger, miming deep thought, as he looked Lucy over. "For a nice girl like you, I think the safest conversational bet is the IUDD—the 'Increasingly Uncomfortable Designated Driver.'"

"Is that you?" Lucy asked.

Dream Boy grinned. "Very perceptive."

"You don't look uncomfortable, though," Lucy said.

"Not now that I'm here with you," he said, holding out his hand. "I'm Shane, by the way."

"Lucy," she replied, slipping her hand into his.

A half hour later, Lucy was deep in conversation with Shane. They'd been sharing stories about their hometowns, which, it turned out, were right next to each other, and celebrated football rivals. "How have I never bumped into you before?" Shane was asking. "At the Pancake Shack? Or Starbucks?"

"Maybe we've passed each other a hundred times on Lancaster Avenue," Lucy said.

They'd talked about Europe, too. Lucy had mentioned her summer trip, and Shane had asked her lots of questions about backpacking and hostels—and especially Italy. "I've been there with my folks," he said. "But I'm saving up so I can go on my own next summer. I'm sick of hotels and guided tours. I want to have a real adventure, the way you did."

Encouraged, Lucy told him about singing onstage at the underground club in Florence, referring to Jesse only as "the friend I was with."

"Whoa! You're my new hero," Shane said. "A rock star and an adventurer."

Lucy couldn't help grinning. She liked this version of herself.

"And pretty, too," he added, in a conspiratorial voice.

Just then, Britt and Sarah appeared at Lucy's side. "We've been looking for you everywhere," Britt said. "I was beginning to worry you'd been kidnapped."

Shane threw both arms around Lucy's shoulders. "I hope you're prepared to pay a hefty ransom," he said. "I'd say she's worth ten thousand at least."

From inside the circle of Shane's arms, Lucy introduced him to Britt and a very wide-eyed Sarah. *Oh my God*, Sarah mouthed in Lucy's direction when she thought Shane wasn't looking. And again, *Oh my God!*

Lucy gave a little apologetic shrug, meant to communicate, *I wouldn't be flirting with Dream Boy, except you were, um, occupied.* And Sarah shrugged back, seemingly happy for her.

"What happened to your new friend?" Lucy asked. "From back on the dance floor?"

Sarah rolled her eyes.

"We were thinking about walking home before it gets too late," Britt said. "Glory says this neighborhood's pretty sketchy at night."

"Why don't I give you a lift?" Shane released Lucy. "My car's right down the street."

"What about your friends?" Lucy asked.

"I'll come back for them. They won't even notice I'm missing."

Lucy's friends took the backseat of Shane's sporty silver car, leaving the shotgun position for Lucy. The girls directed him to their dorm, and when he pulled up to the curb, Britt and Sarah jumped out, leaving Lucy and Shane alone together.

"Your friends are speedy," he observed.

"They are," she said, wondering if she should get out of the car, too. Was Shane in a hurry to get back to the party?

But he shifted in his seat, leaning a bit closer to her. "So I was wondering," he said. "Will I ever see you again?"

Lucy tried to look nonchalant. "We might bump into each other," she said. "Forsythe isn't that big."

"Or we could up the odds." Shane dug in his pocket, pulled out his phone, and handed it to her. "In case you need my party-going expertise."

Lucy found Sarah and Britt waiting in the dorm lobby. "Oh my God!" Sarah shrieked, giving Lucy's arm a little punch. "You have all the freaking luck."

"Do you want to see him again?" Britt asked.

Sarah snorted. "Of course she does. The question is does *he* want to see *her* again."

"That is *not* the question," Britt insisted.

"We exchanged phone numbers," Lucy said, and Sarah squealed and jumped up and down.

"I'd hate you," Sarah said, "if I didn't know how nice you are."

As she followed her friends up the stairs to their suite on the fourth floor, Lucy smiled to herself. She did feel lucky, or at least relieved. Now that she'd met Shane, maybe she could waste less time obsessing over Jesse, wondering what he was up to or why he hadn't written.

After she'd showered the party from her skin, Lucy switched the light off and climbed into bed with her phone. When Jesse's name popped up in her e-mail in-box, she let out a gasp.

"What is it?" Britt asked sleepily from under her covers.

"This really has been some night," Lucy said, clicking through to the message.

To: Lucy Sommersworth
From: Jesse Palladino

Hey there. It made me happy to get your last e-mail. I'm glad you're having a good time at Forsythe. Sorry to be so slow in writing back. Things are changing fast here at the Bertolini. Nello gave notice yesterday. For weeks now, his mom has been calling every night, begging him to move home. Sometimes she even cries into the phone, laying the guilt trip on really thick. So he decided to cave and go back to Torre Annunziata, his hometown. He's such a softy.

Anyway, since Rome, I've been thinking it's time for me to move on, too. The Bertolini won't be anywhere near as much fun without Nello. This morning, he invited me

to come stay with his family in Torre Annunziata—just
until I figure out where I want to go next.

So, next stop: Nello's family home. He's got six
sisters...can you imagine? Lucky for Nello, he has
his own room. Unlucky for Nello, he's going to have to
share it with me.

Ciao,
Jesse

"Oh, crap," Lucy said. "Jesse's leaving the Bertolini."

"What does it matter?" Britt asked.

"I guess it doesn't. Except it makes me sad to think of the
Bert with him not there." Lucy forced a laugh. "I know, foolish,
right?"

Britt didn't answer.

"Should I write back tonight?" Lucy asked.

"Why wouldn't you?"

"Because he takes forever to answer my e-mails."

"Then make him wait," Britt said.

"You're right. I will." And with great resolve, Lucy turned off
her phone and tucked it under her pillow. But she couldn't seem to
keep her eyes shut. At least an hour later, long after Britt's breathing had turned into gentle snoring, Lucy reached back under her
pillow. She turned the phone on under her duvet to keep the light
from waking Britt.

To: Jesse Palladino
From: Lucy Sommersworth

Please send my love to Nello—he was one of the
nicest people I met all summer. I just got home
from my first real college party. It was kind of noisy
and beery and crowded, but I did meet at least one
cool person there, which I guess means it was a
success.

I have to admit, I'm a little bit bummed to hear that
you'll be leaving the Bertolini. The place won't be the
same without you and Nello. But it's very cool that
you're moving on to new adventures. Send me a
postcard or something from Torre Annunziata, okay? I
confess, I don't even know where that is, but I hope it's
great.

So Nello has six sisters? Wow. That's really something.
I'm imagining a houseful of gorgeous Italian girls. *Che
bellezza!* How will you stand it?

When she reached the end of the message, Lucy hesitated,
wondering how to sign off. *Love, Lucy,* she typed, then erased
the words. Jesse hadn't signed *his* message with love. Maybe she
shouldn't, either.

She considered ending with hugs and kisses; she even thought about using something more neutral like *best* or *regards*. After all, *love* wasn't a word they'd used in person. But if what she felt for Jesse wasn't love, Lucy couldn't imagine what love was.

She typed the words again: *Love, Lucy.* And before she could change her mind, she took a deep breath and hit send.

XIII

⚯⚯⚯

*T*he campus of Forsythe University might not be Florence or Rome, but it was beautiful in its own way, especially in mid-September, with the lawns bright green and the leaves just starting to turn. In knee-high boots and a red plaid skirt, Lucy hurried to class, feeling more like an actress playing the part of a college student than an actual college student. She'd chosen the skirt to reflect her mood: optimistic, triumphant. After a couple of days of not hearing from Shane and deciding he probably wasn't going to contact her after all, she'd gotten a text from him, inviting her out for dinner on Saturday night. At a fancy restaurant in Center City, no less.

"An actual date?" Sarah had exclaimed when Lucy showed her the message. "Do people still do that?"

Now a mix of music floated from the open windows of the

dorms she passed on her way to class—rap, country, eighties pop—a sound track to her morning. Silvery chords from an acoustic guitar spilled onto the quad, making Lucy think of Jesse. He hadn't written her back yet. By now, he was probably in Torre Annunziata, living with Nello's six sisters, but she wasn't going to let that spoil her mood today. Even passing the smug brick façade of Marston Hall—Charlene's dorm—didn't bring her down.

She hadn't spoken with Charlene since the long, silent purgatory of their flight home to Philadelphia, though once or twice they had passed each other in the dining hall, each of them working hard to pretend she hadn't seen the other. The last thing Lucy would want now was to bump into Charlene. She picked up her pace, holding her breath until she was safely beyond Marston, then taking the stairs to the Social Sciences building two at a time.

There, at the top of the hill, loomed the ultramodern Theater Arts building. Usually, whenever she passed it, Lucy looked straight ahead, not wanting to catch sight of the drama majors who gathered on the front steps, laughing in a pack. They belonged there and she didn't. But this morning, the plaza in front of the building was quieter than usual. Feeling just a little reckless, Lucy allowed herself one wistful glance at the entrance, which was how she caught sight of a square of neon yellow she hadn't noticed before—a sign taped to the glass door. Curious, Lucy slowed to a halt, then climbed the steps for a closer look.

AUDITIONS FOR *RENT*
WEDNESDAY, 7 PM
EVERYONE WELCOME

Lucy froze, aware of her own heartbeat. *Rent* was her all-time favorite musical. After seeing the movie version, she had listened to the sound track night and day until she knew every single note of the score. Ever since, playing the role of downtown diva Maureen had been one of her favorite daydreams.

Lucy took a step back from the door, then another. She paused at the top of the steps, trying to recapture the optimism she'd been feeling, but it had been replaced by sadness for the things she'd traded away. Lucy felt a sudden urge to head straight back to bed. But her class started in five minutes, so she forced herself onward.

"It's like the universe is tormenting me," she told her suitemates that night. The four of them were lounging around in pajamas, supposedly watching TV, but really talking.

"I don't understand," Sarah said over her mug of peppermint tea. "I thought you never wanted to go on another audition again."

"I did say that," Lucy said. "I meant it, too."

"So what do you care about *Rent*?" The Tweety Bird face on the front of Sarah's nightdress, with its enormous blue eyes, fly-away yellow hair, and tiny mouth, looked comically like Sarah, but Lucy hadn't been able to work out whether or not Sarah herself saw the resemblance.

"Haven't you ever had mixed feelings about something?" Britt aimed the remote control at the TV. Lucy shot her a grateful look.

"Well, you can't have the spotlight and the applause without the auditions and the stage fright," Sarah said.

"Tell her something she doesn't know," Britt said.

Sarah scrunched up her nose. "If she wants to be onstage, she should just face her fears. Bite the bullet." She grabbed the clicker from Britt's hand, settled on a channel, and set the remote down out of Britt's reach. "All those clichés."

Glory, who had been silently doing yoga poses, her glossy black curls tied back in a pouf, made a tsk-tsk noise.

"What's that supposed to mean?" Britt asked.

Glory came out of her downward dog. "She made a promise."

"So?" Sarah asked.

Lucy sat cross-legged, popcorn bowl in her lap, looking from one friend to another as though she were watching a three-player tennis match. If they remembered she was in the room, they didn't let on.

Glory swung onto her belly and went into the cobra pose. "She accepted a trip to Europe in exchange for giving up acting. Her parents held up their part of the deal. She can't back out now."

"Seriously?" Sarah said.

"That's how a deal works."

"This is about Lucy's life," Britt chimed in. "About the thing she loves to do. Does anybody have the right to make her give that up?"

"A promise is a promise," Glory said.

"Technically, she promised not to be a drama major," Britt said. "She didn't promise never to act again. So she wouldn't be *in breach of contract*." She said that last bit tauntingly. Lucy knew that it was only because her suitemates generally got along that they could give one another a hard time like this. Even so, being

148

the subject of their debate was starting to make her feel antsy. She tried to focus on the TV—a rerun of *Friends* was playing—but tuning out *her* friends was impossible.

"So you think she should break her promise? On a technicality?" Glory would make a great lawyer someday, Lucy often thought. She never shied away from an argument.

"I think it's her life," Britt declared. "Promise or no promise. Lucy should do what she wants."

"But what does she want?" Glory asked. "Because at this point I'm not even sure."

All three of them turned their attention to Lucy, who cleared her throat. "I'm not going to audition." She made her voice decisive. "Now can we please just watch *Friends?*"

Maybe Lucy shouldn't have listened to the sound track from *Rent* as she fell asleep that night, so that the songs wove themselves through her dreams. Maybe she shouldn't have looked again at Jesse's picture, imagining what he would say about auditioning. Maybe she should have taken the long way back from her afternoon classes instead of passing the Theater Arts building and stopping to reread that sign.

Back in her dorm room, Lucy sat alone with the lights off, remembering her last, disastrous audition. When Brittany came in, she snapped the lights on and found Lucy blinking, owl-like, in surprise.

"What's this?" Britt asked, closing the door behind her.

"Even if I did try out, they wouldn't pick me for a good role, anyway. Drama majors must get all the best parts, right?"

"What time is the audition?"

Lucy looked at her clock. "In an hour and fifteen minutes."

"There's still time." Britt perched beside her on the edge of the bed. "If you decide you want to give it a try."

"I haven't prepared a monologue," Lucy said. "Or a song."

"But you must know some by heart. Since you've auditioned so many times before?"

Lucy covered her face with her hands. "The last time was such a disaster," she said. "I think I must have over-rehearsed or something."

"So that won't be a problem this time," Britt said matter-of-factly.

"But what if I freeze up again? I'd make a fool out of myself in front of everyone."

"Yeah, in front of a bunch of strangers you'll probably never see again, who will all be so freaked out about their own auditions that they couldn't care less about yours. I can't think of anything worse." Britt tapped her chin and gazed up at the ceiling. "Oh, wait. I can. Sitting alone in the dark, worrying about it."

"But I haven't picked out audition clothes. What if I don't have anything to wear?"

Britt leaped up and flung open the door to Lucy's closet, which was stuffed so full of clothing there wasn't room for one more hanger. "Poor Lucy. She has nothing to wear. Not. One. Thing."

Lucy giggled. "You're really going to make me do this?" She wiped her nose with the back of her hand.

"Ew, girl. Mind your manners!" Britt grabbed a box of tissues from the bureau and tossed it to Lucy. "I'll march you to the Theater Arts building and sit in the front row while you audition, if that's what it takes."

"Don't do that," Lucy said. "If I screw up I don't want anyone I know there. Least of all someone I live with. I would have to ask Campus Life to find me a new roommate."

"Or you could go into the witness protection program."

Britt helped Lucy pick out audition clothes—a red silk T-shirt, a short black skirt, tights, knee-high boots, and her most dramatic earrings. She watched as Lucy dug through the box of her theater memorabilia for sheet music from past auditions. And she saw Lucy off with a big hug and a murmured: "Break *both* legs."

On her way to the Theater Arts building, Lucy rehearsed the monologue she'd used in her last, doomed audition. Strangely, the lines came back to her as though she'd learned them just days ago. *This is crazy*, Lucy told herself as she hurried through the twilight.

The brightly lit lobby of the Theater Arts building buzzed with conversation. Lucy squeezed through the crowd to get to the sign-up sheet, grabbed a handout, then slipped back into the darkest corner she could find to survey the competition. To judge from the excited chatter, everyone there already knew one another, but she didn't know a single soul.

The wait was long and Lucy wished she'd brought Britt along for moral support after all. *If I were a drama major, I'd know everyone here*, she thought. To ward off stage fright, she took deep, cleansing breaths, as the community theater director had taught her. It helped, but only a little.

One by one, people were called into the theater, their friends giving them waves and encouraging smiles just before they vanished. The lobby fell silent, and in the hush Lucy could hear snippets of each audition—piano music or a soprano's voice seeping through the walls. Ten or so minutes later, the would-be cast member would emerge through a second door, looking drained or exhilarated or a little of both.

I've done this before, Lucy reminded herself. *I can do it again.* Just being in the Theater Arts building made the memories flood back—rehearsing, performing, coming out for a curtain call, and soaking up the applause. *Who was I kidding, thinking I never wanted to act again?* Now that she was in this building, surrounded by the competition, Lucy let herself know the truth: Not only did she want a part in *Rent*, she wanted the biggest, juiciest part she could get. But what if that last, horrible audition had jinxed her forever?

When her number was finally called, Lucy inhaled deeply, threw her shoulders back, and stepped into the theater. As she strode toward the stage where the director waited, she was filled with a feeling she hadn't experienced in a while: equal parts elation and determination, the same mix of emotions she'd felt in sixth grade when she'd emerged from behind the curtain in a blue pinafore and headband to become Alice in Wonderland.

"Hello." The director, a slender woman in a gray wool pantsuit, squinted at the sheet of paper in her hand, then looked

Lucy up and down. Her mouth twitched to one side. "I've never seen you before." Was this a good thing or a bad thing? Lucy couldn't tell.

"My name is Lucy Sommersworth." Feeling herself falter, she struggled to recall the tricks she'd learned for nailing an audition: Stand up straight. Fake confidence. Make eye contact. As soon as she'd done those things, she felt stronger. Lucy rattled off the little speech she'd been rehearsing about the plays she'd been in and the roles she'd had, and which monologue and song she'd be delivering for the audition. It was almost as though she'd never given up acting.

"Well, okay, then," the director said. Was it Lucy's imagination, or did she look skeptical? Anyway, there was no backing out now. Lucy settled into the ideal spot on the stage. Then she launched into her monologue.

This time the lines came back to Lucy right away. She relaxed, letting the words and emotion propel her forward.

And though she'd been worried the director would interrupt her mid-monologue, it didn't happen. Lucy knew from experience that this wasn't necessarily a bad sign, but she always preferred getting to the end of her lines, spinning out the emotion she'd called up in herself for as long as possible. When she was through, she paused, breathing heavily. Was that expression crossing the director's face a look of approval?

But the woman wasn't giving anything away. "Now your song," she prompted, running a hand through her white-streaked hair. The pianist launched into the familiar opening bars.

Lucy braced herself as though she were at the peak of a roller coaster, then launched into the song she'd chosen because it fit her range perfectly. Luckily, she remembered all the words. As she sang, she fixed her eyes just above the director's head, willing herself to become the music, to feel its emotions and make them her own. At the end of the song, Lucy exhaled, becoming herself again.

"Thank you." The woman's expression was polite and friendly—but unreadable. Lucy retreated to the lobby to wait for the callback, when the director would have them read in groups. Adrenaline coursed through her veins, making her feel alive in a way she hadn't since that night onstage in Florence. *To think I almost gave this up forever,* she thought, stealing glances at the faces of the drama majors milling around the lobby, waiting for their turns. She had no way of gauging whether she'd been good enough to get a part, but just then it didn't even matter. *I remembered my lines,* she told herself. For the moment, that was enough.

By the time the tryouts ended, the moon was high in the sky, the campus eerily quiet. As the theater majors wandered off in pairs and groups, Lucy reached for her phone, figuring she'd text Britt. *I did it!* she typed. *Are you proud of me?* She followed it up with a smiley face.

When a reply didn't come right away, she fired off a message to Shane: *Hey! Guess what? I tried out for* Rent.

His reply was immediate. *You're an actress? That's very hot! How did it go?*

Good, I think, she replied.

That's fantastic, he wrote. *I'll keep my fingers crossed. Maybe we'll have something to celebrate on Saturday night.*

Thanks. I hope so! she wrote.

Cheered by Shane's message, Lucy started back toward her dorm. She'd made it only a few steps farther when her phone buzzed in her pocket. Surprise! There, at the top of her in-box, was a message from Jesse Palladino. *Perfect timing,* she told herself just before she opened it.

To: Lucy Sommersworth
From: Jesse Palladino

Hello again. How are things? I'm writing to you from Nello's hometown, where we've been for a couple of days. Torre Annunziata is a rough-around-the-edges seaport town—lots of graffiti, crumbling concrete, and unemployment. Not exactly a place tourists are itching to see.

But it's not all bad. Everyone I bump into is friendly and helpful; they hardly ever meet Americans. I'm some kind of novelty. Nello's mother and sisters have been fussing over me, and his tiny white-haired grandmother likes to shout *Mangia! Mangia!* even while I'm stuffing my face with ravioli. They're like I always imagined an Italian family to be—yelling at each other half the time and hugging each other the other half. Only one of

Nello's sisters speaks English, so I'm getting all kinds of practice speaking Italian.

Money has been tight. Since this isn't a tourist town, busking's not an option and jobs are hard to find. But the good news is that Nello's twin sister, Angelina, thinks she can find work for both of us. There's been some turnover at the hotel in Naples where she's a receptionist. I've got an interview in a couple of hours, so wish me luck!

Ciao,
Jesse

In the light of a campus shuttle stop, Lucy lingered over the message, feeling a little worse with each rereading. For one thing, it bothered her that though she'd signed her message with love, Jesse hadn't responded in kind. For another, there was Nello's sister, Angelina, whose name conjured a vision in Lucy's head of the kind of girl she could never compete with: Raven-haired. Bosomy. Exotic.

You're being ridiculous, she told herself. Then she typed a reply, trying to sound breezy and optimistic.

To: Jesse Palladino
From: Lucy Sommersworth

Wow: Naples! I'm excited for you. That's too bad about the busking. Anyway, good luck finding work.

Things have been interesting here. First of all, I tried
out for the college production of *Rent* tonight. I doubt
I'll get a part, but I had to give it a shot, and I'm proud
to say I didn't trip over my own tongue or blank out
on my lines. In fact, it felt really good. I know you'll
understand what a huge, incredible deal this was for
me, so I wanted to let you know. Please keep your
fingers crossed!

Nello has a twin sister? I'm trying to imagine him as a
girl, and failing.

Lucy reread the message. *Should I mention Shane?* she wondered, but there seemed no casual way to work him in. And, now
that she'd already signed off with love once, wouldn't it seem weird
if this time she didn't? She wouldn't want Jesse to guess she was
jealous, or to let on how much he'd hurt her by signing his message *ciao*. So, before she could change her mind, she typed those
last two tricky words—*Love, Lucy*—and hit send.

XIV

⸻❀⸻

On Friday at noon, Lucy skipped lunch, hurrying straight from her eleven o'clock class to the Theater Arts building. By the time she reached the lobby, a crowd had gathered in front of the bulletin board where the cast list for *Rent* had just been posted. Heart pounding, she positioned herself on the fringes. Waiting for a space to open up so she could get closer, she was startled to hear her own name.

"Lucy Sommersworth? Who is *that?*" a girl's voice asked.

"Never heard of her," someone replied.

Lucy gasped, but luckily nobody seemed to hear. They were all too busy looking for their own names on the list—then rejoicing or complaining. "I've had speaking roles in the last three plays, and now I get cast in the chorus?" one girl wailed. "How is that fair?"

"It's a total mistake," her friend replied. "You deserve better."

Wishing she were three inches taller, Lucy craned her neck, trying to see past the heads gathered in front of her. Just then, the complaining girl and her friend stepped away, and Lucy slipped forward to take a look at the list. When she saw her name near the top, her heart skipped a beat. She'd been cast as Maureen, the performance artist-slash-diva. The role of her dreams.

The whole rest of that day, Lucy couldn't concentrate on classes or homework, no matter how hard she tried. At dinner, she couldn't even pay attention to the conversation at her table. Instead of eating, she pushed the food on her plate into little hills and tore a dinner roll into crumbs.

"Lucy, you haven't said a word this whole time. What do you think?" Glory had demanded.

"I'm sorry. I zoned out," Lucy had to admit. "What do I think about what?"

"I was talking about Armand," Glory said. "How I never see him anymore because he's so caught up in a bromance with his lacrosse buddies."

"She could have guessed that," Brittany said. "You're *always* talking about Armand."

"Where is your mind, Lucy?" Glory asked. "It's like you're off in outer space."

"She's thinking about her *boyfriend*," Sarah guessed. "Has he called you back yet?" Her baby-blue eyes took on that faraway look they got whenever she mentioned Shane.

"No," Lucy said. "I mean, yes. We're going out tomorrow night."

"Damn," Sarah said wistfully.

"But that's not what I was thinking about."

Her three friends waited.

Lucy took a deep breath and told them about her part in *Rent*.

"That's amazing," Brittany said.

"Whoa," Sarah said. "This girl I know in Huddleston Hall tried out. She only got a role in the chorus—and she's really talented."

"You're going to take the part, right?" Brittany asked.

"Of course she isn't," Glory said with her usual confidence.

"But why would she have auditioned in the first place if she wasn't going to do it?" Sarah asked.

Lucy's friends fell silent, waiting for her to weigh in. Instead, she reached for another roll, picking it into bits while she remembered how happy she'd been on her walk from the Theater Arts building, buoyed by her audition. Then she pictured herself onstage, in a line of her castmates, singing "Seasons of Love" (one of her all-time favorite songs!) before a rapt audience. Even now, sitting in the dining hall with her friends, she could shut her eyes and see herself stalking the stage in Maureen's high-heeled boots and leather pants.

"Lucy?" Britt was surveying the wreckage on Lucy's plate with a concerned expression.

Lucy brushed the crumbs from her lap and looked from face to face. "Sarah's right," she said brightly. "I'm doing the play." Saying the words made it official, and now that she couldn't back down, she knew for sure she didn't really want to.

Later that night, after Brittany had dozed off, Lucy still couldn't sleep, so she checked her phone. She was surprised to find a message from Jesse in her in-box.

> To: Lucy Sommersworth
> From: Jesse Palladino
>
> You tried out for *Rent*? That's amazing, Lucy. I bet you knocked it out of the park.
>
> Luckily, Angelina is Nello's fraternal twin, so she gets to be much prettier than he is!
>
> I'm at an Internet café, and my time's almost up, so I've got to run. Keep me posted!
>
> Ciao,
> Jesse

Disappointed, Lucy stared at the screen. She could hardly believe Jesse's message was so short. Could he really not have found the time or the euros to type more than a few sentences? Even worse, the comment about *Rent* was overshadowed by the bit about how pretty Angelina was. A vision popped into her mind: Angelina, who looked a little like her brother but much,

much prettier, in skintight jeans and a peasant blouse that bared a perfect shoulder, sliding a plate of pasta in front of Jesse with an enticing smile.

Teeth gritted, Lucy typed a hasty reply.

To: Jesse Palladino
From: Lucy Sommersworth

Thanks for the support. I guess you'll be happy to hear that I got cast in the role of Maureen—the role I really wanted. Bizarre, right? Considering I'd given up acting, that is.

Anyway, I'm glad you've moved on and are making new friends. I'm especially glad to hear how pretty Angelina is. Maybe you two will hit it off?

Oh, speaking of which, I'm happy to report that I've started seeing someone. He's taking me out to dinner in Center City tomorrow night, to someplace trendy and fun. I wasn't lying when I told you that I don't always need to have fancy things and go to fancy places. But every now and then, it's pretty freaking great.

Ciao,
Lucy

As soon as she hit send, Lucy knew she had made a terrible mistake. She groaned, forgetting that Britt was asleep just yards away.

"Who's there?" Britt bolted upright in bed and felt around, probably for the pepper spray she kept in the drawer of her bedside table. Her fingers found something, and she waved it in the air, squinting into the semi-darkness in search of the enemy.

"Oh, God, I'm sorry, Britt," Lucy said. "Don't spray. It's just me." She slapped herself in the forehead, hard enough to hurt. "I'm such an idiot."

"What did you do now?" Britt asked, setting down the pepper spray.

Lucy explained how she'd just fired off the most embarrassing e-mail of all time.

"How bad can it be?" Britt threw her covers aside and padded over to Lucy's bed.

"Pretty bad," Lucy told her.

"Let me see." Britt wrested the phone from Lucy's hand and read the message. "It isn't great," she said finally. "Parts are okay."

"Parts?" Lucy hid her face in her hands.

"What does it matter, anyway?" Britt asked. "It's not like you're ever going to see him again."

"I don't know why it matters," Lucy told her. "It just does." She held out her hand for the phone, but Britt got up and set it out of reach on Lucy's desk. She moved with exaggerated care, as though it were a gun that might go off.

"Shouldn't I send another e-mail?" Lucy asked. "I could say I was kidding. Or that my psycho roommate wrote that message as a practical joke."

"Oh, Lucy, no." Britt sat back down on the bed beside her. "The damage is done. You should just let it go. You never know— maybe he'll think you were kidding?"

"Doubtful," Lucy said.

Brittany yawned without bothering to cover her mouth. "Aren't you going out with Shane tomorrow night?"

Lucy looked over at her alarm clock; its red digits read 1:47. "Tonight, actually," she said.

"So that's a good thing."

"I know," Lucy said. "He's great, right?"

"Great." Britt yawned again, louder this time.

"I'm keeping you awake," Lucy said. "I'm the world's worst roommate."

But Britt was too tired to speak in full sentences anymore. "Need sleep. Morning soon." And with that, she slipped back into her own bed and turned to face the wall.

Britt was right, of course. Lucy needed sleep, too; she had to look her best for that night's date. So she tried to make herself think of happier things—where Shane might take her and what she should wear. In the moonlight, she could make out the photo that hung on the wall above her desk—the one taken on the Spanish Steps. In it, she looked up at Jesse, and he grinned down at her, arms crossed over his chest. But his smile, which once had seemed so warm, now looked mocking.

I'll take that photo down tomorrow, Lucy promised herself. *And I'll never think about Jesse Palladino again.*

XV

‹‹‹≈≈≈›››

*L*ucy's date with Shane was everything she could have
hoped for and more. He showed up on time, wearing a
crisp button-down shirt that played up his silver-gray eyes. "You
look amazing," he told Lucy, who had decided on her black-and-
white polka-dotted dress, her best flats, and a cashmere sweater in
case the night got cold.

"So I was thinking we'd have an all-Italy extravaganza," he
told her as he pulled onto Main Street, driving away from campus.
"Dinner downtown at Ernesto's. And it turns out there's an Italian film playing at the Ritz."

"The Ritz!" Lucy gave a little bounce in her seat. "I've
always wanted to go there. My high school friends never understood why I'd want to trek all the way into the city just to see a
movie."

Shane deftly changed lanes. "Then, if you're up for it, maybe a cappuccino after?"

Ernesto's was sleek and modern, all glass and gleaming wood. Their waiter even had a real Italian accent. When he took Lucy's order, he called her *la bella signorina*, the beautiful young lady. She thanked him in Italian, and he replied with a rush of even more Italian, of which she understood about every fifth word.

"I'm impressed," Shane said when the waiter had moved on. "Will you teach me?"

"I don't know much, really." Lucy took a delicate sip of sparkling water. "Just enough to order in a restaurant. You'd be better off taking a class."

"But what fun would that be?"

"We could practice together." She imagined the two of them in the future, at a corner table in New York's Little Italy, whispering romantic nothings to each other in Italian. Over tortellini with prosciutto, she told him about getting the part of Maureen in *Rent*, and he was every bit as excited as she could have hoped.

"I guessed you were an actor," he said. "I'm always drawn to creative types—actors and painters and poets."

"What about you?" Lucy asked. "Wait. I know. You're a photographer. No...a sculptor."

Shane looked amused. "Keep going."

"A writer," Lucy tried. "A journalist. Or a novelist."

He held up both hands in a gesture of surrender. "I don't have a lick of talent. It's tragic."

"I don't believe you," Lucy said. "Of course you have talent."

Shane reached across the table to lightly touch her hand.

"Well, I'm good at picking interesting friends. You should meet this guy I know—he lives in a loft in Northern Liberties, a few blocks from my apartment. He's an actual hipster, with, you know, the facial hair and the attitude, but he's the real thing. He paints these big, splashy canvases—cityscapes of Philly—and he's made contact with a gallery. He and his roommates throw amazing parties, too. You'd like him."

Lucy dabbed at her lips with her linen napkin to hide her smile; she couldn't help being pleased that he was already making plans for the two of them. "But what about you? What do you do?"

"What do I do?"

"I mean…what's your major?" Lucy felt her cheeks getting hotter. "I know that's, like, a classic campus pickup line, but…"

"Business," Shane said.

"Me, too!" Lucy exclaimed. "But why? If you're so into the arts, I mean."

"I could ask you the same question." He pointed his fork at her.

"You first," she said.

"My parents." He speared the last of his tortellini and popped it into his mouth. "It's not a very interesting story." His hand brushed hers again, for the briefest of moments.

"It is." Lucy leaned in a bit closer. "To me it is."

Shane's smile was wry. "My dad has this company he built from the ground up, selling imports from China. He wants me to work for him after I graduate. I figure he's going to pay me decent money and teach me the business, so why not go for it?"

Lucy nodded. "That sounds great."

"Besides, I'm not one of those guys who has to rebel against his father just to prove a point," Shane said. "I saw how that worked for my brothers. Ryan opened his own mixed martial arts studio, and he's up to his ears in debt. And Randall is in construction, but jobs are scarce." He shook his head. "What about you?"

"Pretty much the same story," Lucy said. On the walk over to the Ritz, through Center City's charming redbrick streets, she told him about the bargain she'd made with her dad, about giving up her Broadway dreams and majoring in business.

"Whoa," Shane said, taking her hand in his. "We've got a lot in common."

A lot in common, Lucy thought, a bit dazed.

Shane interlaced his fingers with hers. Despite the heat, his hand was cool and dry. They held hands through much of the film, a quirky romantic comedy set in Naples. From time to time, when she got tired of reading subtitles, Lucy stole a glance at Shane. Something about his profile, illuminated by the flickering colors of the screen, brought back a memory of Michelangelo's *David* in the Piazza della Signoria—his chiseled face, his swagger. *A lot in common!* she thought again, savoring the words. But then a memory popped into her head: Jesse standing at her side, looking up at Donatello's *David*, his arm brushing hers. Lucy gave her head a shake. *You're here with Shane*, she told herself. *Enjoy the moment.*

She squeezed his hand and forced her attention back to the screen, where the male and female leads were deep in a passionate embrace. *This isn't some vacation flirtation*, she reminded herself. *This is your life.*

Back at the dorm, Lucy's suitemates were waiting up for her in their pajamas.

"Was it fun?" Britt asked.

Lucy did a happy little dance in reply.

"I hate you," Sarah said, hugging her fuzzy pink body pillow.

"Tell us everything," Glory said. "Don't leave out a single detail."

"He kissed you, right?" Sarah said. "Is he an excellent kisser? He looks like an excellent kisser."

So Lucy related the story of her first date with Shane from start to finish. Shane had kissed her good night on the path just outside of the dorm, and he was, in fact, an excellent kisser.

"Was there tongue?" Glory asked.

Lucy smiled slyly. "It was a total movie kiss."

"I've always wanted a movie kiss." Sarah stared off into the distance.

Lucy put a hand on her shoulder and gave it a gentle squeeze. "You'll have one someday," she said.

"I still hate you," Sarah said, squeezing her back.

"Does this mean you're finally giving up on that Jesse guy?" Glory asked.

Lucy felt her cheeks go pink. Though she told Glory and Sarah almost everything, she didn't want to share the story of the embarrassing e-mail; it was bad enough that Britt had glimpsed her at her worst. "I took down Jesse's picture from my wall." She tried to sound casual.

"It's true," Britt reported. "I couldn't believe my eyes."

"He's in my past," Lucy said. "I've decided to face facts."

"About time," Glory said.

"So, does Shane have any single friends?" Sarah asked. "Or maybe a twin brother?"

But the word *twin* brought Lucy another pang of embarrassment. *Angelina*, she thought. *Maybe by sending that terrible e-mail, I've pushed Jesse into her arms.*

Later, as she pulled on her nightgown and climbed into bed with her phone, she thought about how well the evening had gone. Shane had said he would call her soon; he'd even mentioned wanting to go out again next weekend. Still, despite her resolution to forget about Jesse, Lucy couldn't help wondering if he had written her back. What would be worse: if he'd fired off an angry reply, or if he'd simply not bothered to write back at all?

She braced herself and checked her in-box, but there was nothing new in it. *I don't blame him for not answering*, she thought. *But how can I move on when his last memory of me is that crazy e-mail?*

Because she knew Britt would try to talk her out of what she was about to do, Lucy waited until her roommate was asleep to write one last message.

To: Jesse Palladino
From: Lucy Sommersworth

I owe you an apology. I know the last e-mail I sent was straight-up crazy. It must have been obvious I was having a bad night and feeling a tiny bit jealous of your new friendship with Nello's sister. I was even envious

that you're still in Italy while I'm not! As soon as I hit
send I was sorry. If I could have climbed into my phone,
grabbed that e-mail in both hands, crumpled it up, and
tossed it into the trash, I would have. But of course
there was nothing I could do but feel like an idiot.

Still, I just wanted to write you one last time, to let you
know the girl who sent that e-mail wasn't me...not
really. I had a wonderful time with you in Florence and
Rome—maybe the time of my life. I don't want those
happy memories to be smudged out by the stupid
things I've said since then. So can you do me one
last favor and forget everything I wrote in that e-mail?
I want you to remember me the way I was when we
were together—happy and excited—not insane.

I really do wish the best for you. I hope you've found
a good job, one that leaves you plenty of time to
make music. And if by chance you and Angelina do
get together, I hope she treats you right, because you
really, really deserve it.

Love,
Lucy

Lucy read and reread the letter, afraid to hit send. What if
as soon as she did she realized she'd only messed things up even
more? But she knew she had to do something, and this e-mail

was the best she could come up with. Now that she'd apologized, maybe their memories of each other could go back to being purely happy ones.

So Lucy hit send. A second later, when a new message appeared in her in-box, she clicked on it, an uneasy feeling taking hold of her. *Delivery to the following recipient failed permanently*, it read. *User unknown.*

Lucy's stomach constricted. Jesse had changed his e-mail address without telling her? Had he closed his old e-mail account just to dodge her messages? Now she had no way to reach him, no way of assuring him she wasn't as unhinged as she must have seemed. It was official: She would never hear from him again.

Lucy waited a long moment. Then she clicked into her photos, scrolling till she found what she'd come to think of as *the* picture—the two of them on the Spanish Steps, the same one she'd taken down from her wall the day before. It filled her screen: Jesse's smile, her smile. The bright blue sky behind him; the ice-cream cone melting in her hand.

Lucy tapped the little trash can at the bottom of the screen. But when a prompt popped up, asking if she really wanted to delete the photo, she panicked. Maybe she'd never see Jesse again. But that didn't mean she wanted to forget her time with him in Italy. Not yet. Not completely.

Lucy hit the cancel button. Knowing she still could look at that picture if she wanted to—even if it hurt to see it—made her feel the tiniest bit better. *Not that I should even care*, she thought. *What does it matter?* But somehow it did.

XVI

———

A few nights later, rehearsals began. As Lucy hurried through the darkness to the Theater Arts building, she felt as light as a helium balloon. The lobby was bright, warm, and buzzing with the voices of the rest of the cast. Lucy found a quiet spot in a far corner and tried not to look like she was eavesdropping on the conversations around her as she waited for rehearsal to begin. Secretly, she wished someone would approach her and say hello, but nobody seemed to notice her. A few minutes before six, the double doors into the theater opened.

"Welcome, everyone," the director called out as the cast of *Rent* streamed into the auditorium, claiming seats. Elegant in black silk pants and a Chinese-style jacket, she cast her gaze out over the crowd and the room fell silent.

"First of all: congratulations. Competition for parts was

the fiercest I've ever seen it. You all deserve a hand." The cast applauded until the director gestured for silence. "Now the real work begins," she said.

Lucy clutched the arms of her seat, giddy with nerves.

"The first thing I'd like to do is introductions, on the off chance we don't all know one another already. I'm Dr. Marcella Stewart, but you can call me Marcella. And this"—she gestured grandly toward the stage, where a bearlike man in reading glasses emerged from behind the piano—"is Ben Slocum, our music director."

After the requisite applause, Ben said a few words about dedication and hard work; then Marcella did the same. As hard as she tried to listen, Lucy felt herself tuning out the speeches, fast-forwarding to her fantasies of opening night, the audience cheering her performance. She shut her eyes and imagined the scene—Brittany, Glory, and Sarah in the front row, and beside them, her parents. And Shane.

Lucy forced her eyes open. *Get real*, she told herself. *Focus.*

"Because we'll be working very closely with one another over the next few months, we'll need to be on a first-name basis. So when I call your name, please stand, and stay standing."

Lucy's name was the fourth one called. Did she imagine it, or was there a faint buzz among the others when she stood? She tried to gauge the expressions of the cast members turning in their seats to get a better look at her. A couple of faces looked friendly, a few looked less so, and the rest seemed blank. To banish her jitters, Lucy conjured up her queenly smile, the one she'd used when she played Glinda the Good Witch in her tenth-grade production of *The Wizard of Oz*, the smile that said, "I'm above all this." It worked; a few of the faces smiled back at her, and she immediately felt better.

By the time Marcella had reached the bottom of her list, the whole room was standing, and Lucy's heart swelled with joy.

"Now let's get cracking." Marcella handed out the script, the score, and the rehearsal calendar—several weeks of intense work, culminating in five performances near the end of the semester. "Read this over and note it well," she said. "Rehearsal has to be your first priority, no excuses."

As Marcella went over the schedule point by point, Lucy looked around the room at the rest of the cast, wondering if they were all going to resent her—the interloper who wasn't serious enough about acting to even become a drama major.

Fifteen minutes later, when Marcella dismissed them for the night, Lucy scanned the room for a friendly face. This time, a few people were looking at her, but none of them appeared exactly welcoming. Disappointed, she got to her feet. She had almost reached the exit when a tall girl with short, spiky dreadlocks and Doc Martens stepped into her path. Lucy recognized her as the girl who had been cast as Joanne, Maureen's girlfriend. The two of them would be working closely together, singing a duet, and even sharing an onstage kiss. On the list of things Lucy was feeling nervous about, that kiss was near the top.

"Where did *you* come from?" the girl asked.

Thinking she was being challenged, Lucy flushed violently. "Over there." She pointed to the seat she'd just vacated, though she knew perfectly well that wasn't what the girl meant.

To Lucy's relief, the girl laughed. "Everyone's wondering who the mystery girl is. The one who snagged the best role in the show."

"It's not the best role," Lucy said. "*Rent* has eight leads."

"At least three girls in this room were dying to play Maureen," the girl insisted, folding her arms across her chest. "You must be *something*."

Lucy hesitated. She didn't want to come across as boastful, but she didn't want this girl, whatever her name was, to think she wasn't serious.

"Come out with us," the girl said. "For coffee." When she smiled, her eyes crinkled, and Lucy realized she was being welcomed, not challenged.

"Us" turned out to be a clutch of cast members waiting out in the cold, and Lucy's newest friend was Cleo, a junior English major with a minor in theater. They took her to Café Paradiso, a funky little all-night café not far from campus with a jukebox that played the same kind of electronic dance music she'd heard everywhere in Europe. As she listened to the chatter around her, trying—and mostly failing—to break into the conversation, Lucy felt warmed by the music, the company, and the café latte in her hand.

"Are you always so quiet?" This question came from Matteo, the boy sitting to her left. He'd been cast in the part of Angel, the generous and kindhearted drummer, and with his slender build and his nimbus of curly hair, he really looked the part of an angel. "I hope we're not drowning you out."

Lucy opened her mouth to speak but was interrupted by Celia, a willowy redhead from the chorus. "Or maybe we're just not interesting enough for a hotshot like Lucy." Though a moment ago she'd been joking with the others, her voice, like her words, was surprisingly harsh.

The others at the table gaped while Lucy struggled to find her tongue. "I'm no hotshot," she said.

"You're not?" Celia tapped an unlit cigarette against the table, then tucked it into the V between her fingers. "Are you, like, related to Marcella?"

"No," Lucy said, shocked.

"What's your problem, Celia?" Cleo asked. "Why are you being such a bitch?"

The redhead brandished her cigarette. "I'm just trying to figure out how she came from absolutely nowhere to steal the role so many people wanted."

"Steal?" Matteo asked.

"You have got to be kidding," Cleo added.

"Why don't you let *Lucy* speak for herself?" Celia asked, pronouncing Lucy's name with evident scorn.

Outraged, Lucy struggled for words. "I auditioned," she said finally. "Like everyone else."

"Maybe she's just really good," Cleo said. "Ever think of that?"

Celia sniffed. "Well, we'll see, won't we?"

After that someone made a joke, trying to change the subject. But all the fun had gone out of the evening. Lucy excused herself and reached for her coat. She had made it as far as the lobby when someone ran up behind her.

"Wait up, Lucy!" Matteo said. "We'll walk with you."

"What was *that* about?" Cleo asked, zipping on her fringed black suede jacket. "Celia, I mean."

"She's in my voice and diction class," Matteo answered as they swept through the café doors into the night. "She's been going on and on all week about how the role of Maureen was rightfully hers. Asking around about Lucy, and wondering if maybe she slept with somebody to get the part."

"No!" Lucy gasped. "She said that?"

"I told her not everyone's a desperate attention whore like she is."

"You did not!" Cleo squealed.

"Did so." Matteo grinned impishly.

"So that's why she hates me," Lucy said.

"Does it matter?" Cleo asked. "I've never liked Celia. If you think she's insufferable when she doesn't get the lead, you should see her when she does. She was a total diva last year when Marcella cast her as Ophelia in *Hamlet*."

Lucy thought for a moment. "I hate being hated," she said.

"Wear it like a badge of pride," Matteo said. "It means you got what she wants."

"I know," Lucy said. "But still."

"But nothing." Cleo linked her arm through Lucy's. "You need to rub her face in it."

Lucy giggled.

"Show her how a real actor does it," Matteo added, slipping his arm through Lucy's other arm.

"I'll try," Lucy said. *But what if I'm not a real actor?* she thought. She wouldn't want her new friends to know how close she'd come to giving up acting, what a fluke it was that she'd tried out at all, much less been chosen for a part everyone seemed to covet. *What if I blank out onstage and let everybody down?* Lucy wondered, and the thought made her shiver.

"You're cold?" Matteo asked.

"A little," Lucy said. Though Cleo and Matteo hardly knew her, they already seemed to believe in her. The last thing she wanted to do was let them see how little faith she had in herself.

XVII

⚬⚬⚬

*A*fter that night, Lucy's life seemed to be on fast-forward. Instead of long meals with friends in the dining hall, she took to wrapping herself a sandwich and smuggling it back into the dorm; she ate most meals alone, cramming for the next day's exam or studying her lines. That Saturday night, as Lucy was dressing for a date with Shane, Brittany sat cross-legged on her bed, a textbook on her lap.

"I hate how I hardly see you anymore," Britt lamented. "Between *Rent* and Shane."

"The play hasn't even been in rehearsal for a week," Lucy said.

"Now that you're hanging with the cool kids you won't want to be seen with me anymore." Britt jutted her lower lip out in an exaggerated pout.

"Ha! Very funny. Nobody's cooler than you." Lucy dumped

her overstuffed makeup bag on the desk and pawed through its contents for the perfect shade of lip gloss. "And anyway, this is only my third date with Shane. It's not like I'm with him all the time." Midweek, he'd taken her out for pad thai at a charming little bistro not far from campus. It had been a rainy night, and they were the only two people in the whole place. Shane and Lucy had lingered, drinking green tea in the dining room's rosy glow, rain streaking sideways down the plate-glass window. He taught her to use chopsticks, a skill he'd mastered when he was five and his father had taken him to Beijing on a business trip.

"Still, I wish you weren't busy tonight," Britt said. "Glory and Sarah want to go clubbing downtown. I'd feel like less of an idiot if you came, too."

Lucy's fingers closed around her pink lip gloss. "Want me to ask Shane if you can come with us instead? We're going to hang out at his friend's loft in Northern Liberties."

Britt shut her textbook and tossed it onto the pile on the floor. "That's sweet," she said. "But no. It's way too soon in your relationship to be dragging a sad girlfriend along on your dates." The night before, Britt and her boyfriend had argued for hours over Skype about whether they should be seeing other people while they were apart. It had been his idea. And though they'd made up, finally, and agreed to stay exclusive, Britt's eyes had looked pink around the edges all day.

Lucy tried to gauge her friend's mood. "Maybe I should cancel. You and I could stay in and watch a movie."

"What? Are you kidding? Of course you shouldn't cancel."

Britt flopped backward onto the bed. "You really like Shane, don't you?"

Lucy uncapped her lip gloss, stared down at it, and gave a small sigh. "It's like I made a list of all the things I wanted in a boyfriend, and a fairy godmother came along and waved her magic wand. Presto: Shane!"

"Well, that's wonderful." Britt hugged her knees to her chest. "Isn't it?"

"It's pretty wonderful." Lucy bent to feel around the depths of her closet and came up with just one of her favorite black suede boots. "So far, anyway. I mean, it's *soon*."

"That doesn't matter," Britt said. "When you know, you just *know*."

"I guess so." Lucy ducked back into the closet to search for the other boot, not wanting to say what she was thinking. She had been so sure about Jesse, but it had turned out she didn't know a thing.

She emerged from the closet with the missing boot tucked under her arm. "You're sure you don't want me to stay here with you?" she asked again.

"Go," Britt said. "Have fun with Dream Boy."

At the loft in Northern Liberties, Lucy ate take-out sushi and nursed a bottle of Yuengling, listening in while Shane and his friends discussed the merits of experimental jazz. She tried to follow the conversation, but found she didn't have much to add.

After a while, she got up to wander around the loft, taking in the canvases painted by Shane's friend Allen. They were splashy and colorful, but she wasn't sure she understood them, exactly. Allen wore heavy black-framed glasses and had a record collection full of obscure artists. *Maybe if I hang out with Shane's friends, I'll learn to be a hipster, too?* Lucy thought.

Allen's balcony door was ajar, and Lucy couldn't resist slipping outside to breathe the night air and look out over the streets of Northern Liberties. Before long, she heard the door slide open and shut behind her and felt Shane's arms wrap around her waist. "Having fun?" he asked.

"Oh, yes," she said. "Your friends are fascinating. I just needed some air."

Shane's arms tightened. A moment later he was kissing her neck. "See over there?" He pointed to an apartment building a few blocks away, its walls almost entirely glass.

Lucy nodded.

"That's my building," he said.

"Wow," she said, not knowing what kind of reaction he wanted.

"You can see my apartment from here. Fifth floor up, fourth window over."

Lucy looked for and found the darkened window. "Nobody's home," she said.

"We could change that." His hands kneaded her shoulders, sending tingles through her body.

It took Lucy a moment to grasp what he was suggesting. "Um," she said. "That sounds…nice. But I wasn't expecting…I mean, it feels a little . . . soon." She wondered at herself as the words left her lips. After all, she'd slept with Jesse after knowing him for less than a week. And Shane was so gorgeous, so sophisticated, so perfect, really, in just about every way. "I mean, it's not that I don't want to. I do. But . . ."

Shane laughed. "It's okay." He spun her around to face him. "You're right. It *is* soon. It's just that I really, really like you." He kissed her softly on the lips. "Anyway, we don't need to hurry. It's good that you want to wait."

"It is?" Lucy asked, not believing her ears. When he kissed her again, his hands slipped down to her hips, pulling her a little closer.

He smiled with those perfect white teeth of his. "It's smart, actually." He kissed the tip of her nose. "Sensible."

Not long after that, they left the loft, and Shane drove Lucy back to campus. From the passenger's seat she looked over at him—his strong jaw and sharp cheekbones, the suede jacket and expensive jeans that set him apart from the other guys she'd met, who sported hoodies and baseball caps. Had he really called her *sensible?* Nobody had called her that in her life. Considering she'd been listening to her heart and not her head, it was hard not to feel like a fraud. Still, he'd said he was fine with waiting, and waiting was what she wanted. *He's the perfect guy,* Lucy told herself for about the thirtieth time that night.

Shane broke into her reverie. "So how's the play going?"

"It's great," she said. "A little scary sometimes."

"Scary? What would a pro like you be scared about?"

Lucy considered telling him about her terror of freezing up

onstage, then decided to let him go on thinking of her as talented and capable. "Oh, you know what they say. A little stage fright is normal." She tried to sound breezy.

Shane took his eyes off the road to look at her. "Have I told you how proud I am to have a star as a girlfriend?"

Girlfriend? A warm feeling spread through Lucy's chest. "I think you need to see me onstage before you decide I'm a star," she said.

"I already know," he said. "I told you, I have an instinct. Take Allen, for example. I knew he was a genius before I even saw his work. I could tell by how he talked about painting, by how obsessed with it he was. And then I wangled an invitation to his first gallery opening, and it turned out I was right."

Would you like me if I turned out not to be a star? Lucy wondered. She almost said the words out loud, but stopped herself. "Thank you for believing in me."

"It's not something you have to thank me for," he said. "I believe what I believe." They drove on in silence a bit longer. Before they reached the exit to campus, Shane spoke again. "Can I ask you a question?"

"Sure," Lucy said.

"Are we…" He paused, as though seeking the right word. "Exclusive? You're not seeing anybody else, are you?"

"Of course not!" Lucy exclaimed, the words coming out in a rush. "No." Then, after a moment's thought, she asked, "Are you?"

"I'm not," he said. "I mean, I was seeing someone over the summer. Not anymore, though."

"Me, too," Lucy said. "I saw someone over the summer. But

that's over." *It can't get any more over than when a guy changes his address and doesn't send you the new one,* she thought.

Before long, they had reached campus. Shane parked his car and jumped out to open her door. Then he walked her to the entrance of her dorm. In the lamplight, he kissed her for a long time. "I'm glad we're not seeing other people," he said.

"Me, too," Lucy whispered back.

They kissed some more, Shane's hands wandering down to her waist, then up inside her jacket. Before she could object, or point out that they were in public, in plain view of anyone who might pass by, his hands traveled up her body, grazing the surface of her dress in a way that made Lucy's breath catch.

"But I thought..." she whispered, "we were going to wait...."

"We are," Shane said, even as his fingers explored her rib cage. "It's just..." He pulled his hands from her jacket. "It's not easy."

Just then, a trio of guys in Forsythe colors—scarlet and gold— whipped past, making whooping noises. "We won, dude!" one of them shouted in Shane's direction. "Victory!" he yelled, and the other two hollered in agreement.

"I'd better go in," Lucy said.

Shane grabbed her hand. "I was thinking maybe we could go away together one of these weekends. My cousin has an apartment in New York, and he's practically never there. He lets me use it when I go into the city. We could stay at his place, maybe see a play?"

Lucy hesitated. A weekend in New York sounded thrilling, but it would also mean staying alone together. *Overnight.* Hadn't he just said he was willing to wait?

189

"I know it's soon." He caught her other hand, tugging her close again, now that the whooping Forsythe fans were out of sight. "But maybe in a few weeks we'll know each other better, and it will feel right."

Lucy looked down at his hand, so large hers nestled tidily within it. *The kind of hand I can trust*, she thought.

"I'll take you to my favorite place in Little Italy. They make the best cappuccinos in New York. And their cannoli?" He grinned down at her. "Fugheddaboutit."

He's trying so hard to please me, she thought. *And maybe in a few weeks I really will be ready to be with him.*

In the meantime, though, he was waiting for her answer, and she needed to say something.

"Yes." Lucy turned on her brightest smile. "That sounds amazing."

XVIII

⸙

On Monday morning, Lucy's phone rang while she was at breakfast. It was her mother. "I'd better take this," Lucy told Britt, who was eating scrambled eggs and cramming for that morning's history quiz.

"Lu, honey? I just wanted to check in and see how you're doing."

"Oh." Lucy set aside her yogurt. "I'm sorry I haven't called. It's just, I've been busy."

"I know, I know. I remember what college was like. But your dad and I haven't heard from you in over a week, and I couldn't help worrying."

When wasn't Lucy's mother worried about her? "I'm fine," Lucy said. "Everything's great." She shot Britt an apologetic smile and got up from the table so her friend could study in peace. Finding a quiet spot in the lobby, Lucy paced back and forth, phone to her ear. She still hadn't told her parents about her part in *Rent*. She knew her mother would be happy for her, but she wasn't quite sure how her father would react. That uncertainty had kept her from making her weekly call home.

Lucy's mother's sixth sense had apparently been triggered. "I've just had a funny feeling about you lately," she said.

"What kind of funny?"

"You're making friends, aren't you? You're not lonely?"

Lucy laughed. "Yes, I'm making friends." And though she hadn't been planning to mention Shane just yet, she couldn't help trotting him out as Exhibit A. "In fact, I've been seeing this really great guy."

After that, the questions flew thick and fast. Lucy had to reveal Shane's name, his hometown, his major, his hobbies. Though she wasn't at all surprised by the third degree, what came next took her aback. "I've got a great idea. Why don't Dad and I come to campus this weekend and take the two of you out to dinner?"

"Um," Lucy said.

"We could go someplace really nice. I'm sure you could use a break from dining hall food."

"Uh," Lucy said. "That's nice, Mom, but…"

"What about Buddakan? We haven't gone there in ages. I know how much you love their king crab tempura. But maybe Shane doesn't like Asian food? We could go someplace else. Italian's always safe. Who doesn't like Italian?"

"Mom," Lucy broke in, her voice higher-pitched than she'd intended. "Please. Just chill a second."

"What's wrong?"

"Shane and I have only just started going out," Lucy said. "I'm not ready to bring him home to meet the parents."

"It wouldn't be like that," her mother said. "We don't want to interrogate the guy. It would just be a fun little dinner."

"No," Lucy said with as much firmness as she could muster. "It would not be fun."

"Okay, okay. I get the message." But a note of hurt had crept into Lucy's mother's voice.

"It's a very nice idea," Lucy said quickly. "But we're not ready for that yet. Maybe someday," she said.

"You mean after you've announced your engagement?"

"Mom!" Lucy all but shrieked. "Nobody's getting engaged here."

"I was kidding," Lucy's mother said, but she still sounded miffed, and an awkward silence settled between them. Desperate to get the conversation back in motion, Lucy did something reckless.

"Uh, well, anyway, I do have some good news. At least *I* think it's good. I hope you will, too." After all, Lucy's mother had always been happy about her daughter's successes, however small. Why should this be any different?

But her mother's reaction to the news was worrisome. "Oh." Her voice was hushed. "You know I'm glad for you, Lu, but I worry what your father will say about this. He has his heart set on your being a business major, and you *did* promise...."

"But I *am* majoring in business," Lucy said. "That isn't going to change. This is just one play. It's not a big deal. It's something to do in my free time. Like a hobby. Everyone needs a hobby, right?"

"I'll try to explain all that to your father, Lucy. But you know how he is."

And because Lucy did very much know how her father was, she felt too queasy to rejoin Britt and finish breakfast. Instead, she trudged back up to the dorm, cell phone heavy in her pocket. Sure enough, just as she let herself into her room, it rang again. Lucy recognized the number. "Oh, great," she said to the empty room, then steeled herself and took the call. "Dad?" she began.

Even when her father wasn't angry, his voice tended to boom. Lucy held her phone away from her ear, but she could still hear every word. She'd assumed her father would be upset with her, but he was way beyond upset. He began with a dig about how much he'd spent on her "little jaunt through Europe." Then there was a long lecture on how when a person gave her word, she was bound to keep it.

There was no use trying to get a word in edgewise, so Lucy listened in silence until her father said, "What I want to know is what you have to say for yourself." As clearly as if she were in the room with him, Lucy could see the vein that throbbed in his forehead whenever he was mad.

"I *am* keeping my word," she said. "It's one play, Dad. Just one...."

He launched into another lecture about how she was obeying

the letter of the law but not its spirit, and how she knew full well that was a sneaky way to go through life.

"Sneaky?" Lucy felt the vein in her own forehead twitch. "If I wanted to be sneaky, I wouldn't have told you at all. You'd never have found out."

She should have known better. When somebody pushed her father, he always pushed back. "Is that right?" he asked. "What else are you doing that you don't want me to find out about?"

Too hurt to come up with a reply, Lucy yelped as if she'd been stung.

"You'd better pay attention to what I'm saying right now," her father continued. "You're going to drop out of that play today."

"I can't do that," Lucy said. "They're counting on me...."

She scrambled for the words to convince him that dropping out would be the dishonorable choice, that the cast of a play was like a team and she had to be a good team player, but he broke in. "*They* are a bunch of strangers. And *I'm* the guy who pays your tuition."

"But—"

"Listen to me. If you don't quit that play right now, this is your last semester at Forsythe. At any college, for that matter. I won't pay another cent toward your education."

She couldn't reply. For a moment, she couldn't even remember how to speak.

"Do you hear me, Lucy?"

"I hear you," she said, her words coming out still and flat.

"And what are you going to do today?"

Only one answer would satisfy him. "I'm going to quit the play." It hurt to say the words. Lucy knew her father could be brusque—sometimes even harsh—when his employees failed him in some way. But he'd never spoken to her like this before. She'd never given him any reason to. Shouldn't that count for something?

Long after her father had hung up, she stared at the phone in her hand, as if it had done her some kind of injury. Then it rang again. This time Lucy's mother was on the other end, sounding anxious. "Are you okay, sweetheart?"

Angry tears sprang into Lucy's eyes. "No, I'm not okay. You should have heard the way he spoke to me."

"Oh, honey, I'm sorry."

"Can you get him to change his mind, Mom? Can you at least try?"

"You know how stubborn your dad is, Lucy. When he makes up his mind about something..." Lucy's mother's voice trailed off. "But here's what I'll do. When he comes home after work tonight I'll talk to him. Maybe plant a seed. Over time, he'll come around."

"He wants me to quit the play *today*." Lucy sniffled. "Once I quit, they'll give the role to somebody else. You don't understand how important this is to me."

"I think I do."

"You'll try, then?" But Lucy knew it was hopeless. A battle of wills between her soft-spoken mother and her hardheaded father would be like a match between Bambi and Godzilla.

In psychology class, Lucy doodled instead of taking notes. At

196

dinnertime she lost the thread of her friends' conversation, drifting off into her own thoughts. As unthinkable as it was that she might have to give up the role of Maureen, the alternative—having to drop out of school—was even worse. What choice did she have but to quit the play that very night?

XIX

———※———

O n her way to rehearsal, Lucy practiced the words she would say to Marcella. That night's session was supposed to be spent blocking out "Over the Moon," Maureen's big solo number, and Lucy had been really excited about it. Now she would have to pull Marcella aside before rehearsal and ask to speak to her in private. It killed Lucy to know somebody else would be taking over her role. When Britt had gotten home from class, Lucy had cried on her friend's shoulder for a good half hour.

"And you think he really means it?" Britt had asked. "He'll cut off your tuition if you don't quit the play?"

Lucy had sniffed loudly and reached for a tissue. "I think he really means it."

Now, legs trembling, she climbed the stairs to the Theater Arts building. If she could just talk to Marcella before rehearsal started, she would blurt out her apologies and put this whole episode behind her. But that was not to be.

"Hey there, Lulabelle," Cleo's voice sang out from behind her. "You excited for tonight?"

Lucy spun around to face Cleo and Matteo. At the sight of them, her lower lip started to tremble.

"Uh-oh," Matteo said. "What's wrong?"

"Nothing." She looked around the lobby for Marcella, but the director wasn't in sight.

"Really?" Cleo said. "Because you look like somebody's just run over your cat."

Lucy felt that tingling in her nostrils that always meant she was about to burst into tears. She steeled herself. "My cat's holding its own," she said brightly. "Or it would be, if I had one."

"Good thing," Matteo said. "Because tonight you get to show the doubters what you've got."

"Doubters?" Lucy asked, glancing over at Celia Bursk, who was stretching in the corner, surrounded by her friends in the chorus. "There's more than one?" A girl with black pigtails caught Lucy's gaze and turned to whisper in Celia's ear.

"Stupid is contagious," Matteo said.

"Never mind them," Cleo said. "Tonight's your chance to reinvent yourself."

"Create your own legend," Matteo agreed.

"Teach Celia Bursk a thing or two." Cleo pasted a big, phony smile on her face and waved airily at Celia, who glared in reply, first at Cleo, then at Lucy.

"Take cover!" Matteo grabbed Lucy's arm and turned her away. "She's trying to melt your flesh with her death ray." The three of them dissolved in a peal of giggles.

"She *hates* me," Lucy gasped out. This thought was strangely elating...until she realized how glad Celia would be when Lucy dropped out of the play.

I can't quit till I've shown her I earned this part, she told herself. *What will it hurt if I wait until after rehearsal?*

That night, Lucy threw her whole self into her performance, so there could be no doubt about her talent. Even after Celia left the auditorium with the rest of the chorus, Lucy gave everything she had, inhabiting Maureen's confidence, her magnetism. *This is the last time I'll ever feel this way*, she thought. *I'd better make it count.* When the time came to sing, she belted out her part until her own voice echoed against the far walls, filling the space to its brim.

From her seat in the front row, Marcella watched with an unreadable expression on her face. But when Lucy reached the end of the number, the director turned to address the cast members scattered throughout the room. "Hear that, gang? That's how it's done."

Gratified, Lucy scanned the auditorium. From their table at the front of the stage, the assistant director and stage manager were nodding approvingly. Midway back, Cleo and Matteo were grinning broadly. And even farther back, in the shadows of the last row, Lucy spotted a familiar face with an encouraging look in his dark eyes. Lucy smiled gratefully, then did a double take.

"Are you okay, Lucy?" Marcella asked.

"I'm fine." Lucy returned her attention to the director. But as soon as she could, she checked the back row again, only to find that whoever it was she'd seen had vanished.

I'm losing my mind, Lucy thought, struggling to focus on Marcella's praise and instructions. There was no way Jesse was on this continent, much less in this room. Even so, Lucy felt shaken. The feeling stuck with her even after Marcella had dismissed the cast for the night. As Marcella and Ben conferred about the rehearsal, Lucy hesitated at the edge of the stage. She knew she should wait for the right moment, then march up and quit the play. But seeing Jesse's look-alike had rattled her. As the auditorium emptied, she looked around, checking every face. Wherever Jesse's twin had gone, he hadn't come back.

Before she could act, Cleo and Matteo flailed their arms, trying to get her attention.

"Come out with us for coffee!" Cleo shouted.

Lucy took a tentative step down from the stage, then checked over her shoulder. Marcella and Ben were still deep in conversation.

"You owned that song," Matteo said, giving Lucy his gap-toothed grin.

"And you showed Celia and her evil minions a thing or two." Cleo handed Lucy her coat.

Lucy thanked her friends and followed them into the lobby.

"Are you okay, Luce?" Cleo asked. "You seem weirded out."

"I *am* weirded out," Lucy admitted. Through the glass walls of the lobby she could see that the wind had picked up and was whipping dried leaves around the lawn. "This is going to sound crazy, but while I was onstage, I swear I saw this guy I used to know. It was freaky, and now I'm all…" But before she could finish her thought, she noticed a figure across the road, standing in a cone of streetlight. Matteo and Cleo turned to see whatever it was Lucy was gaping at.

But the shadowy person had seen her, too. He was striding toward her now, through the darkness and up the stairs, and she knew, with a shock that began at the soles of her feet and spread to the roots of her hair, that she hadn't been hallucinating. Of all the people in the world, Jesse Palladino—her Jesse, who was supposed to be in Italy—had somehow materialized in front of her. She froze in place.

"Who is that?" she heard Matteo whisper to Cleo.

"No idea," Cleo whispered back. "Is that your boyfriend?" she asked Lucy.

"Yes," Lucy said. Then, "No."

"Which is it?" Matteo asked.

Lucy struggled to find her tongue. "I'm fine," she told her friends. "It's nothing."

"He doesn't look like nothing." Cleo gave Jesse the once-over.

"I'll catch up with you guys tomorrow." Lucy tried to sound reassuringly normal.

Cleo and Matteo looked questioningly at each other. "You're sure?" Matteo asked.

Lucy wasn't sure of anything, except that something momentous seemed to be happening. Jesse, who had fallen off the face of the earth, was walking in her direction. She took a step closer, equal parts thrilled, alarmed, and angry.

"I'm fine," she lied, though her heart was pounding. Lucy hadn't expected to ever see Jesse again, so she hadn't worked out what she might say to him if she did. Should she throw her arms around him or give him the silent treatment—the same as he'd given her? Whichever it was, she didn't want her friends around to watch. "Totally fine," she added.

Matteo and Cleo exchanged another look, then took off through the door, out into the night.

In the brightly lit lobby, Jesse looked familiar yet different. His olive skin was a shade or two darker. *Of course he's tan,* she thought. *He's been traveling all over Italy, having the time of his life, and not even thinking about me.* His hair, still shiny and dark, had been trimmed short. He wore a sweater and khakis, the kind of thing any other boy on campus might wear. Something about these little changes in him felt like a betrayal.

Lucy steeled herself. The expression on his face was eager and nervous. But she wasn't about to forgive him, not after he'd blown her off so completely. Was he expecting her to run up and gather him in her arms? Well, she wasn't going to give him the satisfaction.

"How can you be here?" she asked.

Jesse looked surprised. "I took a plane. And a bus. And then another bus."

"That's not what I meant." Brain on overload, Lucy fumbled for words. "You're supposed to be in Europe."

"Supposed to be?" His mouth twitched in a smile.

Was he making fun of her? Before she could decide, he swooped in for a hug. She stiffened in his arms.

Behind them, someone cleared his throat and Lucy wrenched herself out of Jesse's arms to find Ben, the music director, standing awkwardly nearby. "I need to lock up the theater," he said. "Sorry."

Lucy checked out the window to make sure nobody was watching, then led Jesse out into the night. During rehearsal, the temperature had plummeted; she paused in the shadow between streetlights, fumbling with the buttons of her coat. "How did you find me?"

"It wasn't hard," he said. "I found the theater department's phone number online. Then I called to ask when the next rehearsal would be."

"Oh, great. Now I feel cyberstalked."

"Stalked?" Jesse looked puzzled.

"Well, I thought you were never coming back to the States."

"My cousin got married last weekend," he said. "My parents flew me home for the wedding."

Lucy crossed her arms to create a little wall between them. "What are you doing in Philly, then?" she asked. *On my campus*, she thought.

"I have friends here," he said, wariness creeping into his voice. "I'm staying with this guy I know from high school. Peter Gregorian. He's letting me sleep on his couch."

"You're staying at *Forsythe*?" Lucy took another step back.

"In Bradley Hall. Small world, right?"

"And you just thought you'd swing by and say hi?"

"Sure." Jesse dug his hands into his pockets, looking perplexed, as though he couldn't fathom why she might be angry at him, as though this whole scene were the most normal thing in the world, as though the two of them had been nothing but good buddies and he'd never disappeared from her life without so much as a good-bye.

"But why?" Lucy asked, her voice hard. "Why would you want to see me?"

Jesse frowned. "I just did. I thought you would be happy.... I mean, I thought you wouldn't mind...." He looked down at his sneakers and then back up at her, hurt in his eyes. "Aren't you glad I'm here?"

Hearing the confusion in his voice, Lucy felt a pang. "I missed you." She knew that wasn't the right thing to say, considering Shane and all.

Before she had time to take it back, though, Jesse's arms were around her again, warm and familiar. He drew her closer, and then his lips were on hers and she was kissing him back, unable to stop herself, the feel and taste of him so delicious. For that moment they were back on that terrace in Fiesole, all of Tuscany spread around them, in the middle of a kiss she'd never wanted to end.

"I missed you, too," Jesse mumbled.

"You did?" she asked. She wanted to believe him, but his words had broken the spell, reminding her of all that had happened since Italy. She slipped out of his arms and felt the cold of the Philadelphia night. "Then why did you delete your e-mail account? And without telling me how I could find you?" She fought to keep her

206

voice level. More than anything, she wanted not to give away how much it had stung her when he fell silent. "You dropped off the face of the earth."

"I know," he said, his voice wary.

Lucy hugged herself for warmth. How could he just waltz up to her as though nothing had changed between them and expect her to be thrilled? Her imaginary version of Nello's sister popped into her head—glossy black hair and one bare, perfect shoulder, the two of them traipsing hand in hand through the streets of Naples. "What about Angelina?"

"What about her?" he asked, but something in his voice had changed.

"Were you and she…" It took courage to voice the rest of the question, especially since all she had to go on was a wild guess and her own possibly irrational jealousy. "Did the two of you hook up?"

Jesse looked embarrassed. "It doesn't matter," he said.

"It matters to me," she replied.

He stood before her, not meeting her eyes, until she realized, with dismay, that she'd gotten her answer. "And now you show up at my rehearsal, out of the blue," she said. "As if you thought I'd be waiting for you, like some pathetic loser."

"Lucy." Before she could object, Jesse reached for her again. "I didn't think that," he said, his voice low.

"As if it never occurred to you that I might move on, I might be with someone else," Lucy said, pulling free of his grasp. What would Shane think if he could see her now? She looked around to see if anyone had been watching them, but the street in front of the Theater Arts building was empty.

A few dried leaves blasted past. Lucy looked up at Jesse through the strands of her blown-about hair. "Because the thing is, I *am* seeing somebody."

Her words had their intended effect. Jesse's face fell.

Though Lucy had meant to discourage him, she immediately felt remorse. "I thought you'd forgotten all about me," she added, her voice cracking.

"No," he said. "I could never forget you."

"I had no idea I'd ever hear from you again," she continued. "If anybody had told me you would just appear like this, I'd have called them crazy. I'd say no, not Jesse, he's going to spend the rest of his life hopping from city to city, having nothing but fun."

He shuffled his sneakers in the fallen leaves but didn't reply.

Lucy summoned all the strength she could and pointed up the path, toward Main Street. "So I think you should go back to New Jersey or Italy or wherever it is you're living right now." When he didn't budge, she kept going. "Botswana, maybe. Or Tahiti. Wherever." She looked away, off into the distance, to avoid seeing the hurt look in his eyes. "Anywhere but here."

"If that's what you want." He turned to go, and she fought the urge to change her mind and call after him.

Halfway down the path, he paused to look over his shoulder. "You know, you were amazing back there. Onstage."

Stop being nice, Lucy thought, but her heart leaped at the compliment.

"I knew you could sing, but I had no idea you could act like that. It's so great that you're in the play. In spite of everything."

"Oh," Lucy said, the events of the day returning to her in a rush. "It's not great, not really. I was going to quit tonight, after rehearsal, and then you showed up...." She found herself telling him about her father's latest ultimatum, and he paused, ten steps away, listening intently.

"You can't quit," he said when she was through. "I'm glad I came here tonight, if it stopped you from quitting."

Lucy surveyed Jesse across the polite distance she'd put between them. Why was it so hard to stay angry at him?

"Acting is your thing, Lucy," he added. "Everybody deserves to have their thing."

Lucy hesitated, thinking hard. Her father's decree did seem unreasonable. Did she really have to give up *everything* she loved? Shouldn't she get to make *some* choices when it came to her own life?

"I think so, too," she admitted.

"Well, then." Jesse took a step back in her direction.

"I guess my dad doesn't have to know," she said. "Does that make me a terrible person?"

"Not remotely." Jesse's look warmed her, and for a moment she considered running to him, slipping her hand into his, and following him wherever he meant to go next.

But I am terrible, she thought, remembering Shane.

"I have to go," she said, and she hurried away from Jesse, in the direction of her dorm.

"Wait," he called after her, but she didn't dare stop. Once she started moving, she knew she was doing the right thing. She'd been wrong to let Jesse kiss her, and the longer she stood there in the darkness with him, the more likely she was to let it happen again. *Jesse is the past; Shane is the future,* she reminded herself. She kept walking in the direction of her dorm, imagining its warmly lit lobby and the friends that waited for her there.

Just once, before she turned the corner, she let herself look back, in case Jesse was still standing where she'd left him. But by then he was gone.

XX

*L*ucy was jumpy in the days that followed. She worried that her father would find out she hadn't quit the play. As Jesse had shown, all it would take was some minimal investigation—a call to the drama department or a little Internet sleuthing—for him to learn the truth. And as she walked to and from classes, she couldn't shake the fear that she might turn a corner and bump into Jesse. For all she knew, he was still on campus, lurking in the shadows, waiting to step back into her path at the worst possible time. In fact, it seemed strange that he hadn't come looking for her since the other night. Would he really let her go so easily?

But as the days passed, Lucy had to admit to herself, with a mix of disappointment and relief, that he seemed to have given up.

"I guess I shouldn't be surprised. After all, he didn't fly home just to see me," she told Cleo and Matteo over post-rehearsal cappuccinos. "He was in New Jersey for a wedding. And he probably only came to Forsythe to visit his friend in Bradley Hall. I was an afterthought."

Matteo clucked his tongue against the roof of his mouth. "You can't possibly believe that."

"We saw the look on his face," Cleo said. "That boy's got a serious yen for you."

Lucy looked doubtful. "I'm not the kind of girl people have a yen for," she said.

"You're exactly that kind of girl," Cleo said with a wicked smile. "Don't forget: I've kissed you, so I know." A couple of nights earlier, Cleo and Lucy had rehearsed a stage kiss, during the "La Vie Boheme" number. It had gone well—less awkwardly than Lucy had feared—but ever since, Cleo hadn't missed an opportunity to tease her about it.

"You're making her blush," Matteo observed, which only made Lucy burn an even brighter shade of red. "Face it, Lulabelle, the boy wants you."

"But I told him about Shane, so that's that. He's given up on me."

"Which is good news, right?" Cleo said. "Since, as you keep telling us, you've moved on."

"Yes." Lucy tried her best to sound convincing. "It's true. I *have* moved on."

"Speaking of which," Matteo said, "when are you going to bring Shane around to hang out with us?"

"We want to check him out," Cleo chimed in. "Give him our seal of approval."

Lucy gave a vague little shrug. "Soon," she said. She had a pretty good idea that Shane would like Cleo and Matteo—hadn't he said he was drawn to artsy types? And of course they would like him; why wouldn't they? Even so, the idea made her uncomfortable, though she couldn't have said why.

"You're not ashamed of us, are you?" Cleo asked. "Your weirdo drama geek friends?"

"Of course not." Lucy grabbed each of their hands and gave a quick squeeze. "I *love* my weirdo drama geek friends."

"Then why are you being so...elusive?" Matteo leveled his gaze on Lucy. "Are you afraid we'll reveal your secrets? Like maybe we'll tell your new boyfriend about your Italian boyfriend?"

"Because you can just stop worrying. We'd never do that," Cleo said. "We're on your side, Lu."

"I know you are."

"Besides which, why don't *you* tell him the truth?" Cleo asked her. "It's not your fault Jesse just showed up out of the blue."

"Right," Matteo said. "And it's not like you've seen him since that night. So why not come clean?"

"I don't know," Lucy said. This was the truth. She'd meant to. Just last night Shane had called to confer over their trip to New York, full of ideas about which play they could see and what new restaurants they should try. She'd attempted once or twice to bring up the subject of Jesse. But then Shane proposed that they make their trip the weekend after next.

"I know that's sooner than we planned," he said. "But it turns out my cousin's coming back to town right after that. So if we put off our trip, it could be months till we can have the apartment to ourselves."

"Oh," Lucy said.

"And we don't want to wait that long, do we?"

"Of course not," she said, because it seemed like the right thing to say.

"But only if you're ready. I don't mean to push you."

And Lucy had gotten flustered and forgotten the speech she'd been meaning to give. "It's okay." She fiddled with the diamond stud in her ear. "Don't worry. The weekend after next will be fine."

After that, Shane had sounded happy. "That's great. We're going to have so much fun."

"It sounds perfect," Lucy told him. She worried her earring a little harder, and the back popped off, disappearing under her bed. "Oh, crap."

"Is something wrong?" Shane asked.

"No." On her knees, Lucy felt under the bed with one hand.

"Are you sure? You sound funny."

Lucy's palm found the little piece of metal. "Everything's fine," she said with forced brightness.

"Good. I hope you know, I want our weekend away to be wonderful," he said, sounding so sincere and sweet that Lucy couldn't imagine wrecking his mood by mentioning Jesse's surprise visit. *I'll wait and tell him in person*, she reasoned to herself.

That way he can see from the look on my face how little Jesse matters to me.

"I've been thinking. Why does Shane even have to know about Jesse being here?" Lucy asked her friends now, trying to sound casual. "It's no big deal."

"It's kind of a big deal," Cleo said. "What if Jesse turns up when you're someplace with Shane?"

"Forsythe isn't that small," Lucy said. "Is it?"

"Oh, honey." Matteo took her chin in his hand and tipped her face up so she had no choice but to meet his green-flecked eyes. "Listen to Uncle Matteo. Your life is a house of cards. If you're not careful, a good wind is going to blow the whole thing down."

Matteo's words ringing in her ears, Lucy sat cross-legged on her unmade bed, cell phone in hand. She wished she had Brittany nearby for moral support, but earlier that week, Britt had come down with a fever. Her parents had driven her home to recover, and now the room and the dorm surrounding it seemed uncannily quiet. Lucy typed out a text message, then erased it. The whole business with Jesse seemed too complicated to put into a text, or even to explain over the phone.

Instead, she sent Shane a message suggesting they have lunch together on Friday. A few seconds later, he texted back a yes.

So that was settled. While she waited for Friday, she tried to concentrate on classes, on schoolwork, on rehearsal. She did her best to remember that she had a boyfriend so amazing her friends called him Dream Boy. She tried not to care whether or not Jesse had left Philadelphia for good. Even so, every now and then he would pop into her thoughts. She'd remember how warm his kiss had felt in the autumn night, and, for a moment, she'd forget how she was supposed to be feeling. Falling in love with Shane. Completely over Jesse.

XXI

———❦———

I s everything okay?" Shane asked Lucy when they were almost to the mall. He seemed to survey her through his sunglasses, though they were mirrored and she couldn't tell for sure. "You're so quiet." He'd been telling her about the amazing tickets he'd landed to *Wicked*—fifth row, center—and about the restaurant he'd found for dinner, a Thai place where a lot of Broadway actors supposedly ate.

"Oh," Lucy said. "Sorry." She'd been silently running through the speech she'd prepared: *It's no big deal, really, but the guy I dated this summer—he showed up on campus looking for me. He tried to kiss me, but I wouldn't let him.* Okay, so that last bit was a lie, but the rest was true. *I told him about you. About us. How we're seeing each other now. I told him to go away and leave me alone. I just thought you should know.*

That morning before class she had rehearsed the speech in front of the mirror until she could get through it without her voice trembling. But actually saying the words to Shane was a different story. Lucy was afraid she might blush the way she always did when she felt self-conscious. Would he get the point she wanted to send—that she'd moved on, that Jesse was just an inconvenient bit of her past—or would he get the exact opposite message?

Shane fiddled with the climate controls. "Are you warm enough?"

"I'm totally fine," Lucy said, her words coming out weirdly vehement. *Should I tell him now?* she wondered. But Shane had already returned to the subject of their upcoming trip, listing things they could do before the play—gallery-hopping in Chelsea, maybe, or browsing at The Strand bookstore.

I'll tell him later, Lucy thought. *Over lunch.*

At Pizza Plenty, she cut her slice into smaller and smaller pieces, too anxious to eat.

"You're on some kind of diet?" Shane asked, gesturing at her plate.

Lucy looked up at him, puzzled.

"I hope not. You're beautiful just the way you are," Shane said. His pizza finished, he picked up his fork and started spearing and eating her tiny pieces, one by one.

He's so nice, Lucy told herself. *Why am I afraid to come clean with him? Of course he'll understand.* She set down her knife and fork and took a deep breath. But before she could speak, Shane asked how rehearsals for *Rent* were going.

Grateful for the reprieve, Lucy answered his question in a

rush of words, telling him about the other night, how Celia Bursk and her friends had been waiting for her to fall on her face but instead she'd done pretty well. She described how wonderful it felt to be rehearsing the part of Maureen. "I can't believe I almost quit the play," she added.

"Whoa." Shane put up a hand. "You were going to quit the play?"

"Oh," Lucy said. "I guess I forgot to tell you." She filled him in on the conversation with her father, how he'd threatened to stop paying her tuition if she didn't drop out of *Rent*.

"Wow," Shane said. "That's harsh."

"He's being a total tyrant," Lucy agreed.

"But…" Shane polished off the last of Lucy's pizza. "Why don't you just stand up to him? Tell him the truth. Wouldn't that be better than misleading him?"

"Oh, no," Lucy said. "You don't know my dad. He never backs down from a fight."

Shane didn't reply, and in the silence, Lucy grew flustered. "I'm not usually dishonest," she said. "I don't make a habit of lying to my folks. Or to anyone."

"Of course," Shane said. "I didn't mean—"

"It's just that my father's being totally unreasonable. He thinks he can micromanage my life. Shouldn't I get a say in what I do for fun? Or does he not want me to have any fun at all?" Lucy could hear the pitch of her voice getting higher and higher.

Shane leaned in closer. "I'm on your side, Lucy." He put his hands over hers on the tabletop. "It's just, by not telling your dad the truth, you're running a pretty big risk. What happens if he finds out you're still in the play?"

Lucy, who had been wondering the exact same thing for most of the week, didn't reply.

"Isn't it better to discuss the whole thing with him? Maybe go home and talk to him in person?"

Picturing her dad at his angriest, that vein throbbing in his temple, Lucy flinched.

"Maybe you just need to make him see how much this means to you," Shane said.

"You haven't met my father."

"I could drive you there," Shane said. "Be your moral support."

How could Lucy not be touched by such a kind offer? "That's very sweet. But doesn't that sound really unpleasant to you? Tense, I mean."

He rubbed her hands again. "Sure. A little. But I just want to make things turn out okay for you."

There he went again, being unbelievably kind. How could Lucy bring up the visit from Jesse now? *I can't*, she told herself. *Not just yet. But definitely before we leave the mall.*

After lunch, they wandered through the Galleria. Neither of them had classes that afternoon, and Lucy didn't have to be back on campus until her seven o'clock rehearsal. Finally they wound up in front of Books Incorporated, at the far end of the mall.

"Want to go in?" Lucy asked. Dragging Shane into clothing stores felt awkward, and she'd grown tired of feigning interest in the sports-supply stores he'd wanted to visit. Books seemed like a good compromise.

While Shane stood in line at the bookstore café, Lucy browsed her way through her favorite sections: drama first, and then travel. When she noticed a batch of bright orange spines, she did a double take. The new edition of *Wanderlust: Europe* was out. She pulled out a copy and took it to a table.

"Dreaming of next summer?" Shane set their lattes down on the table and slid into the seat opposite Lucy.

"I wish," Lucy said. "If only I could go back to Europe."

"Maybe someday," he said.

Lucy opened the new *Wanderlust*. "I met one of the authors while I was in Italy. Ellen something. She took me along on one of her research trips." While she hadn't liked Ellen much at the time, in retrospect it seemed pretty cool to know a real author. "I have to check out her section." She found the contributors' page. "Look! That's her. Ellen Lavish. She was writing the chapter on Florence when I met her."

"Cool," Shane said. While he read the latest issue of *Philadelphia Magazine*, Lucy riffled through *Wanderlust*, a plan forming in her mind. What more natural, less alarming way of bringing up Jesse could there be? "I met some interesting people in Europe…" she began, trying for the perfect segue.

Shane nodded, not looking up from his magazine.

"Some of them were great, and others were…" Just then, Lucy found the Florence chapter. "Oh! Here's Ellen's section." She read a passage about the Mercato Centrale aloud to Shane. "This sounds just like her! She was always going on and on about how *authentic* everything was. Authentic this and authentic that. Tell me: How can a plate of pasta or a hotel be *inauthentic?*" Lucy flipped forward to a section titled "Day Trips from Florence." "Look!" she exclaimed. "There's an entry on Fiesole, this town just outside the city. It was the most incredibly beautiful place, with a view of the Tuscan countryside, and Florence off in the distance."

Shane nodded absently. "Sounds nice."

"It's amazing," Lucy said. "I'll show you. There's got to be a picture...." She turned the page and fell silent.

There *was* a picture, captioned *Fiesole Is for Lovers*, of a couple kissing on an overlook, the hills and olive groves of Tuscany rolling away below them and Florence's skyline just visible in the distance. The couple leaned into each other, oblivious to the fact that they were being photographed, his arms twined around her waist, hers thrown back as though the kiss had caught her by surprise. It took Lucy a full second longer to take in the obvious: his longish dark hair, her wild, windblown curls.

She slammed the book shut.

"Didn't you want to show me something?" Oh, sure, *now* Shane was paying attention.

"Never mind." Lucy clutched the book to her chest. "The picture wasn't any good." Only one person could have taken that snapshot; only one person—besides herself and Jesse—had been on that hillside. Eyes shut, she could still see Charlene running downhill toward her, camera dangling around her neck, bouncing with each step. But why? And why would she have given it to Ellen to use in such a public way? *She betrayed me*, Lucy thought.

"Aren't you going to drink your latte?" Shane asked, leaning back, a puzzled look on his face. Good thing he couldn't read her mind.

"Oh. Yes. Of course." Lucy complied, taking a sip and thinking fast. Now there was no way she could bring up the subject of Jesse; she was way too flustered. Her voice would come out all weird and trembly, and then if Shane should decide to glance at the Fiesole chapter, he'd see that picture and jump to all kinds of conclusions. *He'll think I'm upset about Jesse, when it's really Charlene I'm angry with,* she told herself. Not only had Charlene spoiled her first kiss with Jesse, she'd taken that moment—possibly the most romantic of Lucy's life so far—and given it away. To Ellen, of all people. Who had put it in a book, for the whole world to see. *Charlene made me feel like I was being the unreasonable one,* Lucy thought, fuming to herself. *But she was spying on us!*

She jumped to her feet, *Wanderlust* in hand. "I'll put this back."

"You're not going to buy it?"

Lucy mumbled something about the book being a waste of money. But back in the Travel section, hidden from view, she allowed herself one more look. The book fell open right to the picture, and though she couldn't help feeling just a little bit glad that someone had captured the moment on film, she was no less furious at Charlene.

For the whole ride back to campus, Lucy tried to make polite, neutral conversation, but failed, to the point that Shane became concerned. "Are you okay?" he asked, taking his eyes off the road to examine her.

"Oh, everything's fine," Lucy said, maybe a bit too quickly.

"Because you're acting..." Shane struggled for the right words. "Unlike yourself."

Lucy summoned a smile. "I'm fine. Really." But a moment later she fell silent again, fuming and plotting. The minute she got home, she decided, she would call her mother, who could find out Charlene's room number in Marston Hall. And then, first chance she got, Lucy would march over there and tell her a thing or two.

XXII

———

*L*ucy was still furious as she took the stairs two at a time up to Charlene's dorm room. It was just after ten PM but, knowing Charlene, she might even be in bed already, lavender-scented satin sleep mask over her eyes. Lucy knocked on the door of room 415 firmly, to show she meant business. A freckled girl in an oversize Phillies T-shirt cracked opened the door.

"I'm looking for Charlene Barr," Lucy said, and the door opened wider to reveal Charlene at her desk, hands poised above her laptop, regarding Lucy with surprise in her pale blue eyes.

Charlene's room was as tidy as Lucy would have expected it to be, with peach throw rugs and white lace curtains at each window. Charlene wore a fuzzy yellow bathrobe, and her hair was held back by a matching headband. "Lucy?" she said with evident surprise. "What are you doing here?" She looked almost happy to see her old traveling companion, as though she'd forgotten how messed up things had gotten between them.

"I need to talk to you. In private. Is there somewhere we could go?"

Charlene's roommate lunged for the door. "I was just headed to the lounge, anyway," she said, and slipped out.

"Is something wrong?" Charlene had taken in the expression on Lucy's face and was starting to look alarmed. She gestured toward her neatly made bed with its many fussy throw pillows.

Lucy took a seat, feeling some of her fury drain away. She'd never been very good at confrontations. "Yes, something's wrong," she said, sounding more hurt and less stern than she'd intended. "Have you seen the new *Wanderlust: Europe?*"

"Not yet."

"There's a photograph in it. Of a couple kissing on a hilltop in Fiesole. A picture that only one person could have taken."

Charlene paled. "She put that in the book?"

"Of course she did." Lucy's voice rose. "What did you think she would do with it? Why would you give it to her otherwise? Why did you even take that photo in the first place?" Unable to sit still, she jumped to her feet and stalked back and forth in the narrow dorm room. "You violated my privacy."

For a long moment, Charlene said nothing. Exhausted by her own rant, Lucy returned to the bed and waited.

"I shouldn't have," Charlene said.

"Then why did you? *Why?*"

"I'm not sure," Charlene said, her words coming slowly, deliberately. "There was something so ... I don't know ... beautiful about the two of you, kissing like that, with the landscape behind you. I was taking pictures of everything, the way you do when you're on vacation. That night at dinner I showed my photos to Ellen, and she asked if she could have a copy of that one. I didn't think she would use it in *Wanderlust*." She paused. "I feel betrayed."

"*You* feel betrayed?" Lucy's voice rose again.

"I'm sorry, Lucy," Charlene said.

"Well," Lucy said. Now that she'd gotten the apology she'd come for, she wasn't sure what to say next. Though the conversation had been far from satisfying, she stood to go.

"Wait," Charlene said. "Don't leave. I'm sorry about something else, too."

Lucy sat back down.

Charlene reached for a throw pillow and crushed it against her chest. "I've been thinking about how unpleasant things got between us at the end of our trip. And about some of the things I said to you in Italy."

"It's okay," Lucy said automatically.

"It's *not*," Charlene insisted. "I shouldn't have given you the silent treatment in Rome. It's just…it really hurt my feelings when you and Jesse went off together without me."

"Oh," Lucy said.

"And I shouldn't have called you…you know. Spoiled. You were nothing but nice to me that whole trip," Charlene said. "Well, up until you called me coldhearted."

Lucy felt her cheeks go hot again. "I'm sorry," she said meekly.

"I know I must have *seemed* coldhearted." Charlene spoke that last word as though it tasted bitter. "But I didn't mean to be. I just didn't want you to get your hopes up about some guy you met in a hostel."

"Oh," Lucy said again.

"Still, I've been thinking. I shouldn't have told you he was using you. I didn't want to admit it, not even to myself, but I guess I was jealous."

"You were?"

"I could tell you and Jesse had something special. Seeing you together made me wish I'd said yes to Simon after all. That I'd gone with him to Mittenwald, I mean."

Lucy threw back her head and laughed.

"What's so funny?" Charlene asked.

"Lately, I've been thinking you were right about Jesse. And about vacation flirtations—that they aren't meant to turn into anything else. All they do is spoil you for your real life, and mess with your head, and..." Realizing she'd revealed more than she'd meant to, Lucy bit her lower lip. "Jesse's here," she said.

"What?" Charlene asked. "Where?"

"On campus," Lucy said. "Or maybe he's not here anymore, but he came to see me the other night."

"He came all the way to Philadelphia to be with you? That's really..." Charlene seemed to be weighing her words. "Romantic."

"I guess," Lucy said.

"You don't sound so thrilled."

Lucy frowned. "His parents flew him in for a wedding. So it's not that big a deal, really. He was in the neighborhood, so he just decided to swing by and say hi. Maybe he was bored and needed to kill some time."

"Oh, Lucy," Charlene said. "You really believe that?"

"I don't know what I believe." Lucy inspected her fingernails. "Besides, it doesn't matter, anyway. He waited too long. I'm involved with somebody else now." She fished in her pocket for her cell phone and showed Charlene a picture she'd taken of Shane at his friend's loft. He was leaning back in a battered leather armchair, his button-down shirt rolled up to his elbows, a knowing smile on his lips.

"He's good-looking." Charlene sounded begrudging.

"He's wonderful," Lucy told her, annoyed that Charlene was passing judgment on Shane now, too. "He's so smart. But nice, too. And generous."

"I believe you," Charlene said.

"Jesse stopped answering my e-mails," Lucy explained. "He basically disappeared off the face of the earth." She pocketed her phone and jumped to her feet. "Anyway, I'm completely over him."

"Oh." Charlene got to her feet. "If you say so."

"I do." Lucy was almost out the door when something else occurred to her. "Charlene? About that photo? The one in *Wanderlust*?"

Charlene waited, head cocked.

"Could you give me a copy?"

Charlene's mouth twitched. "I'll send it right away."

Lucy thanked her and started down the hall. She'd almost made it to the stairwell when she heard Charlene calling after her and the soft padding of bare feet on floor tiles. "Wait, Lucy. I have to say one thing."

Lucy waited until Charlene caught up with her.

"You should think about what you really want," Charlene said in a tone Lucy recognized. "*Who* you really want."

Here she was again: the superior Charlene who knew better than Lucy about everything that mattered—exchange rates and transit systems and what guys were really thinking. Lucy felt herself bristle. "I already have," she said. "I've given Jesse a *lot* of thought. More thought than he deserves."

"He came to see you," Charlene said. "He didn't have to. That means something."

"Does it?" Lucy asked.

"Why don't you ask him?"

"Ask him what? If he still likes me? If I was more than just a fling?"

"For starters," Charlene said.

"I wouldn't want to give him the satisfaction." Lucy flipped her hair over her shoulder. "Besides, he doesn't even have a phone. Plus, he changed his e-mail address without telling me the new one. That's how much he cares about me. I couldn't talk to him even if I wanted to. Which I don't."

Then she thanked Charlene for her advice and stomped down the stairs and out into the brisk night air.

XXIII

*D*etermined to drive Jesse out of her head, the first thing Lucy did when she reached her dorm room was text Shane: *Thinking of you.*

Thinking of you, too, he texted back. *So excited for our weekend in NYC.*

Me, too, Lucy replied. *Can't wait!* But the truth was that the thought of sharing a bed with Shane in just a little over a week, with Jesse still so fresh in her memory, made her uneasy, a feeling that only grew stronger as the week wore on. Whenever Lucy walked across campus, she kept imagining she might turn a corner and bump into Jesse. Early in the week, she took the long way to and from her classes, just to avoid Bradley Hall, where he was supposedly staying. On Wednesday, she decided she couldn't avoid Bradley Hall forever, steeled herself, and marched past it on her way to class. When she didn't bump into Jesse, she forced herself to pass Bradley Hall on her return trip to the dorm, and then twice more that day, all without incident. *Maybe he's gone*, she thought. She knew she should feel relieved, but somehow she didn't.

That night after rehearsal, with Britt still home in central Pennsylvania, the tiny dorm room seemed cavernous. Wishing she had her roommate to talk to, Lucy tried to find a halfway-decent romantic comedy to watch on her laptop—anything relatively light and frothy, as long as it wasn't *Roman Holiday*. But nothing could hold her interest for long, so instead she lugged her carry-on suitcase out from the closet, spread it open across Britt's bed, and willed herself to start packing for her big trip to New York City. *We'll go to the theater and bop around Greenwich Village*, she told herself. *It will be fun.*

Rummaging through her closet, she found a little black dress, a cashmere sweater, her best jeans, and a pair of boots. So far, so good. But when she thought about the time she would be spending alone with Shane, in his cousin's apartment, she faltered. Looking down at her drawer full of pajamas, she tried to decide which to pack—the baby-doll nightgown, which was pretty but too cold for fall? The plaid flannel pajamas that were warm enough but not exactly sexy? She tried to imagine how she would look to Shane, slipping out of the bathroom dressed in one or the other. But the face that popped into her mind wasn't Shane's.

Somehow, in Rome, she hadn't given a single thought to pajamas. At the Albergo della Zingara, she'd slept beside Jesse wearing nothing—and it had felt perfectly natural. The memory returned, startlingly vivid—the midsummer heat, the breeze that blew across her skin, the slight sunburn on her shoulders, the brush of Jesse's hair against her cheek, her back, her belly. His scent of fresh air, almonds, and crushed mint leaves.

Lucy sank to her bed and rested her head in her hands. *What's wrong with me?* she wondered. *I was perfectly fine until he showed up. Here. On my turf. Messing up everything.*

After that, she abandoned packing. She took a hot shower, then climbed into bed with her laptop, watching *When Harry Met Sally* to get into the mood for New York. But Charlene's words kept intruding: *He came to see you. He didn't have to. That means something.*

What does it mean, though? Lucy couldn't stop wondering. Midway through the movie she hit pause and started clicking instead through the pictures she'd taken of Jesse in Italy. *Not that it matters anymore,* she told herself. *Still, it would be nice to know. For the record.* It made her a little panicky to think that if Jesse really had left campus, she had no way of reaching him, no phone number, no e-mail address. She didn't even know the name of his hometown in New Jersey.

Then a name popped into her mind: Peter Gregorian. *Isn't that Jesse's friend in Bradley Hall, the guy he's been staying with? I can start with him and track Jesse down from there,* Lucy thought, calmer than she'd felt in days.

She knew she probably shouldn't. But she also knew she was going to.

Early the next morning, Lucy arrived at Peter Gregorian's suite and knocked on the door. Nobody answered at first. Just as she was about to give up, a damp-haired, bare-chested guy in a towel opened the door. He looked her up and down as though she were the half-naked one.

"I'm looking for Peter Gregorian," she said.

"Pete's out. Don't know when he'll be back."

"Can I leave a message?" Lucy looked past the guy into Peter Gregorian's messy dorm room. "Or maybe you could help me. It's not really Pete I'm looking for. Do you know Jesse Palladino?"

"The dude who was sleeping on our couch?" He gave Lucy another once-over.

"So he's gone?" Lucy asked.

"Since, I don't know, Monday, maybe. Or Tuesday."

"You wouldn't happen to know his phone number, would you? Or maybe what town he's from?"

"Sorry," the guy said. "All I know is this Jesse guy shows up, asking to crash on our couch. There's hardly enough air in this suite for four people to breathe, you know what I mean?"

"Uh, yeah," Lucy said.

"You could leave me your phone number," the guy said.

But Lucy didn't like the sound of that. "Can't you give me Pete's number instead?" And when he hesitated, she faked a flirtatious smile. "Please?"

Lucy left Bradley Hall with Peter Gregorian's cell-phone number in her hand. As soon as she was out of the building, she left a voice-mail message: "You don't know who I am, but I'm trying to find Jesse Palladino. Please call me back soon." But hours passed with no reply. In English class, Lucy decided she couldn't wait another minute, so she hid the phone under her desk and sent Peter a follow-up text.

Her phone vibrated thirty seconds after class let out, while she was gathering her books. Peter Gregorian's message was short and to the point: *I know who you are*, it read. *Call him. 732-555-2509.*

Lucy gave a little yelp, which caused everyone around her, including the professor, to turn her way. With an apologetic shrug, she slung her backpack over her shoulder and slipped out into the hallway. In the atrium, she leaned against a pillar and dialed.

You've reached the Palladino residence, a woman's voice said. *Please leave a message after the beep.*

"Um, hello. My name is Lucy. I'm a friend of Jesse's." As awkward as she felt, Lucy forced herself to continue. "Could you please have him call me as soon as he can? It's important." She left her phone number, hung up, and inhaled sharply, knowing she'd done all she could. The rest was up to Jesse.

XXIV

⸺⊗⸺

*F*riday night's rehearsal didn't go well. As Lucy ran through her duet with Cleo, she found she couldn't concentrate. Her mind kept wandering to the phone in her pocket. Ever since she'd left that message, it had stubbornly failed to vibrate.

Was Jesse really not going to call her? Even if he'd gone back to Italy already, wouldn't his parents have let him know someone was trying to reach him? Should she have said it was an emergency? Lucy was tempted to call and leave another voice mail, but what good would that have done? Either Jesse's parents would pass her message on or they wouldn't. Either he would want to talk to her or he wouldn't.

He must really hate me now, she thought, hitting a sour note. She told herself to concentrate, but a few bars later she fell out of tune again.

"You okay tonight, Lucy?" Ben, the music director, asked her at one point.

"I think I might be coming down with something. My roommate's been sick. And my throat does feel scratchy."

There was doubt in Ben's eyes. Was he sorry she'd been cast as Maureen? *Get it together*, Lucy scolded herself. She closed her eyes, trying to summon the character's confidence, her flamboyance, her swagger.

After that, things went better. Rehearsal ran late, and it seemed forever by the time Marcella dismissed them, saying, "Go, have yourselves a nice weekend. I'll see your bright and shiny faces Sunday afternoon."

Lucy was buttoning her coat when Matteo and Cleo ran up to her. "Want to come out with us?" Cleo asked. "I was just telling Matteo I could use some binner. You know, breakfast for dinner? I didn't make it to the dining hall tonight, and there's this all-night diner in University City that I'm dying to try."

Lucy had begged off, and now, as she crossed campus by herself, she was having second thoughts. Her dorm room was so empty without Britt in it. She thought about calling Shane, but she wasn't up for faking cheeriness, and how could she explain the bad mood she was in?

The night was misty, the path dark. Lucy jangled the keys in her coat pocket just to hear the sound. The warm lights of the dorms and academic buildings she passed made her feel all the more cold and alone. When she turned the corner and Woodruff Hall came into sight, she sighed with relief. As soon as she got inside she would run up to the fourth floor, tear open the door, and climb into bed.

Lucy was almost to the dorm when she spotted someone hurrying toward her. She recognized the walk and the wiry build before she took in the gig bag slung over his shoulder, the glossy hair, and the olive skin. Her heartbeat kicked into overdrive. It was Jesse, and he'd spotted her; she could tell by the way his step picked up speed. Before she could object, he wrapped her in a hug so warm and snug she knew right away he'd misunderstood her message. *He thinks I want to get back together*, she thought. Though she knew she shouldn't, she melted into his arms, unable to stop herself. But when he drew her face closer to his, leaning in for a kiss, she knew what she had to do, and pulled back.

"No," she said. "I can't. I'm glad you're here, but I didn't mean..."

Jesse surveyed her, his face solemn. "You didn't mean what?"

"I called because I need to ask you some questions."

Now Jesse looked hurt. "Questions?"

"Things I've been wondering about," Lucy said. "Why you hardly wrote to me after I left. And why you deleted your e-mail address without telling me first."

His brow furrowed. "What does any of that matter?"

"It matters to me," she said. "I need answers. So I can move on."

"You said you've already moved on," Jesse said.

"I have," she replied. "I absolutely have."

"With your new boyfriend."

"His name is Shane," Lucy said. Should she tell him about

the weekend she and Shane had planned, how they would be taking things to the next level? *No,* she decided. *It's none of his business.*

For a long moment, Jesse didn't speak. When he did, his voice had an edge to it that she'd never heard before. "What if I've got questions for you? Did you ever think of that?"

Lucy was taken aback. "What questions?"

"Who this Shane guy is," he said, "and what he's like."

Lucy didn't answer. Did he really expect her to stand there and discuss her boyfriend with him?

"How serious are you about him?"

"Very," she said, but her voice came out smaller than she intended.

"Is he good enough for you?"

"Yes," she answered. "He's more than good enough."

"Are you sure?"

"Of course I'm sure. If you really must know, he's great. Fantastic, even." Her words came out in a torrent. "He's cute and sophisticated. He's smart, and he likes to travel and go to nice restaurants. He's a business major and he's got a good job, and a really promising future—"

Jesse interrupted her. "That's what I was worried about."

Lucy's voice rose. "You were worried about his future?"

"It sounds like this guy is someone safe," Jesse said. "Someone your parents would approve of."

His words hit Lucy like a punch in her gut. She recoiled. "He is not. You've got it all wrong."

"Your parents don't approve of him?"

"They've never even met him," she said. "I don't need their approval."

"Lucy," Jesse said. "We both know that isn't true."

His words stung her. "I don't need *your* approval, either," she said, eyes narrowed.

"I never said you did. I would never say that."

"Well, good. Because I don't." She took a step away from him, then another. "This was a mistake. I should never have called you."

"Wait." She could hear him on the path behind her, his voice muffled as he bent to snatch up his duffel bag and guitar.

"Why should I?"

"I'll leave you alone," he called after her. "If that's what you really want."

"It is." Lucy's step slowed.

"But first I should answer your questions. Since that's why you called."

She turned back to face him. "Not here." What if Sarah or Glory came out of the building? Or, worse, what if Shane pulled up to pay her a surprise visit? Not that he ever had, but it wasn't beyond the realm of possibility. Looking for a secluded spot, she led Jesse around the corner to the service entrance, shut at this time of night. She leaned up against the dorm's cold brick, and he joined her there.

"So go ahead," she said. "Explain."

"First I want to say I'm sorry." The unpleasant edge in his voice had vanished, and he sounded like the Jesse she remembered.

"For what?" Lucy stared down at the tips of her boots. It was safer than looking into his eyes.

"For dropping off the radar," he said.

"But why? Why did you just disappear?"

"I was pulling double shifts at the hotel. And on the weekends, I was taking the train out to Sorrento, to do some busking."

Lucy dared a look at him. "Too busy to send an e-mail?"

"You're right; that's not the whole reason." The bright light above the service entrance reflected in Jesse's eyes, making twin crescent moons. With his hands buried deep in his pockets, he looked boyish, vulnerable. Lucy forced herself to look away again.

"I needed to figure some things out," he said.

"Some things?" She raised an eyebrow. From an open window above them, music spilled out, a Top 40 ballad that played under their conversation like the sound track to a melodramatic movie. Lucy willed it to stop, but it only got louder. "You mean about Angelina?"

"She's a good person," he said, his voice a shade more wary.

"And you were...involved with her?"

"For a little while."

"Oh. That's why you stopped writing to me? Why you deleted your e-mail account?" Lucy asked. "Because you were...with Angelina."

"No," Jesse said. "That's not why."

"You started seeing her and forgot about me." Lucy tried not to sound hurt.

"No," Jesse said. "The opposite. I was trying to forget about you, and I couldn't."

What he'd just said wasn't funny at all, but Lucy couldn't

stifle a bitter laugh. "And that's why you blew me off? Because you couldn't forget about me? Sorry, but that doesn't compute."

"I wanted my life back the way it was before I met you." Jesse's words came out in a rush. "I didn't want to give up traveling. Or to fly home and go to college. I didn't want to give my parents the *satisfaction*."

"Then why did you come to see me?" Lucy asked. "And why are you still here?"

He opened his mouth to speak, then closed it again.

"Why?" she repeated.

Jesse moved in closer. "You know why," he said. Then, before she could think better of it, Lucy was in his arms again, standing on tiptoe to receive his kiss. Italy came rushing back to her: the golden sun, the crumbling stone, the crowds, the paper lanterns drifting through the sky above the Arno, the dusty smell of the train station platform where she'd kissed him good-bye. Everything that had happened between that moment and this one seemed to vanish.

"Oh," she said when she could breathe again. "No."

"Don't you mean yes?" he asked with a small, wry smile.

She hesitated, seeking the will to turn him away. But the memories kept coming: the softness of his hair, the feel of his fingertips on her skin, how he'd made her feel again and again in the bed they'd shared in Rome. "Not here," she heard herself whisper.

"Where, then?" he murmured.

The words escaped Lucy's lips before she could think better of them. "My roommate's away," she said. The logistics came to her in a rush. "Room 315, Woodruff Hall. I'll go up first." She slipped from his arms. "Give me ten minutes, then come up."

What am I doing? she asked herself as she hurried away. *It's not too late to change my mind. I could go back and tell him no.*

But with the feel of his kiss still on her lips, she didn't seem able to stop herself. Instead, Lucy steeled herself in case she ran into someone she knew, and kept walking, up the front steps and into the overly bright lobby.

Lucky for her, Sarah and Glory seemed to be out. Lucy left the door to the suite ajar, then slipped into her room, relieved to hear the door click shut behind her. *Who am I?* she thought. *Sneaking around. Kissing someone who isn't my boyfriend. Inviting him up to my room.* Her side of the room, as usual, was a disaster area, especially in contrast with Brittany's. Lucy gazed down at the tangled sheets and blankets of her bed. *Am I really going to do this?* she wondered.

A few minutes later, Jesse slipped into Lucy's room and shrugged his bag and guitar to the floor. She locked the door behind him. A moment later they were sitting side by side on her bed, their bodies touching.

"I can't think when you're this close," she told him.

"Don't think." His hand found hers, and she rested her head on his shoulder.

"But I'm so confused," she murmured.

"I'm not." He pressed her hand to his cheek. A moment later, he was kissing her again, nibbling on her collarbone and unbuttoning her blouse, and instead of stopping him she was helping him tug it over her head. His eyes drinking her in, he slipped out of his leather jacket and pulled off his T-shirt. If she'd said no, if she'd told him to go away, she wouldn't be seeing him like this—so tender and defenseless, and so familiar. She wouldn't be nestling back into his arms, feeling the tickle of his breath on her skin. She wouldn't be letting his hands, his lips, his tongue erase every other thought from her mind.

Though it would have been wiser to send Jesse away afterward, nothing about what Lucy had done in the last few hours was remotely wise. So instead she fell asleep in his arms and woke to find him watching her, the morning sun flooding in through the slats of the pale pink venetian blinds her mother had bought for her dorm room.

"Good morning," he said softly.

Self-conscious, Lucy pulled at the duvet to cover herself. "I must look like a wreck," she said, running a hand through her tangled curls.

"Nothing like a wreck," Jesse replied. "The opposite of a wreck."

"I've got morning breath," she added.

"So do I," he countered. They were kissing again when a knock on the door made Lucy practically jump out of her skin.

"Who is it?" she called when she could speak.

"Did I wake you?" Sarah's voice asked. "Want to go get breakfast with me and Glory? The dining hall closes in fifteen minutes."

"No!" Lucy exclaimed, her voice coming out in a squeak. "I mean, thanks. But I'm going to sleep in."

"Are you okay?" Sarah asked. "You sound strange."

"I'm fine. I'm just…" Lucy sought the words that would send Sarah away without making her more suspicious. "I have a headache." She watched Jesse watching her lie. "I took some ibuprofen. I'm going to stay in bed till it goes away."

"Want me to bring you back something?" Sarah asked. "One of those blueberry-streusel muffins you like?"

Lucy's stomach lurched. "No. Thanks, though. I just need to rest."

That seemed to pacify Sarah. When she was gone, Lucy exhaled audibly. She aimed a small, apologetic smile in Jesse's direction.

But Jesse looked puzzled. "Why did you lie to your friend?" He inclined his head in the direction of Lucy's door.

"You know why." Lucy felt for something to cover herself with and grabbed a satin kimono from her desk chair. "As far as my friends know, I'm seeing Shane." It was hard to even say his name to Jesse. "And anyway, is it any of her business that you spent the night?"

"It just feels weird," Jesse said. "Like I'm some kind of dirty secret."

Lucy jumped to her feet, holding the kimono closed. "It's not you," she said. "It's me. I cheated on my boyfriend. That's not like me. I've never…I wouldn't…" But what more could she say? She would. And she had.

"Your boyfriend?" Jesse looked hurt. "You can still think of him like that?"

Just then, in a cosmic piece of bad timing, Lucy's phone rang.

She fumbled for it, found it on the floor in the pocket of last night's jeans, gave it a quick look, and ignored the call.

"That's him, isn't it?" Jesse said. "Aren't you going to take his call?"

"Right now?" she asked.

"Don't you need to talk to him?"

Lucy looked at him, confused.

"To break up with him?" he added.

"Over the phone? Wouldn't that be cruel?" Though to tell the truth, it felt like it would be just as cruel in person.

"You *are* going to tell him, right?" Jesse asked. "About us?"

"Yes," Lucy said, wondering how on earth she could ever find the words to tell Shane she'd cheated on him.

"When?" While Lucy struggled for an answer, Jesse started searching the floor for his clothes. When he straightened up, tangled jeans in his arms, he noticed Lucy's half-packed suitcase spread out on Brittany's bed. "Are you going somewhere?"

"Oh, God." She sank to the bed and covered her eyes with her hands. "That's tonight."

"What's tonight? Where are you going?"

"To New York." Lucy tried to keep her voice light. But when Jesse didn't seem satisfied, she confessed everything in a rush. "With Shane. It's supposed to be our first weekend away together. He's been planning it for a long time, and he bought tickets to a Broadway show, and the whole thing probably cost him a fortune, and…"

But Jesse was yanking on his pants. "You're not planning on going through with that?" he asked. "Tell me you're not. Not after last night. You can't."

"Now *you're* telling me what I can and can't do?" Irritated, Lucy turned her back to him, yanked the sash of her robe so hard it hurt, and knotted it closed.

"That's not what I meant." Jesse pulled his shirt back on. "You know it's not."

"Because it feels to me like everyone's always trying to tell me what to do," Lucy said, her voice peevish.

"I'm not one of those people." Jesse came to her on bare feet and pulled her to his chest. "Lucy, you know I'm not."

She rested against him for a moment, and when she spoke again, her voice was muffled. "I don't know what to tell him."

"The truth," Jesse replied, his hands smoothing her hair. "Just tell him the truth."

In Jesse's arms, Lucy thought of Shane. He hadn't done anything wrong, not a single thing, and he'd been there for her when Jesse was missing in action. She couldn't imagine hurting Shane. Did he really need to know what she'd done?

"You can't have us both, Lucy," Jesse said.

His words rubbed Lucy the wrong way. "Who says I'm trying to?" She wriggled free from his arms. "And anyway, you haven't said one word about what happens next. Are you going to stick around? Or are you flying back to Italy?"

Jesse jammed his feet into his sneakers without stooping to untie them. "That's what I'm trying to figure out," he said.

"So let me get this straight. You expect me to break up with Shane when you can't even tell me where you're going to be next week?" Lucy's voice got higher with every word.

"Either you're in love with this Shane guy or you're not," Jesse said through clenched teeth.

"It's not that simple," Lucy said.

"But it is," Jesse told her. "Either last night was a lie or it wasn't."

It wasn't, Lucy thought, but she was too angry to say the words out loud. "Nothing's that simple," she said.

Jesse snatched up his leather jacket. "Some things are."

They faced off for a long minute. Was he waiting for Lucy to say more? *I won't,* she thought. *Not until he tells me if he's staying.*

Finally, he reached for the doorknob. "I guess that's it, then."

"I guess it is."

"Don't worry," he said over his shoulder. "I won't let anyone see me leave."

And before she could say another word, he was gone.

"It's okay," Lucy whispered to herself. "It's okay, it's okay, it's okay." If Jesse was going to be difficult, if he wasn't even going to try to understand what she was going through, it simplified things. This way she'd never have to break up with Shane. And nobody would need to know about the night she'd just spent with Jesse. Being with him had been a mistake, Lucy decided. She would learn from it and never do anything that reckless, stupid, and selfish again. Jesse would leave town. He'd go back to playing music in the streets and seeing the world, and before long he'd have forgotten her.

While Lucy showered and dressed, she tried not to obsess over how Jesse was out there somewhere, stalking away from her in the morning sunlight, thinking she was a coward and a conformist. Thinking she didn't care about him. *I do care—enough to let him go back to Europe, where he's happy.* She pulled on the fuzzy sweater she planned to wear to New York City. *I just hope he realizes it someday.*

XXV

———

When Lucy could trust her voice, she called Shane back; together they decided he would arrive at one that afternoon to pick her up. If he heard anything strange or unsettling in her tone, he didn't mention it. Because she couldn't concentrate, eat, or make conversation, Lucy buried the sheets she and Jesse had just slept on in her laundry hamper and lugged it down to the laundry room. While she finished packing, she blasted music, trying to chase all thoughts of Jesse out of her head.

By noon, Lucy's bag was packed, and there was nothing left to do but fret about the coming weekend. She was picking through her jewelry box, trying to decide which earrings to wear, when her phone buzzed. Lucy lunged for it. For a wild, hopeful second, she thought it might be Jesse. She didn't expect him to change his mind, but it would be nice to hear him say he'd at least forgiven her.

But the text was from Shane. *Leaving now*, it read. *See you soon*. That was just the kind of guy Shane was, the thoughtful kind who called to let you know he was on his way. Not the type who fell off the face of the earth and then appeared on a girl's doorstep without warning. It took Lucy forever to settle on her sapphire earrings. As she put on mascara, she thought with rising anxiety of what lay ahead—the two-hour drive to New York City and the Upper West Side apartment where she was supposed to do with her boyfriend the things that she had just done with Jesse. She thought of Shane, who had every reason to expect she was as happy about this weekend as he was. She pictured his silver-gray eyes, the line of his jaw, his hands steady on the wheel of his car.

You cheated on him, she told her reflection. *You should tell him and suffer the consequences.* Her curls were drying into a wild frizz. She gathered them together and twisted them into a bun, trying to look like someone who had every detail of her life under control.

Shane doesn't need to know, Lucy thought. *I'll never do anything like that again. Jesse's gone. I've learned my lesson.* But the girl in the mirror looked back with doubt in her eyes.

Just then the phone rang. Again, Lucy lunged for it.

"Lucy. This is your father."

"Dad," Lucy said. Her father never called. She knew right away this wasn't going to be good news. "Is Mom okay?"

"Yes," he said, impatience in his voice. "Your mother's fine."

"Is something wrong, then?"

"That's why I'm calling. The Forsythe alumni magazine arrived this morning. Are you aware that your photo is in it?"

"Is it?" Lucy's voice came out shaky.

"There's an article about *Rent*. It says you're still in the cast."

Lucy cleared her throat. It would be so easy to tell him that the reporter was working from old information, that the picture had been taken a few weeks back, that she'd quit the play as promised. "I can explain," she began.

"Because I want you to know I wasn't kidding around. If you didn't quit that play, there will be serious consequences. You want a good dose of reality? Try getting a full-time job and putting yourself through college the way I did. You'll see there isn't time for fooling around with drama societies and glee clubs. Maybe you need to work in a restaurant, washing dishes every night, while the other kids at school party all weekend long."

Lucy did a quick calculation. It wasn't too late to turn things around. She could quit the play on Sunday afternoon and her father would never need to learn the truth. "But, Dad—"

"But nothing, Lucy. I'm deadly serious about this. I want to hear it from your own mouth. Did you or did you not disobey me?"

The thundering tone Lucy's father took on when he was mad—like an emperor issuing demands to his subjects—could have sent Lucy into a panic. It always used to, when she was six and spilled her juice box on his computer keyboard, or when she was sixteen and arrived home half an hour late for curfew.

This time, though, she found herself standing up straighter, as if he could see her. "I didn't quit the play."

His voice got even deeper. "What did you just say?"

"I didn't quit *Rent*," she repeated. "I'm not going to." Silence fell between them. She rushed to fill it. "This isn't about you. It's about me. And what I want."

More silence. Lucy kept going.

"I'm going to Forsythe and majoring in business, like you wanted. Why isn't that enough for you? I don't even like business. In fact, so far I hate it." She gasped for air; apparently she'd been forgetting to breathe. "Why do you have to control everything in my life? Why can't I keep this one thing that means so much to me?"

Her father interrupted, his voice cold. "So. You've made your decision."

"Yes," she told him. "I have."

Lucy's father began again, his tone more conciliatory this time. "I thought you were enjoying Forsythe. I got the impression you really love it there."

"I do," she said, not adding that the play was a huge part of why she loved Forsythe so much.

"Well, then," he said, "I don't understand. Why would you give that up just to be in one more play?"

"It's not just one more play," she said. "It's the one I've always dreamed of being in."

Her father gave an exasperated sigh. "I know you, Lucy," he said. "There will always be just one more play you've always dreamed of being in."

So what if there is? Lucy thought.

"We made a deal," he added in the no-nonsense business-man's voice he always used to talk about money. "If you don't hold up your end, I won't hold up mine. That's how the world works. Which means I won't be paying any more tuition."

"I'll take out student loans," Lucy said.

"And how will you pay them back? You'll be in debt for the rest of your life."

"Then I'll transfer to someplace less expensive. Or maybe find a school with a bigger theater department. One that will give me a scholarship."

"Oh, please, Lucy." Now he sounded flat-out exasperated. "Yes, you're moderately talented."

Moderately talented? Lucy recoiled as though he had slapped her face.

"But do you really think you're good enough to—"

Unable to listen to another word, Lucy hung up. Then, in case her father tried to call her back, she turned her phone off and buried it in her purse. She flopped down onto her bed, expecting to have a good cry, but after a sniffle or two, she realized she was too mad for tears. Besides, she didn't have time to feel sorry for herself. Shane would be pulling up soon, expecting her to be on the sidewalk with her suitcase in tow.

She checked her mascara in the mirror and tucked a few renegade curls back into place. *My hair is like my life*, she thought. *Completely out of control.* She remembered the advice Jesse had given her back in Florence: *Make your own choices.* She'd certainly been trying that lately—and look how it had turned out.

By the time Lucy made it downstairs, Shane was already waiting, his car humming at the curb. As always, he jumped out to open the door for her. Then he bent to hoist her suitcase into the trunk. "Whoa! Was your bag this heavy when you traveled around Europe?"

She gave him what she hoped was a convincing smile. "You should have seen the muscles I had back then."

"I wish I could have." He slid into the driver's seat and shot her a second look, studying her with an expression she couldn't quite peg. Could he tell that something had changed? The thought made her pulse quicken.

"Is something the matter?" she asked finally.

"No," he said. "It's just...your hair."

"You don't like it?" she asked.

"It makes you look different. Like somebody else."

As Shane pulled away from the curb, Lucy sank back into the gray upholstery, trying not to blurt out what she was thinking: that she'd just become somebody else—the kind of girl who cheats on her boyfriend. She watched as Woodruff Hall receded from view and thought that soon enough she'd probably have to leave it for good. How could so much have gone so wrong in such a short period of time? Lost in thought, she forgot to make polite conversation. When Shane hit the turn signal, its click-click-clicking echoed in the silence.

"Is everything okay?" he finally asked.

Lucy looked over at him and noticed, for the first time, how nicely he was dressed—in a crisp oxford shirt and a black peacoat she'd never seen before. He was even wearing aftershave. *He's trying so hard*, she thought, guilt washing over her again.

"Everything's okay," she said.

"Really? You seem on edge."

Lucy felt the muscles around her mouth twitch. "You're right. Everything's not okay."

Shane took his eyes off the road. "How so?"

Lucy thought fast. Though she couldn't tell Shane the whole story, at least she could tell him half. She filled him in on the standoff with her dad, and he nodded as he listened, not saying a word until she'd gotten all the way through.

"That's harsh." He reached over to pat her arm.

"I know," she said.

"I'm sure you're very talented," he said.

Lucy forced a smile. "You've never even seen me act," she said, but the minute she said the words, she knew they were a lie. She acted for Shane all the time, trying to seem worldly, glamorous, adventurous, and perpetually upbeat—all the things she imagined a guy like Shane would want in a girlfriend. She was acting for him now.

"I have an instinct about these things." He took his hand back to hit the turn signal and change lanes. "Everything will be okay."

"I don't see how," she said.

"Lots of people put themselves through college," Shane said. "If they can do it, you can."

Lucy looked out the window at the landscape rushing past, then down at her knees—anywhere but at Shane.

"I know what," he added. "Maybe I can help you find a job. I'll ask my dad. He might know someone who's hiring."

"That's really sweet," Lucy said. "But you don't seem to understand. Forsythe costs a fortune. I should know; my father mentions it every chance he gets." She picked a loose thread from her coat and forced herself to sound matter-of-fact. "Job or no job, I'll probably have to transfer to community college."

"So you'll go to community college," Shane said. "It's not the end of the world, right?"

Lucy nodded, but she was thinking of Britt, of Sarah and Glory, of Cleo and Matteo, of Café Paradiso, and of the Theater Arts building and the plays that would be put on there without her. She thought of the bell tower that rang the song's alma mater every day at noon, and the blueberry-streusel muffins at the dining hall, and her little pink and white dorm room, which she'd come to love though it was barely big enough for one, much less two. And remembering her room brought another image flooding back: Jesse lying under her pink-polka-dotted duvet.

Lucy shook her head vigorously, as though she could shake the memory from her mind. "I'll need to start looking for a place to live, too," she observed glumly. "Oh, God. I'm sorry. I'm no fun at all today."

"Can't you live at home?" Shane asked. "Then you wouldn't have to worry about rent."

"After the way my dad talked to me today? I'd rather live in a roach motel downtown." She thought of Shane's neighborhood, funky and bohemian, bustling with young professionals and artsy types. "How much does your apartment cost?" she asked. "If you don't mind my asking." When he told her, she felt the glumness descend again. "That much? How on earth can you afford it?"

"My parents help out." Was it Lucy's imagination, or did Shane sound a little defensive? She didn't know what to say in reply, and Shane, deep in thought, didn't speak again until they were on the turnpike. "You could live there with me," he said, out of the blue.

Lucy gaped at him, stunned by the offer.

"If you can't find a place of your own," he added.

"Oh," she said. "Wow. You mean live together?" She could barely get the question out. "That's really...thoughtful. But we haven't even...I mean we don't know each other that well yet. Do we?"

"That's what this trip is about, isn't it?" The sun came out from behind the clouds and Shane reached for his sunglasses. "Listen, you're right; it's soon. It's not like I'd be asking you to move in under normal circumstances."

"Oh," Lucy said.

"But these aren't normal circumstances. You need a place to live. So we can just try it out for a little while, and if it doesn't work, it doesn't have to be forever. Who knows? Maybe living together will be great."

And maybe it won't, Lucy thought. She had the sudden, bizarre urge to fling the car door open and jump out.

"You wouldn't even have to pay rent." Shane took one hand off the wheel to give Lucy's shoulder a reassuring rub.

"I'd want to," Lucy protested. "That would only be fair."

Shane returned his hand to the wheel. "Well, then, you could chip in whatever you could afford."

Lucy looked back down at her own hands, palms-up in her lap. "You're like a dream boyfriend," she said.

Shane chuckled.

"No, seriously. You are so, so, so nice." *I should tell him about Jesse*, she thought. "I think maybe I don't deserve you," she said.

But Shane was lost in the details. "It'll be great. We can split groceries. We'll keep each other on track. Who knows—maybe you'll wind up saving some money."

"I don't see how that's possible," Lucy mumbled.

"We'll put a little aside every month. Then you could even come with me to Europe next summer. Wouldn't that be great?"

"Europe?" Lucy asked in disbelief.

"We can do it on the cheap," Shane said. "Stay in hostels, the way you did last year. Get student rail passes. Think how great it would be. Planning a trip would give you something to focus on. Something to look forward to."

"But I'm going to be dead broke," Lucy said. *Does he really understand the situation I'm in?* she wondered.

"Well, then, if we can't afford a whole tour of Europe, we could just stay in one place for a while. Find a cheap sublet. Live like the locals. Wouldn't you like that?"

Lucy was dumbfounded. "But..." she began, then trailed off.

"In Rome, maybe," he said. "Or Florence. You really liked Florence, right?"

"Yes," Lucy said. "I loved Florence." And though it all seemed so crazy, she tried to calm herself by shutting her eyes and envisioning Florence. She tried to imagine wandering its streets with Shane—pausing to look in shop windows, drinking wine at a sidewalk café in Piazza Santo Spirito, lingering on the Ponte Vecchio, looking out over the Arno. The mental snapshots were all so vivid—but in each one, the person she kept seeing at her side was Jesse. She tried to picture something more immediate instead: the apartment that awaited them in New York that afternoon, the bedroom they would be sleeping in that very night. But when she tried to conjure Shane's face beside her on the pillow, the face she saw was Jesse's.

Just then, Shane hit the brakes and the car slowed almost to a halt. "Oh, great."

Lucy's eyelids fluttered open. They'd hit a traffic jam. She glanced over at Shane and found him fiddling with his GPS, punching its buttons. "Must be an accident up there."

"I'm sorry," Lucy said.

"Ah, so you caused this?" He gestured toward the traffic in front of them, ground to a complete standstill. "You must have superpowers."

I'm sorry for everything, Lucy thought, the words echoing in her head until she was tempted to say them out loud. "I can't go to Europe with you," she said instead.

Shane sighed. "I know how hopeless everything seems right now."

Lucy peered ahead, trying to spot a way out of the traffic jam, but the next exit was nowhere in sight. "Everything *is* hopeless."

His smile faded. "Don't you think you're being a little... dramatic?"

She wriggled, her seat belt too tight. "You don't understand."

"Maybe I don't," he said. "Maybe I've always had it pretty easy. Maybe I've never had to pay my own tuition or rent." A silver SUV was trying to wedge itself into their lane; Shane gave the driver a weary wave. "But I shouldn't have to apologize for that."

"Of course not," Lucy said. "I didn't mean..."

"I'm just trying to cheer you up. And you're not...you're not..."

"I'm not what?" Lucy asked.

"You're not making it easy."

Lucy looked at him—really looked at him, past the mirrored shades and his whole handsome surface, to the person he was, the guy who wanted to make her feel better. The guy who was willing to let her move into his apartment even though—let's face it—he hardly even knew her. *He deserves better than this*, she thought. *Better than a girl who wants to be with someone else.*

A moment later, the traffic started moving again; they passed a fender bender and a patrol car, its red lights flashing a warning. Soon they would be hurtling at full speed toward New York City and Shane's cousin's apartment. Somehow the thought was unbearable.

Though she wasn't at all sure what she was going to say next, Lucy knew it was time to say something. "I know my timing is terrible, but I can't help how I feel," she began. "About us. I mean, I like you. I really like you, but..."

"What?" Shane's voice was full of disbelief. "It almost sounds like you're breaking up with me." He laughed, and when Lucy didn't laugh along with him, he asked, "Are you?"

Lucy grew flustered. "No!" she said. Then, after a moment's thought, "Yes."

"Are you serious?" Both his hands left the steering wheel in a gesture of frustration and confusion. "Have I done something wrong?"

"No," she said. "You've been nothing but wonderful."

"Then why?" In what felt like slow motion, his hands returned to the wheel.

"Because I'm in love with somebody else." As soon as she spoke the words, she knew they were true. Jesse was probably already on a plane back to Europe, and she might never see him again, but that didn't change the fact that she wanted to be with *him*—not with Shane, or anybody else.

Now Shane was looking at her with something like horror in his eyes.

"I only just realized," Lucy said. "Really, it's got nothing to do with you." Her words tumbled out. "You're really, truly great. Most girls would feel incredibly lucky...."

"But not you." His voice was flat.

"I'm sorry," she said.

"Who is this somebody else?"

"Nobody you know," Lucy said, though that much was already obvious. It wasn't like she and Shane had many friends, or even acquaintances, in common.

"And you fell in love with him while you've been going out with me?" Shane's voice got harder. "Have you been cheating on me this whole time?"

Lucy flushed. "He's somebody I knew last summer. I didn't think I'd ever see him again. But then he came to see me. And things just...happened."

"*Things?*" Shane sounded exasperated. "What kind of things?"

Lucy bit her knuckle, unable to answer.

"I can't believe this. Tonight of all nights. We have reservations at Tiger Lily at eight. And fifth-row tickets to *Wicked*. Do you know how hard those were to get?"

"I'm sorry," she said again. Now that she'd started confessing, she wanted to keep going, explain every sordid detail. But while spilling her guts might make her feel better, she knew it would only make Shane feel worse. "I didn't mean for any of this to happen." *I wanted to love you*, she thought. Though she was tempted to reach over and pat his hand, she held back.

"What happens now?" Shane's knuckles were white against the steering wheel. "What do we do?"

"Could you take me back to campus?" Lucy asked. "Please?"

He looked at her, almost uncomprehendingly, for a long moment. Then he punched a few more buttons on the GPS and veered abruptly to the right, cutting off two lanes of traffic, aiming for the next exit.

XXVI

⸺❦⸺

*T*he drive home was excruciating. When the silence between them grew unbearable, Shane turned on the radio, restlessly scanning from station to station. Lucy had him drop her off at the edge of campus to cut the trip a few minutes shorter. The day had grown gray and cold, and she dragged her overstuffed suitcase behind her, its wheels noisy against the pavement. The sight of Barton Hall, where her English class met, ordinarily wouldn't have filled her with emotion; today, though, it reminded her of how little time she had left at Forsythe. And walking past the Theater Arts building, which was quieter than usual, made her father's words ring in her ears: *Moderately talented, moderately talented, moderately talented.* He couldn't have said any two words designed to hurt her more.

Today I lost everything, she thought, buttoning her coat against the cold. *Jesse. Shane. Forsythe.* She hadn't realized how much she loved Forsythe, but the thought that she would soon have to leave it gave her an actual pain in her stomach. *I'll lose Cleo. And Matteo. And Britt.* Tears sprang to her eyes at the thought of her roommate. *I have to tell Britt.* She rummaged in her purse for her phone and turned it on.

Immediately, it rang in her hand.

"Lucy?" The voice on the other end of the line was, of all people, Charlene. "Where are you?"

Lucy stopped mid-stride. "In front of the Theater Arts building. Why?"

"I'm coming to pick you up. Stay where you are."

This was a strange development. Beyond strange. The line went dead in Lucy's hand. What on earth could Charlene mean? Lucy tried to call her back, but the call went straight to voice mail. She tried a second time and was leaving a message when a slightly battered gray sedan pulled to the curb next to her. The driver—Charlene—leaned across the front seat to throw the passenger door open. "Come on," she said.

"Where are we going?" Lucy asked, climbing in and buckling her seat belt.

Charlene was as breathless as if she'd been running toward Lucy instead of driving. "To the airport. To stop Jesse."

Lucy struggled to find her voice. "What?" she asked finally.

"I saw him. This morning. Stomping away from your dorm. Lugging that guitar bag of his. So I asked him where he was going. He said to the airport. Then he kept walking."

"Wait. What?" Lucy asked again, unable to get beyond one-word questions.

"So I got in my car. Drove around campus. I found him at the bus stop. Asked him why he seemed so mad." Charlene gasped for air. "Said the two of you had a fight. And he had an open ticket. To Naples via Rome. Tried to get him to wait. To think it over. But a bus pulled up and he got on."

The car screeched onto the highway and Lucy clutched the dashboard. "He's leaving today?"

"Tonight." Charlene said. "He didn't say what time. But he mentioned his ticket was with Etruscan Airways, so I checked the schedule online. I think his plane leaves at six forty-five. Flight 376, nonstop to Rome." Charlene leaned on the horn and passed an Oldsmobile going the speed limit.

Even though last summer they had hiked up mountainsides and climbed medieval bell towers, Lucy had never once seen Charlene this out of breath. "Are you okay?" she asked.

Charlene nodded. "When I panic, I forget to inhale." She shot Lucy a look that was almost accusatory. "Where have you been hiding? I've been trying to reach you. All afternoon."

Lucy checked her voice mail. Sure enough, she found five messages from Charlene.

"Call him," Charlene urged.

"I would if he had a phone," Lucy said.

"Who doesn't have a cell phone?" Charlene asked. "What is he, some kind of monk?"

Lucy tucked her phone back in her purse. "I don't understand, though. Why are you this worked up about Jesse?"

"Because he came all the way from Europe. Not for his cousin's wedding. That was just an excuse. He came for you. He said so."

"He did?" Lucy asked. "Why didn't he tell me that?"

"Who knows?"

"But . . ." Lucy said. For all Charlene knew, Lucy was still going out with Shane. "Why do you care so much?"

"I figure I owe you one. After Fiesole. After giving your photo to Ellen." Charlene switched lanes to zoom around a slow-moving Buick. "But that's not even the real reason."

"It isn't?"

"It would be wrong to let him get away." Charlene tore her gaze from the highway just long enough to meet Lucy's eyes. "He *loves* you."

Lucy felt her heart speed up. "You think so?"

"He said so."

"He told you he *loves* me?" Lucy's voice came out in a squeak.

"He didn't want to admit it," Charlene said, "but his bus was late, so we had some time to talk, and I broke him down with my expert interrogation skills."

Lucy couldn't help but smile. She'd seen Charlene in action and could easily believe she'd bent Jesse to her will. "You're terrifying," she said.

"I know." Charlene grinned back, pleased with herself. "But that's beside the point. I think *you* love him, too. Don't you?"

"Yes," Lucy said. "Yes."

"Well, then," Charlene said, "when we hit the airport, I'll drop you off at the terminal. You can run in while I park. Maybe you can catch him before he gets on that plane."

In the romantic comedies Lucy adored, there was almost always a scene at the end in which the hero realizes he loves the heroine and races to the airport to catch her before she gets on a plane and flies out of his life forever. Or sometimes the heroine would run after the hero, kicking off her high heels, barreling through the crowd, pushing other travelers out of her way and getting to the gate just in time. But in real life, Lucy soon discovered, a person couldn't just beg her way through security.

"You could buy a ticket," the uniformed TSA officer told her when she reached the front of the line.

As she ran to the ticket counter, Lucy dug in her purse for the credit card her parents had given her when she left for college; maybe her father hadn't canceled it yet. At this time of night, the line was surprisingly short. But when the ticket agent called out "next," Lucy remembered her passport, which was sitting in the top drawer of her desk back at the dorm.

"Oh, crap," Lucy said. "Can I get through security without a passport?"

The ticket agent pursed her lips. "I'm afraid not," she said.

"But you don't understand." Lucy's voice cracked. "There's this guy. He's getting on a plane to Rome. I need to stop him."

The ticket agent looked at her appraisingly, then reached for her phone. "What's his name?" she asked. A moment later, her voice was echoing over the PA. "Paging Etruscan Airways passenger Jesse Palladino. Jesse Palladino, please report to a courtesy phone in Terminal A."

Just then, Charlene arrived at Lucy's side. "They won't let you through?" she asked.

"No passport," Lucy said.

"Why didn't I think of that?" Charlene bonked herself in the head. "Anyway, I checked the monitors," Charlene said. "His plane is boarding."

"What if he's on it already?" Lucy asked.

Charlene addressed the ticket agent. "Can we reach a passenger who's on the plane?"

The lady looked doubtful. "Only for an *actual* emergency." She glanced down at her watch. "Besides, by now the plane has probably left the gate."

But Charlene, who never backed down from a fight, wasn't about to wimp out now. "Probably?" Her nostrils flared grandly. "Can't you tell for sure?"

The lady noisily clicked a few computer keys. "Flight 376 is listed as departed," she said.

Lucy slumped against the counter. "Never mind," she told Charlene. "We did our best."

"Maybe 376 isn't even his flight," Charlene said. "Is there another flight to Rome tonight?"

"Not with Etruscan Airways," the woman said. "Maybe you should try another airline." *And leave me alone*, her expression said.

"He said he was flying Etruscan," Charlene said. "And that it was a direct flight to Rome."

"That must have been the one, then," Lucy said sadly.

"Could you check the passenger list to make sure he got on

board?" Charlene asked. "He might have gotten stuck in traffic," she said to Lucy.

"Not likely," Lucy answered.

"But possibly," Charlene said.

"There was no traffic. Remember how quickly we got here?" Lucy said.

The woman looked back and forth between them, following their conversation, her gray hair so lacquered into place it didn't move when her head turned.

"Let's have the *nice lady* check anyway," Charlene told Lucy.

Charlene's sarcasm wasn't lost on the ticket agent. "I'm not permitted to give out that information," she said, her voice acidic. Then she looked past Charlene and Lucy to the handful of passengers who had gathered in a line behind them. "Next," she called.

The ride back to campus seemed to take forever. Now that there was no need to beat the clock, Charlene was back to her usual self, driving in the slow lane and speaking in full sentences. "You could probably track down Nello's family in Naples," she said hopefully. "The Bertolini might have their number. Nello might know how to reach him."

"Who are we kidding? He won't want to hear from me." Lucy flopped her head back, letting it rest against the vinyl seat. "He was so disappointed in me this morning." She sighed. "Maybe we just weren't meant to be."

"You really believe that?" Charlene asked.

The reality of the situation—that she would never see Jesse again—hit Lucy like a cold ocean wave, making it hard to think or even breathe. She looked at her friend, panic in her eyes.

"It's a long flight," Charlene said. "By the time the plane lands, he'll have had plenty of time to cool down. A few phone calls, and you'll have his number."

"This has been the worst day." Lucy filled Charlene in on the conversation with her father.

"Your father won't really make you drop out of Forsythe, will he?" Charlene sounded shocked. "After all that business about wanting you to go here in the first place?"

"He's a big believer in keeping his word," Lucy said.

"Where will you live when the semester's over?" Charlene asked.

"I don't know," Lucy said. "I'll figure something out." All she could think of was Jesse flying over the dark Atlantic, believing she didn't care enough about him to break up with Shane, getting farther away from her with each passing second.

Charlene stopped the car in the circle in front of Woodruff Hall.

"Thank you." Lucy leaned over to give Charlene a hug. Whatever had been difficult between the two of them was now in the distant past. "I really mean it. What you did today was just..." She trailed off, unable to find the right words.

"I'm sorry we couldn't catch him," Charlene said. Then she chuckled. "I should have climbed over that ticket counter and put that woman in a choke hold."

Despite herself, Lucy laughed. "You definitely could have

taken her." She released her friend, opened the car door, and stepped out into the night.

As Charlene drove off, Lucy waved good-bye. The campus all around her was eerily quiet for a Saturday; it seemed everyone but Lucy was off somewhere, partying. Lucy was feeling in her clutch for her key card when she heard steps behind her on the path. She whirled around to see someone tall and masculine, with dark hair and a long-legged stride, hurrying in her direction, his face obscured by darkness.

She held her breath. Could Jesse have missed his plane after all, either deliberately or on purpose? She thought of the other times he'd stepped out of the night to surprise her, times when she'd been more alarmed than happy to see him. If only by some miracle this was Jesse, she would run to him, throw her arms around him without reservation, and tell him how she felt, holding nothing back.

The guy drew closer, saw Lucy watching him, and shot her an overconfident smile. No, he wasn't Jesse—not by a mile. She looked away quickly, fumbled with her key card, and stepped into Woodruff Hall's lobby. It was empty except for the motherly guard behind the desk.

"You in for the night, sweetheart?" she asked Lucy. "It's so early."

"It's too late for me," she told the guard, and her words had the ring of an awful confession.

XXVII

On the opening night of the Forsythe University Players production of *Rent*, Lucy waited backstage, paralyzed with terror. To dispel the preshow jitters, Cleo, Matteo, and the other cast members were joking around, playing pranks on one another, while Lucy stood in the wings, trying to summon her inner downtown diva. Even her costume—black leather boots, skintight pants, and a sleeveless leopard-skin blouse—wasn't helping. *I should have dropped out of the show*, she thought, doing a nervous little dance in place. *What if I ruin it for everybody else?* Ever since that terrible phone call with her father, his words would echo in her ears at the worst possible times. In the middle of rehearsal, or at two AM when she couldn't sleep, she'd hear them again: *Yes, you're moderately talented.* Maybe somebody else would be happy to be called that, but not Lucy. She'd always prided herself on being truly talented—on being real Broadway material—but what if she'd been wrong? What if she seized up again and ruined the play? More than once she'd given serious thought to stepping aside and giving up acting, for good this time.

"You can't do that," Britt had told her over the phone, and then in person when she finally came back to school. "This play means everything to you. Now you want to throw it away?"

The only thing that had gotten Lucy through dress rehearsals had been Britt, Matteo, and Cleo urging her onward, telling her she was good, really good. Whenever she started to panic at the thought of opening night, Britt would urge her to take deep breaths, promising that everything would work out okay if she only believed in herself half as much as all her friends believed in her.

But Lucy worried, and not just about *Rent* and her acting abilities. She worried about what would happen when the semester ended and she had to find a job and move out of her dorm. And sometimes she worried about Jesse, and how she would never see him again. She'd taken Charlene's suggestion and tried calling the Bertolini to get Nello's phone number in Naples, but the desk clerk she'd spoken with had refused to give it out. Besides, even if she could have found a way to track Jesse down, what could she possibly say that would make up for her hesitation, her failure to choose him over Shane?

Jesse was gone for good, and Lucy knew she needed to get on with her life, and let him get on with his. But how could she when he kept making cameo appearances in her dreams? Over and over, she'd wake up and be forced to remember how she'd hurt him. Still, Lucy had managed to get through the last several weeks of school and rehearsals. She'd even convinced herself she would be fine once the play opened. But she hadn't counted on her usual opening-night jitters turning into full-blown panic, the kind that closes over a person like a tidal wave, washing her lines clear out of her mind. Now she paced back and forth in the backstage shadows, too preoccupied to think how crazy she must look.

Cleo's voice came from behind, startling her. "Hey, Luce. Why are you lurking here all by yourself?"

Lucy read concern in her friend's warm brown eyes. "I'm just psyching myself up," Lucy said. "Trying to become Maureen."

"That's what you're doing?" Cleo sounded unconvinced.

Lucy nodded, a little too vehemently. "I always pace," she lied. "It's my preshow routine."

"If you say so." Cleo pointed to where Matteo was giving them both a little wave. "We'll be over there if you need us."

Lucy waved back at Matteo. "I'm fine," she said. "I swear."

But as the moments ticked away, Lucy realized she was distinctly not fine. She could hear the blood whooshing in her ears, could feel it speeding through her veins. *There's no backing out now*, she told herself, too frightened to even pace anymore. *Become Maureen*, she ordered herself, picturing the downtown performance-artist diva she'd always wanted to be.

Just after eight, the play began. Lucy waited for her cue. Eyes shut, she prayed over and over again that the magic would somehow happen.

Surprisingly enough, it did. When Lucy stepped onto the stage, her walk wasn't her own; it was Maureen's slow, high-heeled strut. When she spoke her first line, her voice rang out to the back of the theater, and the play itself—the gritty, bohemian, East Village world of *Rent*—seemed to open its arms and gather her in, the way she'd desperately hoped it would.

When Lucy looked out into the audience, she kept her gaze above the heads of the crowd. Only once did she let herself scan the crowd for familiar faces. But she didn't see a single face she recognized. Where was Britt? Where were Sarah and Glory? It hurt to know that for the first time ever, her parents weren't in the audience, proud of her, wishing her well.

Don't think about that now, Lucy commanded herself. *Don't lose focus.*

One heartbeat later she was Maureen again, intent on reciting her lines and hitting her marks. The rest of the play passed in a flash. When the cast gathered onstage for the show's final number, their voices blended and built to fill the theater. Lucy looked to her left and saw Cleo singing her heart out; she looked to the right and met Matteo's eyes. *This is my family now*, she thought.

Only when it was all over and she was Lucy again, when the audience had jumped to its feet and was applauding, when she ran out, hand in hand with Cleo, for her curtain call, did she allow herself another sweeping look into the crowd. This time, she saw them in the center of the auditorium: Britt, Sarah, Glory, and even Charlene, all on their feet, applauding. Nearly swooning with relief, Lucy blew her friends kisses while the applause went on and on and on. And then, farther back, not far from the exit, she caught sight of a face she hadn't dreamed she'd see in the crowd: her mother's, smiling almost shyly.

Backstage, Lucy didn't waste time changing out of her costume, washing off her makeup, or even chatting with her castmates. Though she was flushed, sweaty, and covered in goop, she dashed straight into the hallway where the audience was filing out and milling around. Still in Maureen's high black boots, Lucy craned her neck to see over the crowd. She spotted her mother standing near the glass double doors, anxiously twirling her silver watch around and around on her wrist. When she glimpsed her daughter, her face lit up.

Lucy struggled through the crowd. "You came," she said. And though she'd spent the last two hours projecting her lines to the back of the auditorium, her voice now emerged in a whisper.

Lucy's mother flung her arms around her daughter. She smelled like Chanel No. 5, and the scent—so familiar from childhood—made Lucy's heart twist with love. "I sneaked out. Your father thinks I'm at my book club."

But you're a grown woman, Lucy thought. *You shouldn't have to sneak out. You should be able to go wherever you want.*

"He'll come around sooner or later," Lucy's mother continued. "I've been planting the seeds, but he has to believe it's his own idea. You know your dad." She patted her handbag. "Besides, I've got a secret weapon now." Her brown eyes twinkled. "I used my camera to take a video of you performing. You were so beautiful up there, sweetheart. And you did such an amazing job, really professional." She brushed a stray curl out of Lucy's eyes. "I'll wait till the moment's right and show it to your father. He'll come around."

"Will he?" Lucy asked. "Do you really think so?"

"Oh, honey," her mother said. "I know so." On tiptoes, she kissed her daughter's cheek. "It's so good to see you, Lu. I've missed you, more than you can know. But I need to get home. My book-club meeting usually breaks up by ten."

As Lucy watched her mother walk away, tears filled her eyes. But then Cleo and Matteo ran up, laughing, engulfing her in a double hug. Before long, Britt, Glory, Sarah, and Charlene surrounded her, too, and Lucy was introducing Charlene to her castmates and suitemates and absorbing everyone's congratulations, her heart swelling with their praise. Of course her friends would only say good, kind things about her; of course they weren't objective about her acting. But in her heart of hearts, Lucy knew she'd done well. She believed—no, she knew—she was more than just *moderately talented.*

Lucy was glowing with pleasure when she happened to look up and see another familiar form. A clutch of vivid yellow sunflowers tucked in the crook of his arm, he took a step closer, his gaze darting from face to face, finally landing on hers.

It was Jesse. But how could it be? Lucy fumbled for words and, not finding any, threw herself into his arms and buried her face in his leather jacket.

"You're really here?" she asked. "Tell me I'm not imagining this."

Jesse didn't answer, but she felt his warm breath on her neck and smelled crushed mint and almond mingled with the green, summery scent of sunflowers.

"Charlene said you'd gone back to Italy," she said. "We tried to catch you at the airport."

"You did?" Jesse's dark eyes scanned the small crowd sur-rounding Lucy. *He's looking for Shane*, Lucy realized. She opened her mouth, but before she could explain, Jesse was telling her how he'd meant to leave for Rome that night, how he'd gone to the airport and even passed through security, but at the last minute he couldn't make himself board the plane. Instead, he'd caught a bus to his parents' house in New Jersey. He'd holed up in his bed-room writing songs and trying to work up the desire to return to Europe.

"But I couldn't go," he concluded. "I had to stay until opening night, even if I was just some guy in the back row. Even if I had to see you with your boyfriend afterward. I had to be here, even if it hurt."

While Lucy's friends looked on as if this latest development was just a final, surprise act in the evening's performance, she con-fessed how she'd broken up with Shane that very day, how she'd finally realized she didn't love him and never would. "I wanted to tell you," she said. "But I waited too long. And then you were gone."

"Tell me now." Jesse's voice was husky.

So she did. "I've never loved anyone but you." And then, not caring what onlookers would think, she wrapped her arms, crushed sunflowers and all, around Jesse's neck. Losing herself in his kiss, she hardly even noticed when her circle of friends burst into a round of applause.

Coda

Florence

The Bertolini looked just as Lucy remembered it—the plush, cherry-red carpet, the old-fashioned light fixtures, and the brochures fanned out near the entry. When she and Jesse stepped up to the check-in desk, the woman on duty greeted Jesse like he was family returned from a long journey, exclaiming in rapid Italian. Jesse answered in only slightly less rapid Italian, with Lucy following along so intently she almost didn't notice when they switched to English.

"This is your girlfriend?" the woman was asking. "The one you wrote me about?"

Jesse smiled and nodded.

"Look at him, so shy!" The woman winked in Lucy's direction. "I'm Renata Bertolini." She held out a hand for Lucy to shake. "Where you two met?"

"Right here." Lucy told her. "Last summer."

The woman smiled and clapped her hands together. "Firenze is the place for love, no?"

Lucy and Jesse beamed back.

"I will upgrade you to our best private room." Renata glanced down at the desktop computer. "On the top floor. With a most beautiful view of the piazza."

Lucy smiled to herself. "A view would be perfect," she told Renata. "*Mille grazie.*"

The climb up to the fifth floor, knapsacks in tow, was harder than Lucy remembered. "I need to get my backpacking muscles back," she gasped as they paused on the landing, Jesse fiddling with the key.

"We both do," Jesse said, then pushed the heavy wooden door open with a flourish.

The room's window had been left open, and a robust breeze blew back the lace curtains. For June in Florence, it was a relatively crisp day, the electric sky over Piazza Santa Maria Novella dotted with clouds. Someone had filled the square with many boxes of red flowers, creating a makeshift garden. Lucy knelt on the window seat for a better look, and Jesse joined her.

"It's like seeing an old friend," she told him. "An old friend I never thought I'd see again."

Jesse's new cell phone chirped in his backpack. He dug it out. "Speaking of old friends," he said.

"Nello?" Lucy guessed.

"He says he'll meet us here on Friday. He can't wait to show us around Naples."

"I never thought I'd get to see Naples," Lucy said.

"Maybe we can lure him to Venice afterward. He says he has to get back to work on Monday, but I bet we could talk him into taking a few more days off."

Venice. Lucy sighed happily at the very idea and shut her eyes. When she opened them, Jesse was closer than he'd been a second before. "Of course, it would be okay if it's just us in Venice," he said, bending to kiss her. His hands spread to encircle her waist, the breeze from the window ruffling his hair as well as hers. "More than okay."

"This is so much better than last summer," she told him when she could speak. "Not that last summer wasn't great…"

"Isn't it, though?" he murmured, undoing the barrette that held back her cascade of hair.

Lucy made a sound deep in her throat, then pulled away. "Shouldn't we be getting to work?" She gestured out the window. "We've got music to make." They'd been rehearsing together ever since the final performance of *Rent*—that wonderful night when Lucy's mother had managed at last to talk Lucy's father into attending the play. Though he'd been too proud to speak to Lucy after the show, her mother had reported back the next day. "Sweetheart, I wish you could have heard your dad on the ride home." Her voice deepened in her best impression of her husband. "'I have to give her credit, Elise. She's stubborn like her old man. When she wants something she knows how to work for it. I'm starting to think she could do anything if she sets her mind to it.'"

Though Lucy had already reconciled herself to finding a job and leaving school, at the last minute her father had paid her tuition on the condition that she get a part-time job to learn, in his words, "the value of hard work." Lucy had readily agreed, relieved that she could stay at Forsythe and keep rooming with Britt after all.

Though Jesse had found himself a job in the campus copy shop and had started searching for an apartment he could share with Lucy, he was fine with the change of plans. Within a week he had found a room in a reasonably affordable apartment just off campus. By fall, he would be a part-time student at Forsythe, slowly but surely working toward his degree. He hadn't settled on a major yet, but he and Lucy agreed there was plenty of time for that.

By the middle of Lucy's second semester, she had signed up to be a drama minor. Soon after that, she landed the role of Cecily in the school's spring production, *The Importance of Being Earnest*. When she wasn't studying or rehearsing, she and Jesse worked up a repertoire of popular songs and even a few Broadway show tunes, the two of them taking turns on melody and harmony.

"We have to make money," Lucy said now, a little breathless from all the kissing. "I need to pay my dad back for my plane ticket."

Jesse fiddled with one of her curls, holding it under his nose like a mustache. "We have all summer," he said. Jesse had been playing guitar around Center City in Philadelphia on weekends to pay for his own share of the trip. "Starting tomorrow, we'll get serious." He kissed the tip of her nose, and then her chin. "For this one day we can relax and just be together. In Italy."

Lucy leaned forward for another look down at the piazza. "In

Italy," she parroted with satisfaction. Then she pointed. "Look! Over there. Those two girls checking out the menu," Lucy said. "The petite one in the blue T-shirt and the tall one in yellow." From their body language, it was pretty clear they were arguing over whether or not to go into the restaurant.

Jesse looked bemused. "What about them?"

"Don't they remind you of anyone?" Lucy smiled. "It's like looking at Charlene and me. And look over there." She pointed at a red-haired woman sitting cross-legged in the grass, staring down at her iPad. "It's Ellen Lavish, taking notes, planning an article for next year's edition of *Wanderlust*."

"Or maybe she's just checking her e-mail?" Jesse guessed.

Lucy pursed her lips and shook her head. "That's absolutely this year's Ellen. See how she's frowning, trying to think of something clever to say about how *authentic* the piazza is?" She scanned the scene. "And look over there!" She pointed at the base of the obelisk, where a young man with shaggy hair was opening his guitar case. "I don't have to tell you who that is, do I?"

Jesse laughed, wrapped his arms around her waist, and pulled her so close she could feel the heat of him through his T-shirt. "I can't believe your dad let you come here with me," he said.

"Me, neither," Lucy admitted. In January, when she had taken Jesse home to have dinner with her parents, her father hadn't been thrilled. He'd even made a comment afterward about Jesse being a "scruffy underachiever." Still, he'd been polite enough in Jesse's presence, and on subsequent visits he'd seemed almost friendly, offering to help Jesse find a decent used car at a reasonable price. "He may be the most stubborn man in the universe, but he's not blind." Lucy clasped Jesse's wrists, one in each hand, and gazed up at him. "He sees how we feel about each other."

Jesse looked solemnly back at her, not quite convinced. Lucy struggled for the words to make him believe.

"I'm serious. He's beginning to understand.... When a person really loves something...or someone..."

"Yes?" Jesse asked, softly, his lips brushing her ear.

"You just have to..." Lucy looked away, over to the sun-drenched piazza, then back into Jesse's smiling face, into his warm, searching eyes, and the words came to her. "You just have to stand back and let them."

Acknowledgments

As I worked on this book, I had not one but two amazing editors, Pamela Garfinkel and Julie Scheina. Thanks to both of you for believing in Lucy and helping her reach her destination.

A generous summer research grant from Saint Joseph's University allowed me to revisit Italy a few summers ago. Without that assistance I simply would not have been able to research and write this book.

Thanks also to the many others who helped me along the way:

My agent, Amy Williams, whose honesty and expertise I cherish.

Ann Green and Ted Fristrom, for giving me crucial feedback on an early draft.

My mother, Grace Lindner, who brought me back to Italy for a follow-up visit, and my sister, Melody Lindner, who knows Mickey Mouse.

Laura Pattillo, Renee Dobson, and the Saint Joseph's University Theatre Company.

My Facebook Brain Trust: Heather Goldsmith, Gina Tomaine, Lauren Boyle, Clare Herlihy Dych, and especially Mike Zodda, who schooled me in the anthropology of the college party. Gregory Dowling, Alicia Stallings, Eric Coulson, Emily Hipchen, Melissa Goldthwaite, Sharon Dyson-Demers, and Amy Montz, who helped me with air-travel logistics and imaginary airlines. Fly Etruscan Airways!

The Tent in Munich, for the most memorable hostel experience in all my travels, and for letting me return three summers ago to wander the place and take pictures. You're still as magical as you were the first time I visited.

My husband, Andre, for being even more excited about my writing projects than I am, and for being eager to watch *A Room With a View* and *Roman Holiday* with me—over and over and over. We'll always have Rome.

My sons, Eli and Noah, for putting up with my wanderings.

Finally, everyone I have ever met on the road, for fellowship and inspiration. While writing this book, I looked through my photo albums and thought fondly of every face I saw there. I hope your travels have been happy ones.

Not ready to say good-bye to Jesse and Lucy? Find out
what happened while Jesse was in Naples in April Lindner's
digital-original novella *Far from Over*.

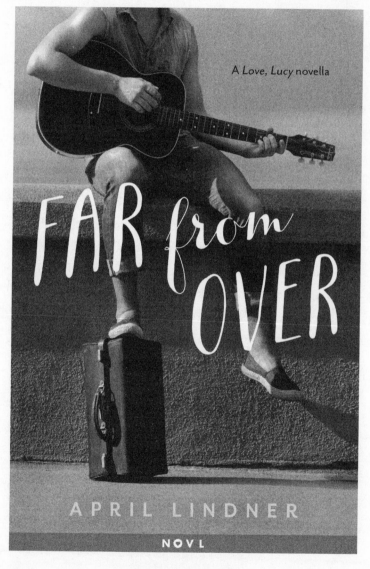

Available now.

APRIL LINDNER

is the author of *Catherine* and *Jane* and a professor of English at Saint Joseph's University in Philadelphia. Her poetry collection, *Skin*, received the Walt McDonald First-Book Prize in Poetry, and her poems have been featured in many anthologies and textbooks. She plays acoustic guitar badly, sees more rock concerts than she'd care to admit, travels whenever she can, cooks Italian food, and lavishes attention on her pets—an elderly Lab mix, a formerly stray cockapoo, and two rescued guinea pigs. April lives with her husband and two sons in Pennsylvania. Her website is aprillindner.com.